DISCARDED

FINGER PLAY

by

Robert Wallace

LONDON
VICTOR GOLLANCZ LTD
1991

First published in Great Britain 1991
by Victor Gollancz Ltd,
14 Henrietta Street, London WC2E 8QJ

© Robin Wallace-Crabbe 1991

The right of Robert Wallace to be identified
as author of this work has been asserted by
him in accordance with the Copyright, Designs
and Patents Act 1988

A CIP catalogue record for this book is
available from the British Library

ISBN 0 575–04902–2

0042520

WESTERN EDUCATION
AND LIBRARY BOARD

Typeset at The Spartan Press Ltd,
Lymington, Hants
Printed in Great Britain by St Edmundsbury Press Ltd
Bury St Edmunds, Suffolk

FINGER PLAY

By the same author
TO CATCH A FORGER
AN AXE TO GRIND
PAINT OUT

'The Indian who smiles while being tortured, is he defeated?'
                              Paul Gauguin

Chapter 1

Groggy, hell! And I couldn't see.

What's this, Essington?

My body might have rolled, perhaps that's what woke me. Was it waking? More like consciousness returning to a knocked-out mind. As it will do, thank God, given half a chance. In the long run the mind's as hard to cancel as the body: it'll fight back, even with all the messages scrambled.

There must have been blood. But I couldn't taste it, or smell it, not blood, not anything. I was gagged. And it being so dark in there that even without a blindfold I couldn't see. Not straight after coming to, I couldn't. With my head hurting from where it had been . . . the curious thing was I had no recall of what had happened.

I'd try and put a picture together, or some sequence of action — nothing.

I was turned over again by the motion, but by what motion? This time feeling my cheek flatten against the ridges and valleys of a pressed metal floor.

Still I couldn't get the picture, or make sense of the bumping; the hollow, reverberative drumming sound. The continuous vibration of walls and floor was like the beat of a steel hummingbird's wings — some hummingbird with murder on its mind.

It wasn't me playing games, making myself roll around inside wherever I was for the fun of it. I was being flung by unknown forces from one side of the metal box to the other, and unable to do a thing about it. I cracked my head — how many times was that? Holy Jesus! Wanting to chuck my guts because of it! Each blow causing me to lose touch with whatever sense I'd been starting to make of my situation.

My skull slammed against the floor and I had to begin all over again, trying to put the pieces back together.

Did I try a thousand times? And with what varying number of pieces?

Sometimes I could smell petrol, the fumes. Not strong, but there. And, as well as the drumming, I picked up the constant drone of a motor sounding behind everything else.

Except it wasn't so constant. Not when you came to concentrate, to think about it. It changed, both the pitch of the note and the volume.

Like being locked inside a synthesizer devoted to the minimalist cause.

There were times when I'd slide forward in the metal compartment, six foot of me like a ramrod, taking the full impact on my skull.

I was an insect, or a mole: some hapless creature in a box stuffed into the pocket of a boy on a motorbike.

There is no way of telling how long I spent in there. Consciousness came and went like a model train on its track: entering black tunnels, emerging again into the light. Mostly I'd lose consciousness with some sudden change of direction in the box's movement.

Or maybe what I was experiencing was a compacted equivalent of the passage of days I might have lived to the full under normal conditions: life speeded up so you don't get it. Except there's nothing normal about being bound and gagged. And for me the sun didn't rise, didn't pass across the firmament, nor did it set. It could have been minutes instead of hours that separated relatively lucid moments from those when the old Holt mind had been out of play.

Of course, there are those among us who'd reckon that my thoughts are never quite on the ball, that they're always behind the game trying to follow what's happening out there in front.

When I look in a mood to see the joke they'll tell me that to my face. Well some people will — those who reckon I love them well enough to take it.

Even if I am slow I've never been so out of it as I was boxed up in that steel hell. Nothing made sense in there! Like how I got inside in the first place.

Where there might have been a smile across my stupid face, now there was the strip of sticking plaster. I was almost choking on the cloth it held in place, drawing in air through my nose, but panicking, as though there wasn't enough getting to my lungs. The more I thought about respiration, the worse it got. Till there was a crazy thumping at the centre of my being — where they'd more or less claim the soul ought to be located — and I'd think I was going to explode. As if the spiritual thing people talk about was a bundle of gelignite.

Then the steel box was rattling from side to side as though it was a pan full of pay-dirt in giant hands washing after gold. Except a pan is round and it doesn't have a top. I was being kept in the dark, the lid was in place.

Almost in the dark. There was a vertical slit in one wall, white light showing through that.

So with extended periods of consciousness I had something I set myself to do, a task. With the box bouncing as it was, and me getting thrown about, I decided to try at turning myself around. Not so easy with your hands tied behind your back and the ankles trussed up as well. Attempting to get my head down to the end where the light was, that was when I discovered I was trussed up with one piece of rope, my ankles and wrists were joined so I couldn't bend forward at the waist.

Wriggling like a caterpillar I eventually got my head to that wall with the slit of light breaking through. A couple of times during the manoeuvre I was tossed about by the box's movement and the Holt head suffered more heavy blows. I was conscious enough to notice that I wasn't the only thing in there. I had for company a couple of unidentified flying metallic objects: a car jack, tyre lever, shit like that, I guess. If I thumped against the side these had a go at me from behind.

The contents of my stomach were coming up; I wanted to puke, needed to. I could feel it, the acid burning at the back of my throat. And me trying to swallow it down despite the gag. I reckoned a mouthful of sick was all it would take, then I'd choke, drown on the contents of my own stomach. The more I thought about that one the worse it got.

Next I reckon I was thinking about the metaphysics of the

situation: me being in the middle, the box working from the outside, those acid juices from within — each, after its fashion, hell bent on my destruction. Isn't that the mad thing about calamity, the way the mind will freewheel? It will hunt about for some crazy notion, some idea to start playing with, as though that's a pre-coded means of escape from when reality gets too rough.

My wife, Karen, she'd say: 'Not metaphysics, Essington.' And she'd screw up her nose as though metaphysics had gone off at the back of the refrigerator.

Karen wasn't being bounced about inside a metal container, was she? Karen was back at home with Pietro, snug, warm. She was getting off on the smell of talcum powder, of those lotions you rub in to stop skin chafing, on the burps left hanging in the air.

Pietro is the baby.

Pietro equals Peter; on that rock we were going to build our relationship.

Rebuild our relationship.

When at last I got my head to that one slit of light in the box the next problem was to line up the Holt eyes so they could see out. That meant getting my body to stop jiggling along with the movement. By then the thing wasn't so much a metal box any more; it was starting to be the back of a van. And I reckoned we had to be belting along some back road, with a surface like that! The big bumps were potholes. The periods when my limited world seemed hell bent on shaking itself to pieces. I started to believe in road corrugations when that happened.

My mind was forming memory fragments into pictures, piecing them together. There was some sort of understanding forming. And I was thinking of Pietro as well, of his dark brown eyes. Like while I was lying there swallowing back on my vomit those eyes were scanning my face, asking questions, wanting to know that he could trust me, that it would be all right, safe, to have some faith in another human being.

Maybe it would, little Pietro, but then maybe it wouldn't.

Because, whatever, there's no saying what being in a metal box will do to the human mind. I was shoving my face up to the slit, my nose hard against cold metal. Suddenly, bang! The whole lot — Holt body, metal box, unidentified flying objects —

came to an abrupt stop. I slid, smashed against the front wall, luckily feet first this time.

There were voices.
 I thought: Voices!
 Then: Save them, Essington, for later. Because these bastards, you are going to have to kill them.
 Funny, I'd never thought that before, about anybody. So clearly, too.
 Then back to Madam Reality. It occurred to me: Save yourself first . . . if you can.
 Voices! To concentrate on them was to come one step closer to mind control, to establishing bearings.
 Suddenly the slit of light was a rectangle, the day's glare as intense as an electric welder's flash. That zap burnt out what mind I'd put together while the box had been closed.
 And the nightmare world back there seemed infinitely nicer than the new one: this illuminated hell. I shut my eyes, feeling as if I was a child's doll preferring the gloom within gift wrapping to the thumping I was certain to get at the hands of a spoilt infant.
 It was one of those voices out of southern Africa. The British reckon it's the accent of the Boers. But they develop it themselves down in those parts, in Rhodesia, for instance — when they still had the nerve to call it Rhodesia — so maybe it's something in African soil that attacks the vocal chords.
 It frightens me, that accent, always has. I gather plenty of people get the same chill feeling from hearing our Australian intonations. Me, Essington Holt, I talk Australian.
 I opened eyes slammed shut against the glare. There was a face close to my face. Zooming in on an ear I could see two gold earrings in the lobe.
 A voice from outside the van asked: 'He isn't choking?'
 And, first off, I was wondering if they'd said 'joking'! Shit!
 Two hands grabbed me by the collar, dragged me as though I was a sack of wheat. I was lumped up against one of the side walls of my metal box. Opening my eyes again I could see the face up close to mine, the pale blue eyes — like ice — focused. I was being examined.
 For what?

The flat of a hand shot in on the plane of my vision then was pulled away again.

'He seems right in the eyes. There's reflex.'

'Once he's dead we're wasting our precious time.' That other voice wasn't from Africa, it was London. And it wasn't East End either . . . tending more to the la-di-da, I would have thought, but a bit rough around the vowels here and there.

I was watching the blue eyes hovering in front of mine, noting the red veins breaking the white that surrounded it. Weathered, I thought, a touch of coachman's eye on the cornea; I know about that, I have it myself. The skin around the eyes was weathered too, and tanned. Crow's-feet. They might have been a deck-hand's eyes. The sandy hair, a sense of sun bleach, was cut short and spiky on top and left long down the back of the neck.

Trying to talk through the gag, I was attempting to tell the man to take the thing off, that I was going to suffocate.

As though I believed he cared!

Now hadn't the man with the eyes — they were intense with that pale blue — hadn't he seemed to change from regarding me as he might a sack of grain? Had he suddenly noticed that, as though by some magic, I'd become a member of his species?

I guess that's why he gave me a crack over the ear. The human touch, see, for no reason. For no reason!

Then he smiled. I had pleased him in some obscure way. I hate to say it but even then, that early in the ordeal, I was rewarded to see him happy.

And I blew into the gag, puffing out my cheeks.

The other man, the one with a tutored voice, he said: 'Is he all right or isn't he? We have to keep on going, Tony, old boy.'

'No names, I told you no names . . . never. It isn't worth it, the risk.' Sudden anger, on top of which there was the harshness of that Boer pronunciation.

The van doors were closed on me.

I heard the motor start up, they took off. I fell sideways with the movement, cracked my head; consciousness went down the gurgler.

Chapter 2

I'd caught a glimpse of a rocky and infertile landscape out there beyond the van door while they'd been checking my condition. There had been a sense of stunted trees, of dry undergrowth, pale yellow and buff ochres, some calcareous rock showing almost white. I reckoned that we were well east of Paris, possibly heading south, quite a long way south. That gave me an idea of how long we'd been going. It couldn't have been much less than five hours, maybe six.

Where the hell were we headed?

Could be we were into Italy. The geography follows pretty much the same pattern there as in France. But if Italy . . . who'd drive across a national border with a trussed-up body in the back, even one still breathing?

Answer: Anybody who had a mind to do it. They don't check.

We stopped again, I was subjected to the indignity of another examination, and a fresh clip across the side of my face. Great fun that, you could see the pleasure it gave Tony . . . Wasn't it Tony who had two earrings in his right ear and none in the other?

The second man stayed out of sight as before.

What did I make of me and them . . . I mean at those moments in the journey when I could make something of anything? I decided that the voices, the differing accents, indicated roles, the structure of their relationship. The posh voice belonged to the schemer. The other guy was the muscle, which was why he liked taking a poke at me. He was the man of action. That was what I deduced from a pinch more than nothing.

So I was yet to be introduced to the main player; something to look forward to.

During the second stop I noticed another detail: that Tony had a snake tattooed on his arm, on the left arm. It was in red and blue, with a tail flattened like an oar. It had to be a sea snake. That went together with the deck-hand skin. I managed to file those details away with the rings in the ear.

I was dealing with a born-again pirate.

Mostly I lost track of my thoughts, fighting instead for some regulation of my body, of the beating of my heart, the expansion and contraction of exhausted lungs. Fear batting at my temples.

We seemed to be right into the back blocks. From the movement of the van I figured the road was winding. There were right-angle corners as well, ones you could misjudge. I knew that because we'd pull up too suddenly, skidding; I'd pick the noise pattern as the driver changed down then planted his foot, impatient for more speed. Surely wheels were still dropping into potholes. Each time that happened my skull flicked against the steel floor and my companion objects would relocate themselves.

Torture.

Next my consciousness registered more light, entering now through several cracks. And the old body wasn't taking a bashing any longer. I could breathe too, breathe and swallow.

The floor was cement. I was lying on it. On the oil that had been absorbed into its surface. I could smell that garage smell. My hands and feet remained tied and the same length of rope still joined them together. My pupils must have been at full aperture because, despite the lack of light, I was making out details of the interior, stuff like the work bench down one end that was two lengths of thick wood resting on blocks cut direct from the trunk of some tree. There was tin nailed over where there might have been a window or just some opening in the cement block wall. Most of the light leaking into the shed came from around the double doors. These were of timber, planks with cross pieces and diagonals bolted into place, and there was a low door set into one of them so that a man could step through. I sensed I'd seen a man do just that, step through, then go out again. That had been after I'd been dumped from the van. Dumped then thumped over the back of the head with something heavy but soft, like a sock filled with wet sand. Smack, then I was out of it again.

Next thing had been when hands were fiddling with my face, getting the sticking plaster off so the gag could be removed. Peeling up a corner then ripping the plaster away. Taking a layer of skin at the same time.

I'd watched my visitor exit through the door.

There must have been a night which passed. And then there had been an infinite day; my mind turned minutes into hours like it says in the song, don't ask me which song. It would have to have been someone singing about love time . . .

. . . Which seemed an eternity ago.

In the shed there wasn't any love, not flowing either way, nor the milk of human kindness, either. They say that you can grow to love your captor in some perverse fashion, there are stories of occasional Jews getting to be like that in the concentration camps. I tried to keep the requisite psychological shift at bay, yet knowing that given time things would come to that unhappy pass. And with tears running down my cheeks I'd thank these bastards for every one of ten thousand blows to the head.

Once already there'd been a desire to have this Tony approve of me. It's just so crazy that the mind can perform these tricks against its best interests.

But gratitude wasn't what I had in my thoughts right then, coming to on the oily floor, nor revenge. I guess I was just hoping, hopelessly, to escape, and thus to survive. I'd eye the work bench, wriggle across the floor to it, ease my way on to my knees, kneel there as though before an altar. With my eyes I'd search for something, for anything, that could assist me in my purpose.

In what purpose?

They do that in the movies: dark screen, just a touch of light on the face, vaguely defined objects; and then our hero discovers a file, maybe a key, or a pistol someone conveniently left behind.

My shed was devoid of useful items. And even if there had been something I simply didn't have the dexterity to make use of it, not with my wrists and ankles tied as they were.

When it came to evening, and the light fading so cracks around the doors slowly receded back to become part of a general gloom, thirst took control.

I took it into my head to shout for water.

Starting mid-range, then working up; finding pleasure in the activity, in the noise itself, in the defiance it represented.

The illusion of defiance.

I wouldn't know how long I kept up the hullabaloo, but I ran out of voice before any angels of mercy responded to the call.

Chapter 3

Christ, it was a long night. I must have slept, but you never know. The impression was of lying there, awake, shivering with the cold, with disorientation; pissing myself, feeling the warm damp of that. And thrashing against the cement block walls with my torso, my shoulders.

Also I have this memory of me growling like a leopard caught in a net.

The night crawling past, its meteorological, its astrological events unobserved — well, at least by me. The dawn was ultra cold. It always is because you've let most of the life out of you by then; that is if you didn't pass away altogether at three a.m. I figured the chill factor had to mean we were high up, some location where the atmosphere doesn't retain the heat. It was the month of May, and in my neighbourhood, down on the Côte d'Azur, there were people swimming already.

I heard a motor.

Was it the van? It could have been the van.

A vehicle arriving, didn't matter much which one, it had to mean something.

The question was, what did it mean?

With the first light I'd dragged myself across the floor and tried looking out through the cracks around the doors. All I could make out was a landscape falling away, some stunted trees, the apricot dawn sky. No other buildings. Maybe there was a track sweeping down with the surface of the hills, it was difficult to tell for sure. I'd pressed up against the crack, I'd looked for so long — for too long — looked till my eyes, tilted like that, started to play games, to shift out of focus; there'd been electric green spots drifting across their surface.

You can stare at something as we weren't intended to do, say through a narrow aperture, till you just don't know if the image you receive is real any more.

And then, turning into the dark interior, I had suffered disorientation: the light still there within me, my eyes brim full of it, holding it back as though reluctant to let go.

In response to the car's arrival I was wriggling towards the door to take a look. For hadn't I been right through the still night with no sound except a fox barking, its dry cough call shifting about the place. Maybe there'd been two foxes out there, keeping in touch, letting rip with a love duet.

I was most of the way back to my position for spying on the world when the door swung open.

In came Tony. I was dazzled by the light surrounding him, delineating his outline even though in that flash of illumination I picked up a duller, more leaden sky where it met the profile of the hills. And trees strangely detailed, though so far away, minutiae registering on my retina so I got the impression of reading each of the leaves as a separate entity.

Tony pulled me up on my feet by the shoulders.

'Pissing ourselves . . . dirty boy.'

I wasn't gagged, yet I couldn't muster a response. Not in any shape or form. Most of my voice had been thrown away with that burst of maniacal screaming I'd indulged in at the beginning of the night. I knew the taunt about pissing myself was an invitation to stand on my dignity, and thus to invite another of his gratuitous head punches. Perhaps my eyes told him my thoughts, I don't know. How the hell would I know? About that . . . about a thing! What was it they expected of me, anyway?

The door was open still. I looked past Tony at the lowering sky, at the grey spreading across what had been a pure, cerulean blue dome. At the same time I noted the presence of another man. He was small, limping; wasn't that a built-up shoe?

And then a woman appeared.

She was carrying a tray on which there was a jug, a bowl. Jesus, it was feeding time for the animals.

'Mister,' she said, only in Italian, waiting, standing there just outside the open door. 'The food.'

I don't have much Italian, but I can get about, order a meal and a bed.

'Leave it there,' Tony responded in English, pointing. She put the tray down on a smudge of oil just inside the door.

'Get on with it.' The educated voice. The man with the built-up shoe had taken himself out of sight but I knew it was his voice. Why? I don't know, just that it fitted with him not undertaking the heavy work. Maybe the way he was dressed, too: a waisted sports coat, more a riding jacket, in something close to Prince of Wales check. Had they been fawn twill trousers?

Quite a different kettle of fish to our Tony who went for the international uniform of T-shirt, jeans, Reeboks.

Reeboks!

Bare arms so I could see the sea snake. It was striped, the red and the blue bands alternating. And tough, Tony, he didn't mind the early morning chill, probably he reckoned it was good for you.

So I remembered the sea snake, filed it away in case there'd be a future use.

Tony had it in mind to repackage me. He had chains for the task. It looked like it was to be the shackling first, then the feeding. The tray stayed where it had been placed while he padlocked a chain around each ankle, tight. After putting handcuffs on my wrists he untied the rope. Finally, he padlocked a linking chain between the hands and the ankles, but this time it was in front. So were my hands. That was an improvement. I could stand. I could even move my arms about in a restricted sort of fashion.

Up on the wall there was a steel ring set into mortar between the cement blocks. I saw that Tony was looking at it. And there was still a length of chain in his hand; he swung the loose end about, entertaining himself with its serpentine movement.

I said: 'What are you keeping me for?' My voice scratchy, almost inaudible.

The answer: I got the chain full force across my face.

'Fuck you,' I would have screamed. But it came out a trickle of dry sound. I brought my hands to my face, protecting myself.

He'd rounded on me. I was free to move, even with my hands and legs chained. I took a step towards him, stumbled, fell. He laughed as he came towards me.

I lay there, seething, uncertain, half shit-scared. I guess I thought I might get somewhere if I could bring him down on to the concrete floor. I'm a big boy, heavy, strong enough for that sort of play. If I could just get a hand on him the game might even out . . . a little.

I could see in his eyes, see the way he was responding to the challenge, how he was spoiling for a fight.

And me lying on the cement, not even moving, waiting now for my chance.

'Hurry up in there.' The other voice, impatient. 'It's starting to rain . . . What are you up to now, Tony?'

'Don't use my fucking name! I told you once, so don't do it.'

I kicked out, keeping both legs together, bringing them up high, putting as much power into the action as I could. But it was nothing more than a glancing blow catching him above the knees.

He stepped back. 'What's this, want a go, do we, sport?'

I didn't say a word.

'We'll see about that.'

He kicked me in the face, the Reebok instep catching along one side from chin to temple. The blow stunned me, there was nothing but shock inside my skull. Then I felt what was like a pile-driver connect with the back of my head.

'Hurry up in there; it's starting to rain, Tony.' When I came to and found myself attached to the ring high up in the wall I remembered those words, or something like them. Funny, the guy not wanting to get wet!

It was a sufficient length of chain, so I could only just lie down. And, standing, was permitted four paces up and down on my tether.

The food had been shoved within reach. That was kindness, their style. I was going to find time to get used to it. I went for the water first, pouring it down my throat, gulping, spilling it over my chin. Then I was biting into peasant bread and the lump of cheese. Not high cuisine . . . but, Jesus, the way things can taste depends on your state of mind.

It rained for three days. I could hear it on the roof, see it driving in under the shed's doors. And the air was cold. I was dressed in a light cotton jumper, cotton slacks, socks, shoes, a shirt. I was shitting at the end of the chain's reach. Most of the time I was shivering, with teeth chattering as though they were trying to work themselves lose in my head. I was sick, feverish too.

The woman came in once a day, wrapped up against the rain. She'd place the tray on the floor out of my reach, push it in with a stick.

She avoided meeting my gaze.

On the third day she put a folded blanket under the tray, pushed the lot in, then fled. I shouted at her, in English, in French, in Italian: 'Pity,' I implored. I got no reply. She certainly wasn't on the point of coming over to my side of the argument. And charity was a blanket to keep me warm, nothing more.

I was glad of the blanket. I ate that day's ration — some small local olives were added to the cheese and the bread. I drank a portion of water. Afterwards I wrapped myself in the blanket and, propped against the wall, set to sitting out another unendurable passage of hours.

My shit was a disgusting pile a couple of metres away from where I lay. It was attracting scavenger insects. I could smell myself in my excrement. I was feeling like a penned animal must feel: some wild creature forced to adjust to a cage and bars.

It was while I was there like that, wrapped in the blanket, taking comfort from the warmth it afforded, I first believed I understood what was going on. I was kidnapped, wasn't I, and being held for ransom. Why else would I be kept like that? I was a hostage and while I was chained to that wall negotiations were going on.

Who was doing the negotiating . . . on my side?

And what chance does a kidnap victim have?

The way I saw things the answer to the second question was none. All the time I kept on remembering that Italian politician — was his name Moro? Aldo Moro? How they'd turned him up dead in the boot of a car.

Because there isn't any incentive for kidnappers to return the goods, not unless, intending to do business again, they want to demonstrate their bona fides. I sensed that I was a oncer for this lot, they wouldn't be wanting to come back for any second deal. It was going to be cash somewhere, in a luggage locker perhaps . . . that's the way these things were resolved. And then they'd dump the body, my body, out on some lonesome road. It always ends the same way, because the kidnapper has all the cards, and the initiative.

So I had to lose.

Some game!

Well, there was one consolation prize, I guessed, I hoped. Our baby, Pietro — it hadn't been him they'd snatched. Maybe I should have felt grateful for that in some crazy way.

Snatched! To comprehend how they'd got me I had to find the means to remember. And that was exactly what I hadn't been able to do since becoming aware of myself in the back of the van.

I simply couldn't think it out, where I'd been just before whatever happened. I couldn't get hold of a reconstruction of the action. To get a grip on that might have led to understanding these people. What they were after. Like, if it wasn't a kidnap, then . . .

I came to believe knowledge was the key to survival.

Headaches, they came and went, together with a continuous sense of nausea. Maybe it was exposure, or being held in the dark. Most probably both. I knew I'd taken a lot of knocks on the head. It was sore on the outside, and inside, as well. Each a different type of hurt.

I would get myself down on the floor, lower my head between manacled hands and investigate its surface with loving fingers as though it was all I had in the world.

My own skull, with wounds on it where scabs had formed under blood-glued hair.

There were times when I'd just weep. For the pity of it all. I'd shed tears for the world's madness, for my own predicament; for life itself, that it couldn't have been in some other form.

Of course I knew what chance I had. None. Except, perhaps, a faint possibility of salvation through this woman who had brought me the blanket. That way she had of never meeting my eye or entering into any form of communication, it had to mean something.

That she had her own unstated doubts, maybe?

I'd have to try some of the Essington charm on her.

With my shit piling up there, and fumes of ammonia building from my urine, a fat chance I had of sweeping her off her feet.

But where did she come from, this woman? Which country were we in? Was it definitely Italy? And the food, it didn't fall like manna from the sky. Surely, eventually, someone else might notice something of my presence, start to investigate, discover a human being was kept chained to a wall — and begin to ask the question, why?

Day four, or six — it felt like day three hundred. The woman approached again, bearing the tray. As always her gaze was fixed on a point somewhere above my head. It struck me that rather than avoiding eye contact with the captive she might merely have been checking on the condition of the ring set in the wall, the one to which my chain was fastened.

I went into the old routine: 'Pity,' I said, in Italian, and dropped my face into my hands. 'Pity,' I repeated, that time followed with a muffled sob.

Watching her between my fingers I saw that the play-acting had no effect. Art she could do without. The bitch was getting about her business, placing the tray on the ground, taking up her stick so the food could be shoved across that no man's land of possible contact. I had gone silent then, fixing her with a doleful stare, hoping that the look itself could penetrate her soul.

Do they have souls, those thick-set peasants with round and ageless sallow faces? You read sentimental stories in which they are accredited with every human quality bar the urbanity to make a display of their own virtues.

I could pick up nothing from those dark eyes which were like currants stuck on a child's pastry man, or beads stitched to the face of a rag doll.

Next thing I became enraged. From standing against the wall directly below the ring I lunged forward, howling, taking the few steps allowed by the chain. All of my substantial, if diminishing, weight was in that rush, my frustration too . . . and in the animal cry. The chain came taught, suddenly, dragging my wrists down into my groin because that was where the leash was attached, at the wrists. I pitched on to my face, shouting with pain, and with anguish at the total searing hell of the situation. The woman retreated, surprised but unmoved.

The cow! The fucking witch! Her stocky little body, the stupid peasant face, that hair dragged into a bun at the back. Everything about her expressive of a simplicity of mind, of no mind, of total, God-given stupidity. It was plain as the nose on your face that while keeping me under these conditions she was remaining in daily and uncomplicated contact with her deity . . . or at least with the Blessed Virgin.

How would it be? *Mea non culpa* . . . some shit like that. Trusting in the Lord!

In the Lord who conceived, even at the beginning of time, that I should be chained to that accursed wall.

They can do that, those wilder peasants of the mountains, they can slit the throat of a grandmother and still stay on great terms with the Virgin.

I hated her then, the Virgin, like I hated this squat expressionless biddy who brought the food.

Ignoring the tray I lay where I had fallen after being pulled off balance by the chain. I noticed the rain had ceased, yet outside the door the sky remained an unpromising grey, the landscape unchanged.

Funny that, I got a fix on the weather. Like, just to know what was happening as far as clouds were concerned, that became important to me.

Later on I set about working at the ring in the wall. It wasn't easy because I was attached to it with the chain running between my legs and I couldn't lift a leg over on account of the hobble between my ankles. There simply wasn't a position from which I could apply pressure to the fastening without causing myself pain. Yet, pain or no pain, it was an activity of sorts. To try and work the ring free was a symbolic act of hope and thus, in some fashion, contributed to my capacity to endure the confinement.

I thought of Samson and of his super strength as long as he had hair on his head.

Well I had hair, albeit thinning at the crown.

The ring in the wall had responded a little to what work I'd been able to put in; it was pulled out of shape, but not very much. At the start I'd banked on it being a shank set into the mortar between the cement blocks. That was before I'd noticed that there was a corresponding ring at the same height on the opposite wall. Which meant at some stage there must have been something tied between them, I guessed a cable capable of supporting weight — otherwise why go to the trouble of putting the rings up there in the first place? And if weight, then, most likely, there'd be a steel plate on the outside to stop the shank of each ring from pulling through. That's the way they do that sort of thing, with the threaded shank going through a steel plate on the outside and a nut securing it there. No way I could pull that sort of a set-up loose. The only possibility was to open up the ring itself.

Some hope!

My technique was to go in close to the wall, place one foot on the tether chain, draw it tight, the foot anchoring it against the concrete floor, and then to bash at the chain with the other foot, each kick straining the ring a fraction.

A fraction! Futile!

Sure. Yet there is this story of a man — wasn't he called Icarus? — who pushed a huge stone up a hill and each time he reached the top was doomed to watch the thing roll back down again. That is what life is, shoving the stone, forever. Getting nowhere. So the story would have us believe. Or did Icarus fly too close to the sun? No fear of that with me.

But maybe one day, I dared to hope, they'd tell of Essington Holt and the ring in the wall. They could recount the tale to Pietro, my adopted son, so he would understand.

Understand what?

Chapter 4

Before I'd been captured — and no matter how hard I tried I couldn't recall what had happened — before that we had been up in Paris for a couple of weeks.

We, meaning the whole bunch of us, the entourage. That is Dawn, of course, Dawn Grogan, and my wife, Karen; then the baby. And there was Jodie out of the Midwest of the United States of America. Jodie's job was to look after Pietro so that the rest of us were only exposed to his best side. It was the time of the Autumn/Winter *Prêt-à-Porter* parades put on in the Jardin des Tuileries by the rag trade.

Dawn and Karen were right into the fashion industry because they'd managed to sell a range of silk prints to Makihei, a young Japanese designer who was making his Paris debut. Their input consisted of prints based on the Western Desert paintings of certain Australian Aboriginal artists, people who had adapted traditional earth pictures to the medium of paint on canvas. There was a growing global interest in these pictorial creations and Karen had bought the rights to use several as fabric prints.

This Makihei was a wild-looking man: very small, long plaited hair, extremely eccentric, and with a penchant for drunkenness.

'There was a Buddha in China who is drunk all his life, that is how he becomes His Holiness.'

I liked Makihei, we'd fish together in the Seine; he reckoned he got inspiration from fishing. We hooked plastic bags, condoms, syringes, stuff like that. Each catch had Makihei shrieking with laughter, whipping the top off another can of Heineken. He'd go for the booze, get red-eyed; his skin would come up in goose pimples.

'Plastics, rubber . . . the condom . . . I think the condom is . . . how is it the Americans say? The bottom line of fashion.'

'Or the front line, Makihei.'

Maybe he was the Buddha of the fashion world. The international press took to Makihei. There were shots featured in the daily papers of those fishing expeditions of ours, but leaving me out. Who was I anyhow? And I have this habit: I'll turn away from a probing lens given half the chance, even family photos.

The silks Dawn and Karen had produced were used as linings for a curious range of asymmetrically designed, camel hair winter coats which had one shoulder huge, padded, and the other following a natural line. Or there were sou'wester hats made of the quilted silk. A great deal of quilting in Makihei's range, lots of bustles done with straggly knots of quilted lengths so that the models looked as though they were celebrating steatopygia.

On most days Jodie, the baby minder, stayed back at my apartment in the Sixteenth Arrondissement, looking after Pietro. But not on our big day, when the Makihei parade was on, then she came along with us. This had been at Dawn's insistence. It was Dawn who had chosen Jodie in the first place. An unusual choice. Normally us affluent couples with live-in baby minders go for plain girls who won't put the old man off his domestic duties. And, I guess, the same girls act as a foil, so that Mrs can shine by comparison.

Well, Dawn, having a weakness for the flesh of her own sex, had picked us what I expect in the drug-stores of Jodie's home town they might have called a 'living doll'. Or maybe that's *passé*. Still, there is no denying beauty: beauty is beauty. And Jodie was it, wrapped up in cellophane. The looks carried with them a certain power. You just couldn't turn to her and tell her to do something. You tended to ask, as though she was going to be executing some favour. That is unless you were my wife, Karen, then you barked commands and gave the girl the cold eye. Jodie respected Karen for it, did what she was told, el quicko.

But with Dawn all over Jodie, and me tending to go soft and watch her, just for the entertainment, the baby minder was getting a cushy ride.

It was like having a mini Bo Derek in our midst. Not that I was 'having' her. And nor — age having wearied it — was the idea floating about too buoyantly in my mind. No, with me, Jodie was simply beauty for beauty's sake, an invention of the Lord's curious imagination.

So it was Dawn who'd urged that Jodie come along to view the Makihei parade. Which meant that we had a problem with little Pietro. Well, we did and we didn't. There was a solution: how about the doting father? There we had it. I was to wave them off in their taxi and then sit about the apartment twiddling my thumbs, hoping that the baby didn't come up with problems his middle-aged daddy couldn't handle.

A complication arose when Makihei himself could be heard at the security door downstairs, asking that he might come up.

Suddenly there he was in our midst, resplendent. Even if size-wise he seemed to be in competition with Azzedine Alaia to win the smallest designer in the world award. The difference between them was that Makihei didn't carry a dog. Instead he carried a long staff with feathers attached to one end, as though it was associated with the worship of bird ancestors.

Karen asked Makihei why he wasn't already at the Jardin des Tuileries putting the final touches to cut, fit, and accessories?

'There are more people than one of me.'

'You mean, you divide . . . like an amoeba?' Dawn asked while popping a jaunty green hat on top of Jodie's perfect head; pecking her on the nose as a reward for allowing the job to be done right.

A shrill giggle from Makihei, admiring Dawn's work: 'It is so wrong it is wonderful!'

Me protesting about waking the baby.

'No . . . I make my entrance . . . I am thinking of it all yesterday . . . I have the perfection.' Makihei's face lit up with inspiration.

He was dressed in baggy black, so that he looked like a clown. He was a clown, I guess, that was his style. And on his head he wore a tam-o'-shanter sporting an over-large pompom on top. He had his arms akimbo, and was spinning so that the loose pants flew wide like a skirt.

And Karen was laughing.

Smiling, laughing . . . there hadn't been much of anything else since Pietro had come into our lives ten months earlier. It was joy, joy, joy. Sprinkle a bit of Makihei on top and what have you got?

So I was laughing too, happy that life should be like this. Because earlier there had been problems between us, baby problems, old husband-young wife problems. Karen had not been able to conceive and, as a result of this, there'd been recriminations. Somebody always in the wrong. And the same with approaching adoption, tensions there as well, worse because they had been to do with the immovability of bureaucrats.

That phase was over. We had baby, we had Pietro. Our future was built on his delicate, dark-eyed head. Pietro had been adopted out of the alleys of Naples, down in what the Italians call the *mezzogiorno*, and absorbed into the luxury of my house out on Cap Ferrat.

He held our hearts in his keeping.

'But, Essington, you must be coming also. Together we are the fishermen.'

It had occurred to Makihei that our plans and his were diverging.

Dawn: 'Makihei, what are you going on about? This is our day . . . yours, Karen's, mine. Go to it! It's going to be very terrific.' Dawn enjoyed her superlatives.

Now the small Japanese man's face had become the tragic clown's mask: il Pagliaccio: 'No Essington, no show.' His hands were held up, ringed fingers spread wide.

It was touching, to be wanted. There was generally the opposite sentiment around the place: the idea that the show ran better when my ill-fitting bulk was safely shoved out of the way. Yet here was this little whiz-kid of the cutting table insisting on my presence.

'I look after the baby today, Makihei.'

'Essington' — with Makihei it sounded like 'Effington' — 'this baby, it is life. This is the force . . . to be baby. We take the baby . . . it's our show.'

'Makihei, come on,' complained Dawn, 'they'll be wetting themselves at the Jardin des Tuileries.' One arm loosely around Jodie's shoulders, the tip of her nose just touching the full, golden cheek.

'Ah . . . but the hat!' Dawn's urging had missed Makihei altogether. It struck me that he was stoked on something to get through the day, he was that unworried. For now he was thinking only of that blasted green hat; he was standing in front of Jodie, reaching up, gripping the felt brim in two clenched fists, dragging it out of shape, shoving the front up for comic emphasis. Now making a theatre of looking at a watch which wasn't there, rubbing his hands together: 'Where is baby, our little Peter-pitter-pat?'

'No, I'll look after him, it's no trouble,' I protested. 'To disturb him now would be the worst thing we could do.'

It finished up fun to be all there together in one of the three matching scarlet Rolls-Royces that Makihei had hired for the occasion. They were blocking traffic in the narrow street outside my apartment building. And there was a chorus of car horns sounding . . . was it Parisian approval of the extravagance? Or complaint at interference with the flow of automobiles? You can't tell which way they'll jump in the French capital, where the population always goes for a bit of style despite their streetwise impatience.

The day was under control. There in my street was a tall Japanese gentleman standing by the passenger's door of the lead Rolls, speaking into a walkie-talkie. And the press was assembled before us as well! In their tens, with movie cameras, still cameras, videos; reporters were clutching microphones like kids might hold on to lollipops, but talking into them instead of licking.

And we had walked out into all of that. Me holding baby in my arms. Me dressed in a lightweight, deep blue, double-breasted suit and sporting a red rose in the buttonhole. Makihei had inserted it there, his *haute couture* touch.

And on my head nothing but a mop of dark brown hair swept back to cover the growing bald patch. Karen had done that for me, with her brush, as I'd changed out of my house clothes. Karen laughing, making jokes about bald men in general, about me in particular.

And then they'd put the baby into my loving arms.

As I stood there chained to the wall of the shed it struck me how a photograph had caught the eye of one of the colour weekly's pictorial editors. It had been fate dealing a blow. For there I was three days later, on every news-stand: the tall Australian millionaire holding his baby. We'd displaced Princess Caroline, even the public's beloved Princess Di. It was us that day, the Australians and our small Japanese superstar friend.

What must have caught the editor's eye most was the incongruity of the child in my arms. Mind you, even I have to admit, all together like that we filled the star bill. My own gentle self, maybe it was the shock of that battery of cameras, I was staring angrily at the world, looking ready to rip it apart. And the expression gave me something of an edge. I reckoned even Jodie must have noticed: old daddy had some zap in him yet . . . almost Mr Spunk.

Well, in the photographs at least.

And that was what there were, not 'a photograph' but 'photographs'. Several spreads of them with accompanying scrambled articles detailing fictitious relationships, business and otherwise, between all of us who had poured forth from the entrance to my apartment building in a very exclusive part of the genteel Sixteenth Arrondissement.

From unknown Aussie expatriate with an interest in the visual arts, even a collection to call his own, I became Mr Fast-on-his-feet, the Super-mega-rich-man. Essington Holt, the guy who had just focused his interest on the world of fashion and thrown his weight behind the brilliant designer, Makihei.

Jodie wasn't identified by name in the articles accompanying the pics. But at that moment when the shutter caught me for the cover shot Jodie, not Karen, was at my elbow, her big mouth open in an Americo-Scandinavian smile such as Hollywood had yet to dream about. That fraction of a second had her frozen, for an infinite instant, as a new erotic fetish.

So the Australian with the baby in his arms, still a breeder, had this scrumptious beauty at his side in full colour. While in behind that enchanted pair was Karen, her doll-like face turning, mouth a fraction open, the pale apricot hair ruffled across her forehead. She had star quality too.

Dawn wasn't in that shot. Maybe they cut her out deliberately because she took a sartorial lead from Joel Grey in the musical *Cabaret*, the black suit, the white shirt, the bow tie. And Dawn had her hair standing up, spiky, gelled. Her eyes were round as marbles.

We were a set.

Left-anarchists might have exploded at the sight.

Several days chained to a shed wall convinced me that any response I might have had to going public against my will would have been futile and too late. And made me certain that those shots of us, and the reportage accompanying them, were the reason for my being snatched.

No question about it, I had to be up for ransom.

The big problem was I couldn't remember how or where this Tony and his little pal had got their hands on me. I'd work on it, chasing through the dim-lit alleys of my mind, but nothing and no one scuttled out of the shadows.

Except that there, in my head, I had this feeling about Pietro, of him being close at hand.

But when close at hand?

Once when catnapping in what had become my sty—so maybe I was pig-napping — I dreamed I heard his cry in the room next door. But, suddenly awake, there wasn't any room next door, there was only my prison and beyond it mountains stretching to the ends of the earth.

Another day, and above me the iron ring. It was futile to continue to try, yet I did keep at it, perhaps precisely because it was futile. I stood on that chain and stamped with my other foot, counting out a rhythm at the same time.

What tended to happen was rather than get far with opening up or dislodging the ring, I dragged myself along closer to the wall with each jab of my foot on the chain, so that it was necessary to return to my starting position every few minutes.

I kept at it for what must have been half an hour or so and then I heard a hum some distance off. I stopped the stamping, stood still, listened. For some unaccountable reason the sound of an approaching motor caused me to hope . . . when fear might have been the appropriate response. Fear or dread.

I heard wheels grind to a halt on the dirt. By that time I was arranging myself, standing with my back to the wall, regretting my shit, my piss, the stench. It's true, I was embarrassed. I wanted nothing more than to present my best face to the new arrivals. You get that way, chained.

The little door opened. It was my friend! It was Tony!

Why do I write 'my friend', without irony even? Was that how he appeared to me at that instant?

The horror of it!

He was dressed as before, except, because the weather had turned cold with the sky remaining overcast, he was wearing a snappy, zip-up, black leather jacket, soft. An expensive little number.

'How have you been keeping?' A voice to reward my optimism, almost friendly.

I was unable to form a word in reply. The machinery wouldn't function. Instead I let out some ill-defined noise, like that of a dying animal.

Tony stood there, half-way between the open door and where I was attached to the wall. His hands were on his hips.

'Still alive?'

Shit, wasn't that a great joke of a thing to say?

Did I laugh? To please the bastard?

'We *need* you alive.'

They wanted me alive! Pitiful the succour I took from that. After so long on the planet it was enough to be '*needed* alive'. The question of 'what for' never entered my mind. It doesn't, you see. It's not like that, the mind, it has switches inside there which it throws in its own way. Under pressure they are difficult to control, you try and isolate them from activation and, against your will, the mind itself flicks them on and off. It's terrible.

Me standing there weeping, loud sobs. My body shaking with emotion.

Tony, legs apart, lighting up a cigarette, watching me over his fingers. I'd picked up every detail of that, the packet of Camels, him tapping it the way they do, the slender white cylinder slipping out. And the lighter, one of those gas-filled, throw-away jobs some slob inflicted on the globe.

'Can't have you fading away.'

Fading away! Of course I was fading away.

I tried to say, to tell him that I couldn't take much more. Again no words.

The other voice, the educated one, it shouted something from outside. I didn't catch what it was.

I'd considered how the other man liked to keep out of sight. There had been moments of fantastic dreaming in which I turned these two against each other after first wooing Tony over to my side, making him see that with me he was on to a better thing.

I had money, I could promise him riches he wouldn't need to share.

Though through the filth he couldn't connect with what I had to offer. Not through the tears, the sobs, the stubble on my face, the weeping sores that had begun to colonize my body.

He said: 'There's a bit of clerical work for you, sport.'

Sport, he had actually called me sport! Again.

Clerical work! The words whirling about inside my brain, and me seeing, hearing, nothing but promise in them.

'We want you to sign on the dotted line.'

He hadn't made another move, but stood there, legs apart as before, occasionally the hand that held the cigarette would be brought to his face, he'd take a drag, then it would return to hang loose by his side. Like a method actor.

I managed three words: 'The dotted line,' I repeated.

'That's right, a letter, sport.'

If it was a letter, part of me registered the fact that it would be used to prove I was still alive. But the other part of me only desired to please the nice man. I reckoned I'd do anything for that.

He dropped the stub of the cigarette on to the cement floor, ground it out with the toe of his shoe. It was a contemplative action, Tony took his time about it. Then he reached into his back pocket and brought out an envelope.

'To your near and dear ones.'

I wanted to read it, believing that simply by doing so I would break out of the isolation and a part of me might sail off through the ether like you see the Holy Spirit rising in some Renaissance paintings, taking the form of a white bird.

'Only thing is how do I stop you playing tricks, you know what I mean?'

Tricks! No, I didn't know, I couldn't understand what he was trying to say to me.

'Ripping it up, that kind of smart arse caper, Mr Holt.'

I didn't respond. The idea that I could have a trick left! It was too much.

Curious, at that juncture I began taking control of myself. Warning voices were nattering away inside my head. This is the main play they are preparing, the voices said. Collect your wits, Essington, concentrate on the moment.

But being too far gone, it was really useless for me to try.

Tony was taking a sheet of paper from the envelope, he was opening it out. That would be the letter. Christ, it seemed so professional, the folds just right, neat.

'I tell you what I reckon's the best system for this, sport: why don't I just clip this pen to the paper, so, then slide it in to your cozy corner?'

There was laughter in his cold eyes. Maybe it was supposed to be nice for me to observe it there.

He did just as he'd suggested. He used the woman's stick. Going across to where it was leaning against the far wall as though he'd put it in that particular spot himself. He slid the paper in and as I approached I saw it become discoloured by some of my mess.

'You are a dirty bastard, aren't you? Money pouring out your ears, but a fucking animal, that's what you are inside, sport . . . You know you're a fucking pig, Mr Big-shot Holt.'

I only half listened. My eyes were on the paper, already I was trying to read its message.

What message?

Surely it was blank sheet!

'What am I signing?' I was crouching then, grabbing at the paper.

'Screw about with me, sport, and it'll be your death warrant.'

No smiling in those eyes now.

Later, of course, I realized how it made sense, how it hung together, in fact it was rational what they did. But at that particular moment, all I could make out was that games were being played. And I experienced a surge of indignation at the idea of this Tony thinking me stupid enough to sign a blank sheet of paper.

See, that's how out of it I must have been, believing there was some connection still existing with the regular business practice of our world. Inside my shed! Or inside my head.

I stood up, the paper and the ball-point in my hand. I was laughing at Tony by then, laughing at him standing right over there, so far away, out of reach.

And then I crouched down, flattened the paper with a sweep of my hand. Still laughing, maybe hysterically, I scrawled 'Essington Holt' right across the whole sheet, pressing so hard that the ball-point tore the paper when it reached the end of the word 'Holt'.

Chapter 5

The *Prêt-à-Porter* fashion extravaganza had us gadding about all over town: cocktail parties, dinners, stand-up-and-stare dos of every description, ladies watching each other for signs of decay, us men checking status by counting the stitches in lapels. Mainly the parades were held in three gigantic tents erected in the Jardin des Tuileries down the western end of the Louvre. But there were certain design houses which preferred gilded Second Empire interiors for the display of their wares. Thus we were bussed backwards and forwards between locations, the whole bunch of us pretending to be friends: comparing notes, laughing, chatting, standing still.

Our team was Dawn, Karen and me. Oh, I didn't mind at all: like with Jodie, beauty cannot be denied and I was perfectly content to watch the mannequins strut the cat-walk, to enjoy the colour and texture of the clothes they were wearing, effects of choreography, the lighting. For they were no ordinary parades these, and the competition between houses was fierce; thus there were musicians playing, lights flashing; dancers, jugglers. A jungle of kitsch. And no expense spared. Dazzling, if meaningless. A series of gorgeous acts of reverence to the gods of consumerism. For what we were watching pass before our eyes, cleverly pinned to anorexic dolls, would finish up displayed in stores in Tokyo, Rio, Dallas, at the Galeries Lafayette, at Harrods, in Milan, Berlin, Athens, Helsinki.

I was giving myself over to these decadent multi-sensory delights while, most days, back in the apartment in the Sixteenth, Jodie was attending to Pietro's every need in her clean Midwestern manner. So, for her, going to Makihei's show was a special treat, courtesy of our Dawn Grogan.

Dawn and her girls fascinated me. Back in Nice Farah was

running the shop Dawn and Karen regarded as their business base. She'd been selected by Dawn for the job. I mean, if I'd chosen Farah someone would have blown the whistle, screamed 'sexist'. But Dawn, she could do it, get away with it. Hell!

And then it was Jodie being recruited as an addition to the string. Dawn touching her, watching as she went about her chores with the baby, even assisting. Dawn! What did Dawn care about babies? Yet there she was shoulder to shoulder with Jodie changing diapers as though she had just discovered some lost vocation.

Then came the photographs taken as we stepped out on our way to Makihei's parade. Me suddenly becoming visible all over France.

There's something about invisible wealth, about keeping the secret to yourself. For one thing people treat you better if they don't know. Suddenly, thanks to that barrage of photographers, I was one of the media's people. Mr Megabucks! On the first occasion there had been the line of scarlet Rolls-Royce cars, the chorus of sounding horns. After that, for a couple of days at least — which seems to be the paparazzi's concentration span — the bastards were watching and I'd attract attention if I nicked out to buy a packet of disposable diapers, a tin of baby food. The shots taken were used to fill up holes in the newspapers. During that week of parades it seemed as though every pressman and woman in the world had descended on Paris to catch up with the stars. No doubt that meant I too was well recorded and Essington Holt stories were growing like Jack's beanstalk.

None of which was what Karen and I declared we were about.

Karen has a head for business. She enjoys it. Thus the silk shop, the printing of lengths of fabric, the involvement with Makihei . . . thus bloody near everything.

And me, I possess the raw material: the cash.

Take the Holt money, process it time and again through the Mrs Holt mental faculties and you finish up with compound growth that's more than satisfactory. Karen played with what I had like you'd juggle tennis balls, creating companies registered in the island tax havens of the Pacific, buying chunks of real estate in its myriad forms, bonds and stocks, too. Even our collectable cars accumulated value faster than they used gas.

There were moments when I half tuned in to words like gilts, equities, options, futures and the ubiquitous junk-bond.

And we had art, quite a lot of which I inherited from my aunt, Mrs Fabre. She'd been a collector living on the Côte d'Azur like any sensible rich Australian widow ought to do.

After Aunt's death I continued to pick up the odd picture here and there, adding to the collection in a fairly unspectacular fashion. With me it had been what you might call an interest. That's what you finish up with once necessity flies out the window, you finish up with an interest.

People said: Good old Essington, he's got his art.

Karen found yet another example of my limited world vision in the pictures. I'd whip up to Paris to an auction at the Hôtel Drouot, pick up maybe a small Pissarro drawing, cart it home as a trophy.

'You've heard about real estate, Essington. It's position, position, position, that's what you look for.' She enjoyed lecturing me on stuff like that, it was a game with us which had turned into a ritual within our relationship: the ageing bull with the loose marbles, and the smart young wife.

'Pictures, Ess, it has to be the same, doesn't it?'

'The same?'

'Certain ones you ought to go for.'

'It's not to make money, Blue.' Don't ask me why I called her Blue. 'I couldn't care less about that angle.'

'You can't say that, it's just not true.'

And she was right. Of course I used the money, I enjoyed it. Suddenly to be without my comforts would be unthinkable. Still, I liked to imagine that at least where art was concerned it was the images that grabbed me. That and the surprise of discovering them.

'Ess, if you didn't have the fare, not to mention the spare time, you wouldn't have been to Paris to buy this in the first place.' That was the Pissarro drawing, a peasant girl in an apron sitting under a tree. 'So, why not pick on something big. Take van Gogh for instance, all of a sudden certain business interests go for him for his flowers. They get into the market, set to work on the price, pushing it up, doubling it every few months. They're constructing their own hedge against inflation by putting the price increases over into an area where there can't be too many players. The crowd thins out, Ess, once you reach the fifty-million-dollar range.'

It was true, true if sad.

Maybe I'd be relaxing, back from walking the dog down by the sea, or just sitting in the sun sucking at the cool rim of a glass of rosé: 'Essington, you ought to check out the art index.'

'Art index?'

'Impressionists, Post-Impressionists, modern American, these paintings have done better than three times the S&P 500.'

'The S&P 500!' My mind tried to work it out.

'Standard and Poor, Ess.'

'They wouldn't be poor if they'd kept up, would they? Or standard even.'

'Never mind.'

'Karen, but I do mind!'

'The problem with you,' she went on — the dog and I, we were watching my earnest young wife, paying proper attention as she lectured us on the art index — 'you're a pair, you can't concentrate, you won't concentrate . . . not for more than five minutes.'

The dog wandered off. Hell, why should she put up with abuse when she could be down on the fence talking to the poodle next door?

You could say I was driven to it.

There was more urging on other occasions, Karen keeping at me: 'Think of an artist neglected by the pundits. There's only a certain quantity of money, so, if it's pouring into one area there has to be something else that's being ignored. They pay the premium for a van Gogh . . . who's being left out then? Modigliani, for instance.'

I shook my head: 'Not Modigliani. He's popular, almost too popular.'

'Well, who?'

I said 'There's Gauguin.'

'I don't believe it, but I love Gauguin!'

'It's true, to an extent, say, compared with van Gogh. Gauguin has been out of favour for quite a while, simply because none of the fashion makers have concentrated on him. Also being mad about women hasn't helped, not in our puritan climate . . . the ideologues don't like the idea of physical beauty.'

'Did they ever?' Karen can hit the nail right on the head. But vacantly, as though the thought has come from nowhere.

'All right,' she narrowed her eyes, 'there's Gauguin.'

'But we'd be talking about a great deal of money.'

'What sort of money?' Suddenly she was grinning, knowing I balked at breaking a five-hundred-franc note.

'In dollars,' I said, 'millions.'

'Millions,' she snorted, 'ain't what they used to be.'

'Neither am I, Blue.'

'You'll do me,' she said, rising now to get on with a busy life.

There were times when I almost regretted being a drone: tippling, basking in the sun, hunting through my philosophy for a subject for thought.

How could I know that bidding six million US dollars for a minor Gauguin would cost a finger? And more scar tissue than you'd think a soul could build.

With so many of the people who were anybody in Paris for the fashion parades some keen lad at a leading London auction house decided to stage a star sale. Karen followed it up, secured a catalogue, pressed me into demonstrating interest.

She'd fixed on Gauguin. Impressionists, Post-Impressionists, she reckoned they were the thing. Karen had limited her investment studies to that area. And turned up interesting statistics. Interesting, that is if you don't find this money–art nexus too disquietingly vulgar.

Did I have the constitution for the game? It's a big jump from buying the occasional minor gem to going up a hundred thousand a bid.

I'm not an inflation baby and I've got this old-fashioned notion that somewhere there are a set of real values that have been lost sight of. Some time soon, I believed, would come the day of reckoning.

But maybe that's theology, not economics.

There I was in Paris, photographed but yet to be made famous through the reproduction of that shot on the front cover of the colour weekly.

And doomed to head for the art auction.

First to the viewing the afternoon before sale day.

You can't tell what life's got up its sleeve for you. And that day I wasn't thinking of anything other than the quality of this Gauguin. I'd looked at the reproduction in the catalogue, and liked what I saw. It had those fully pigmented sombre hues which characterize the best of late Gauguin. Judging from the date in the catalogue, 1893, it was a Tahiti or a Papeete painting.

Gauguin set up house with a thirteen-year old girl named Teha'amana in the summer of 1892, round about the time that he was badgering the governor to get him a free passage back to France. I bet the arsehole didn't tell Teha'amana he was plotting his departure. In 1893, May of that year, he and the girl went to Papeete.

The provenance in the auctioneer's catalogue had my picture coming out of a collection in Compiègne, one M. Renouard. The work had been held by the Renouards until the present moment when it was being put up for sale as a result of the family dying out.

How could you ascertain the truth of that? The trick with a provenance is to make it look good and to have everybody dead so that checking is difficult. The vast majority of art works put up for auction have been doing the rounds of the dealers, sometimes for years, value going up each time, real financial settlements made out of the auction room. Every now and then along comes Mr Right who waves his finger in the air and provides the economic story with a happy ending . . . for the dealers that is.

Was I going to be this time around's Mr Right? Or was it true that the work had suddenly been dropped into the ring by some provincial notary acting on behalf of distant and financially impatient relatives of the dead?

The Gauguin, it was beautiful. How he'd gone for those Polynesian women, become obsessed by their natural beauty. For him the islanders were what we all should become.

My Gauguin — that's how I thought of it from the start — was simple: a woman sitting on a beach looking out at the white crests of waves breaking among conical islands. Most of the composition was the back view of the woman, in semi-silhouette against chrome yellow sand. Near her buttocks there was a leaf, a deep red flower, and a conch shell: as though symbolizing her genitalia. A plait of hair had fallen forward over her shoulder and, judging by the position of her elbows she was holding this in her hands. The sea was green turning to a black blue-purple which became also the colour of her hair. Her skin was somewhere between deep gold and mahogany.

As displayed by the British auctioneers the thing shone. Yet it had no frame, instead there was brown paper stuck to the sides of the canvas where it was pulled over the stretcher.

I might have been observed going to the plush rooms that had been selected as a venue for the auction. Certainly I wasn't visible on the day of the sale itself. Instead I put in my bids by telephone from the apartment in the Sixteenth while Dawn and Karen were out watching a parade . . . Kenzo, or Gaultier, Ungaro, Givenchy . . . what's the difference?

It was just me, Pietro and Jodie — the baby making sure we got our money's worth out of Jodie. I shut myself off from their din, rang through to the auction, held the line waiting for my moment. Which was still some time off. They'd instructed me: that was the way you did it. And I'd told them the bids had to remain anonymous. If you're a real collector you don't want *hoi polloi* knowing what you've got, otherwise vulgar little dealers pester you to the grave, hoping you go weak in the head and hand the collection over to them as a gift, or better still, pay them to cart it away.

Half an hour after I'd picked up the phone I offloaded six million US dollars and purchased myself more trouble than it could ever be worth.

When I made it on to the cover of the colour magazine the accompanying article indicated that the journalist had been tipped off that I was the mystery buyer of the Gauguin.

Essington Holt, baby Pietro, Gauguin and all. A real catch.

For someone.

Either I was the catch or it was meant to be the baby.

All that hadn't taken place so long before Tony picked up the paper with my signature scrawled across it off the shed floor. He held it by one corner, between thumb and forefinger.

'You ought to be ashamed, letting yourself slip like this,' he said. Humour, Tony style, delivered in that chilling accent. My one moment of arrogance hadn't fazed him.

Then he said: 'It'll do, sport.' And abruptly walked out of the shed.

There was talking on the other side of the wall, I could hear it as a murmuring; occasionally I thought I picked up a woman's voice as well.

Must that have been the peasant who'd been carrying out her instructions like a zombie?

No way of telling.

The woman saying: 'No!' Repeating it again and again. And a man's voice, raised now. But I couldn't make his words out. There was the chance of it being Italian they were speaking.

So, we were a polyglot lot, were we? Well, maybe not the woman.

Whatever that was worth as knowledge, chances were I wouldn't get the opportunity to use it or to sell it.

That was where I was up to when I saw the man come in through the door. It was the other one this time, and he was holding a shotgun under his arm. He smiled at me as though he was about to offer insurance at a cut rate. Life, or the sort of policy to guarantee comfort in old age.

In what old age?

I was looking at a long face, the sort you might expect to find on a small starved horse waiting on the bare dirt of a knacker's paddock. I didn't like the face, nor the smile, either. And a whole lot of old responses came to me, ways I'd developed for dealing with life. But you don't have much option when someone's holding a shotgun on you. And you think you've heard a woman repeating 'no' outside.

You put two and two together. Well, at least, I did.

So I abused him. Not much to lose, see. I told him there were friends of mine scattered all over the world who wouldn't stop till they were wearing his guts for garters. Maybe I was raving, certainly it wouldn't have been too convincing, the abuse, not out of a derelict like I'd become. Clothes and grooming maketh the man, that's what they reckon.

This cool little bastard wasn't aiming the gun, mind you. He was holding it like the true sportsman he fancied himself to be. Pointing at the stained floor, the twin barrels not so far above the built-up shoe of his game leg.

Acne as a teenager, from the texture of his skin. That morning he'd cut himself shaving in a couple of places! I was sure there was a spot of blood on the collar of the viyella check shirt. Again the waisted hacking jacket.

His hair was neatly brushed, a bit like that of a choirboy, a sense of it still damp from a morning bath.

Something of the child about the man. A great deal of the killer about him as well. That he could stand there like that, gazing at what was left of me, and display no concern for my condition.

I hated him.

I continued raving: the empty threats, promises of retribution.

Then Tony entered. Funny the relationship I'd developed with Tony. It was still there, the bond between us, my wanting to please, needing him to like me, to approve. Possibly delirious, I was feeding Tony with my contempt for the one with the gun. Grinning at him as well, trying to coax him into taking my side.

And Tony calling me 'Essington'.

I couldn't believe it! I was getting somewhere, wasn't I? I tossed my head, confidence growing with each passing minute. While I heaped abuse on the other man, on his skin, his short leg, his fucking voice!

Tony smiling: 'Sure Essington, you and me both.'

It was Tony and me. See? That was how it was going to be.

And the other one simply standing there, taking it, holding on to the shotgun. Of course it didn't occur to me that he was the one with the weapon, therefore he had the power. Hell no, all I could understand was that I'd got between them. Surely there was a rift, and I was going to profit from it.

Next Tony was stepping across in my direction. He was holding out a hand in greeting. I was all the way forward, my feet together, leaning out, supported by the chain still attached to the wall. I was holding out my hand too, eager to seal the pact, to establish the bond of friendship.

Tony's other hand, the left one, was stuck in a back pocket.

That was the way he was, he'd stand like that, just the fingers shoved in. He took my hand in his, a human touch, you can get to long for it.

But then he swung around, his back to me, he was pulling, hard, as though he'd rip my arm out of its socket. The other hand wasn't in the back pocket any more.

He was saying, 'Cover him,' and the barrels of the shotgun came up level with my chest.

I'd just registered the gesture.

It was on the instant when expecting to receive the blast that I felt — my memory says it was secateurs, like the orchardists use — my little finger snipped off like last year's vine growth.

Initially I felt it separate, at the second joint, then I registered the fact.

Next came the agony.

Followed by a blank, by a total blank. Till, waking in the closed shed, there was the dull pulse of pain from the wound beneath a strip of torn cloth that somebody had tied in place to stem the flow of blood.

It was losing the finger that brought back my wits.

Something had needed to do it.

Not that wits are that much use if you're chained to a wall.

Chapter 6

They were professionals, had to be. Subsequent, albeit inexpert, self-investigation revealed I'd received an injection in the arm; that was the only explanation I could come up with for the prick mark and sense of bruised tissue. At first I thought this must have been the administration of something to knock me out, but that wouldn't make sense, wasn't logical. The finger had come off with the patient in full possession of his senses, so why render me unconscious afterwards? And then I figured it must have been an antibiotic of some kind, probably long lasting, just to make sure I didn't die of blood poisoning. Hell, I was the goose, wasn't I? The one that could lay a golden egg. When the time came to cash me in they'd be expected to show their prize live and well . . . show it from a safe distance. Then we'd take the final walk to the slaughterhouse.

Don't call me pessimistic.

The woman came and went, quicker now than before, eyes still averted, shoving the tray across no man's land, then bolting. Was there evidence that she'd become less happy in her work?

I'd abandoned trying to force the ring to which I was attached; I'd more or less abandoned everything. Most of the time I lay against the wall, shivering, letting myself vanish into the fever that had taken hold. It was almost pleasant to become like that: head slumped, chin caught on my shoulder, the workings of my mind losing track of themselves while hunting about in their own secret corridors. Periods of peace. Possibly a form of self-defence for a brain casting about for explanations, envisaging outcomes, continually reassessing my chances of getting through the business alive.

My chance of surviving? Reason came down on the side of death. I would die, nothing surer. Probably that was what society wanted anyway, because it's neat. And when I was found, dissected and stuffed in a freezer, or whole in a culvert, wouldn't all the press photographs on the files of the newspapers which had bothered to follow the movements of the Australian multi-millionaire, wouldn't they then come in handy?

I couldn't work out exactly how the journalists had got on to the identity of the mystery buyer of the Gauguin nude. But the thing was that they had. Maybe one of the employees of the auctioneers, or an insurance man . . . they'll do that in insurance in the same way as they'll lift information off the files for thieves to know where to look. Generally I don't carry insurance, certainly not on paintings. But with the Gauguin I'd taken out a cover at least until I got it home. That, I expect, had been an act of cowardice on my part, but never before had I spent so much money on an object of such diminutive size — or on anything. It frightened me to have done so. I'd arranged the insurance with a reputable company whose down-at-mouth representative had been hovering about in the wings all through the sale day and after.

Chained, convinced I was in line for a premature death, the exact details of who had leaked the information of my purchase to the press should have seemed of little importance.

What my mind returned to all the time though was the fact that the information *had* got out. Because it was positive proof I was loaded.

There had to have been someone hanging about, knowing details of my life. Such as, that I'd spent time in the apartment on the end of a telephone bidding blind for a Gauguin.

X number of days after my finger had come off, while dull pain still throbbed at the joint, and sharper spasms shot up my arm at regular intervals, I was blessed with another visit from my captors. I guess by then I'd totally lost understanding of the passage of time, even of when it was to become light, when dark. But my impression that it was early morning proved correct. They were wearing working togs this time, the pair of them swinging straight into it, into business.

'Right Mr Holt, sport.' Always that facetious edge when Tony used my name.

The other one, now dressed in a boiler suit, stood at a distance and pointed the shotgun in my direction, on the offchance that there were tricks left in me. His short leg stuck out at an angle, sort of comic-grotesque. He'd cut himself shaving again; there was a wee triangle of paper tissue stuck to the spot.

Unsteady hand, I reckoned.

Padlocks were undone, chains fell loose, every one of them.

Tony took me by the scruff of the neck, steered me across the shed floor, out of the way of the mess I'd made and through the open door. I stood in the blessed outdoors, blinking at a clear day's brightness, at blue sky, seeing even a solitary bird up there, flying as if on a mission.

'Strip.' That came from the small man who was keeping the gun at the ready. Still the phony posh voice but a brittle tone to it.

With numb hands I set to undoing buttons, unzipping; getting the order wrong, falling over, mumbling. Pitiful stuff, perhaps, but then there wasn't anybody there to display pity.

Outside that shed was a wide levelled area on the far side of which two cars were parked: a Ford van, possibly the one in which I'd been transported in the first place; and a pale blue Audi Quattro that looked as though it had seen better days. There was no other building, not the stone house I'd imagined to be close by, the place where the woman should have lived. Nothing. The shed was set within an area defined by a chain wire fence with three strands of barb running along the top. We appeared to be on the crest of some hill with the land falling away in three directions. In the fourth, up behind the shed, there was a ridge running away level with where we were standing. The enclosure had two gates: one leading off that way, along the ridge; the other straight in front, pretty much in line with the shed's doors.

So, I wondered, as I removed the last of my clothes, where had the woman come from, bringing that tray of food each day?

Only a part of my mind addressed itself to the question, the rest was concentrating on doing as it was told. Tony still had that power over me. Even though I was, by then, conscious of hating him, of wanting nothing but the revenge I had promised myself at the start of my incarceration: I would kill the bastards, but slowly. True fulfilment of that resolution would be to cut his fingers off, one at a time, and to watch them fall. There had even been moments when I'd imagined each digit wriggling on the ground like the tail shed by a lizard escaping predators.

Yet I was taking off my clothes, and then standing, dressed in nothing other than the blood stained rag tied about my finger's stump.

Instructed to bend forward, I allowed a bucket of ice cold water to be thrown over me. Then another. 'Can't have you looking less than beautiful, can we?

That was Tony again, he was the talker all right. The other man remained tight-lipped: your average still-waters-run-shallow type of a fucker.

The water was a shock. After the dousing I was thrown a stained striped towel. Funny the way the mind will fix on a thing like that, on the orange and green stripes of a towel. Watchful, I dried myself. It was dawning on me that while clearly I remained in a hopeless position, at least it was a better one. Or is that one of those absurdities the philosophers play about with? Can hopelessness come in grades: good, better, best?

I willed my mind to pull itself together, to regain some control, to consider. Consider for instance the twin barrels of the shotgun! They were a fact.

It must have been true that me dead would represent total failure for Tony and his little pal — if, that is, I was to be swapped for a ransom. And if they couldn't afford to kill me just yet, how would they go about stopping me heading off into those beckoning hills?

The gate nearest me was shut, but the other one? Surely I could outrun a man with a short leg. Which left Tony. Well, a fight hand to hand, it would be worth a go. The physical, that was what they'd always said I was good at.

But then my mind drifted away from the possibility, it just sort of wandered.

Tony grinned at me. I grinned back. I was dry, naked. It was weird, like a death camp with me the only inmate.

I finally broke and ran.

My thinking had been right: no shooting. They wanted me alive. I was heading for the gate beyond the shed, the one that gave on to the track running along the ridge. The only problem was that it was closed, and there was a man standing there, on the inside. He was watching me running at him, naked! I expect I was so out of it I didn't even bother to change direction but simply put my head down, charged like a bull.

Calm as you like the man watched me, a flickering intelligence in his dark eyes. He was waiting. Next he let me have it, a blow into the stomach as he stepped to one side the way a toreador might. I buckled and fell.

They dressed me in fresh clothes, Tony making a game of it, saying 'that's nice, sport,' and 'just wait till we get this buttoned up straight, won't you?' Acting the fairy. Well, somehow it went with the deck-hand eyes: Mr Frilly Knickers crossing the equator.

I was bundled into the back seat of the Audi, my hands and ankles tied. The man who'd belted the wind out of me got in at my side. Tony was going to be driving the van so the little shit with the built-up shoe slipped behind the Audi's wheel, putting himself where I could study his neck. Dream of breaking it.

We were off.

My minder was more the peasant woman's type. He wore a pair of dark green, velvet cord trousers, a white shirt buttoned right up but with no tie, and an old suit coat over the top. He was big, and solid. Sitting there I sensed the hardness of his muscles, as well as picking up the disinterested fashion in which he regarded the actions of the other players.

Almost, one might have thought, an aristocratic unconnectedness.

He was too much for me.

As was the silence within the cabin of the Audi. I felt as though I was being taken to my execution, and very aware that there was no reason to mistrust the hunch. We were missing the priest, that was all.

The Audi Quattro's four-wheel drive got us, sure-footed, down a narrow track out of the mountains. We stayed on that till we came to a junction with a made road, the centre lines and edges marked. Built-up shoe swung right. I was taking note of all this, as best I could, trying to fix detail in my mind: bridges we passed, perched villages away in the middle distance hanging over valleys where melting snow had filled the beds of streams with frothing water. I tried to remember direction signs, place names, distances, the nature of the vegetation. Yet, my concentration was poor. I was feverish still, trembling. I'd take in some detail and the next minute find it gone. I'd fix on the name of the place, repeat it, only to have it evaporate. And the light was burning holes in my wounded brain. It didn't escape me that they wouldn't care what I remembered of our route. So, what could that mean other than they were confident I'd never try to retrace the journey?

The dumb bastard sitting at my side was watching the country slip past the car window like it was interesting for its beauty and for nothing else.

Interesting!

His near ear was misshapen, the shell of it came down half-way and then looked as if it had been sliced off at an oblique angle, so the lobe wasn't there at all. Looking more carefully, I observed that this must in fact have been the result of a knife fight because there was the indication of a scar running on the same angle across the man's cheek.

Funny, I kept that ear detail in my memory but lost the directions of our route.

Later in the journey there were moments when my fellow passenger came to life. They were preceded by some remark from the driver. Italian speak. Then a hand would grab the back of my neck, push me forward and down so all I could see was my bare feet and the grubby carpeted floor between them. The fingertips biting into my flesh; I could sense the pleasure they derived from giving pain.

It was a long drive, taking several hours. I judged it as best I could by the car's clock, the only problem being that the thought of doing that didn't strike me till we had been on the road a while.

Chapter 7

I guess, seeking escape into other moments, I drifted off. My mind kept on throwing up images of the people with whom I'd shared my recent life. As though I needed to visit them once more in the hope that the real nature of our relationship could be made clear by doing that. Was there some purpose in our existences and a reason why the way we lived had been modified by *this* friendship, by *that* animosity.

Dawn and I had got along all right. There was ribbing, sure, her getting at me for what she regarded as sexist attitudes, me setting up those situations because her ideological purity was like a red rag to a bull. Still, we seemed to have the same taste in women, which was something. Only I suspected that Dawn was the one elected by the gods to collect the cherry each time. I was married. Even happy to be so. And disinclined to do anything that might upset the happy home.

Which isn't to say that beauty doesn't interest me: middle aged Essington watching life and its potent forces set like the sun over a personal horizon.

There are times, even when I'm not on the way to my execution, when I'd reckon beauty is everything.

I never make a point of censoring my reactions. Girls on the beach, the dog Desdemona crouching, a horse rolling in sand, dolphins leaping — they do things for me.

Farah: Dawn's all-enduring girl Friday. I could watch Farah for hours, her brown eyes, the sense of olive skin turning a grey blue around them, the dark curve of her eyebrows, a nose of such a shape as might be found in Egyptian tomb paintings of dancing girls. She was a constant pleasure.

Dawn knew how Farah's magic worked on me, and she played with that fact.

But then so did Farah herself.

Perhaps sexual responses are the beginning of politics.

What I'd really found hard to take was Dawn's growing interest in astrology, and the way in which she tried to inflict it on the rest of us. What it amounted to was predestination theory. Yet, under the guise of astrology, predestination seemed to have taken on a new respectability.

Poor little Pietro really got the treatment. Once we had adopted the baby into our house there were charts drawn up by Dawn, predictions made, it was discussed what he had on the cusp.

On the cusp for Christ's sake! I don't even know what 'cusp' means.

Dawn worked on Karen as well, trying to get her to follow the stars in her buying and selling on the financial markets. As was consistent with her character, Karen took it all in when it was given — the propitious moments, the prophecies of failure and success — smiled as though it was interesting, then chucked it out with the bath water. The result, ever increasing wealth. Because instead of gobbledegook Karen looked at what she thought to be general trends, examining ways the collective psyche of the investment community responded to economic conditions. Then she would examine alternative strategies, weigh them up, try one. She claimed you could rely on the fact that the majority of people were wrong most of the time. Yet the one time she turned her economic attention to art she went with the mob. Strange that.

When we were together down there in the south, Dawn, Farah, Karen and myself, there wasn't anyone other than me to block this astrology garbage of Dawn's. And there was Pietro to egg her on, just by the fact of his existence.

He was born in April. In fact at the time of my abduction he was just past a much-celebrated first birthday. His precise date of birth was invented since his entry into this world had passed unrecorded in the stone jungles of Naples. Dawn fixed on the eleventh, it was a number she claimed to like.

'I would have thought you'd go for sixty-nine,' I quipped.

'Very fantastic, Essington, months don't have so many days.' And then she grinned, the expression telling me that I wouldn't have a clue.

*

Driving towards my death in the pale blue Audi, thinking about people, events, this peasant arsehole sitting totally relaxed at my side. And nothing I could do because my hands were tied, literally . . . I was heading for where? I found other stuff inside my mind as well. I suppose some kind of automatic scanning was going on in there, random searching, a part of me wanting to know the why, and the how.

Suddenly there was a visual moment, but as though at the periphery of my vision. I had a sequence of pictures of it, out of focus, imprecise. I'd glimpse them, try to go back, to arrest an image in the frame, but with each attempt at grabbing hold of these fragments they'd slide away out of my grasp.

There was a sheet of glass in there somewhere, as a part of the illusive picture.

Back in the real world again. The car was coming down out of the mountain ridges and now the road crossed a valley with orchards, and stock grazing in neat fenced paddocks. The grass was extraordinarily green, lush, like the pastures of heaven. Even touches of other colours, pure mauves and yellows where wild flowers grew.

Next in my uncertain memory there was a face behind the remembered pane of glass. Then my mind's eye was zooming back, getting a long shot, setting the glass into the frame of a door!

The Paris apartment in the Sixteenth Arrondissement is set on a narrow street that heads south from the Avenue Paul Doumer — the curious thing is that I've never bothered to find out who Paul was or what he did. Still his street exists, and so does the one on which I live when in Paris. If you walk on down past the apartment block you finish up close to Radio France, and over the road are the murky waters of the Seine, where, in better times, I'd fished for life's debris with Makihei, the designer.

When I say a narrow street I mean a narrow street.

Wait a minute! In the Audi heading for my execution I was catching other information stored away in the Essington Holt mind, I was getting snaps of one of the photographers who'd been standing out in front of the apartment that day I'd emerged, baby in my arms, to get into one of the line-up of scarlet Rolls-Royces. I had this camera in my mind's eye, and behind it a long face. Sure, the face was half obscured and generalized, it could have been any face.

But could the built-up shoe have been any shoe? I tried for the texture of the skin, couldn't get it, the hair was nondescript, shit coloured. No joy in that either. But I had it, the shoe. And, not connected though, I had this pane of glass set into . . . yes it was the security door of my apartment block. And there was somebody on the other side of the glass, inside the building. I could pick up the idea of a face, of eyes. An expression in the eyes, as though the face knew something of what was about to happen.

But surely they were memories from different days.

'Not long now.' It was our driver's plum-in-mouth voice.

Not long now to what?

I didn't need to know the answer to that one. Yet the Holt mind went for it, for the fact that time was running out. I was resisting acceptance of a truth, wasn't I? And trying to escape, wanting to travel back to the street, to the face, to the photographer with the built-up shoe.

I dropped my head on to my chest, pressed my eyes closed, concentrated. Nothing more came, no linking image. And even the detail I had already managed to conjure up with so much certainty began to dissolve.

My eyes were open again to see us in the Audi climbing up the far side of that fertile valley, going in among more mountain tops. There was snow capping the farthest peak. The driver was nattering in Italian to my companion in the back, talking fast like a machine gun.

He got monosyllabic responses, grunts.

And in my mind another day recalled; there he was again, the man with the built-up shoe, camera raised! This time I was looking out the window of a cab while arriving at the building where the art up for auction was on display. The lens was aimed at me! Of course, at the time, I hadn't made anything of that, assuming the press, or at least some stringer desperate for a shot to sell, was working shutters on a percentage basis. You have a viewing of art works that are going to get up into the millions, so someone who is somebody is pretty likely to chance along to take a peep. A stringer's celebrity shots will always find a buyer.

So I'd been photographed as well in case I turned out to be a somebody. Well, in the end I did, didn't I? More fool me. I was that somebody who bought the Gauguin, who made a big man of himself. Who got kidnapped for his trouble.

A reluctant big man. It had been Karen's idea. She couldn't leave it alone. Suddenly I thought that. I was tense, and sitting in the back of the car with Mr Half-an-ear; I thought that it was all her fault. She'd ripped that much money out of the stock market, wanted to dump it in something solid enough to ride out an anticipated period of uncertainty she'd been going on about for some time. Bloody Karen. Firstly she sold before the crash of October 1987. Then she bought back in, at the bottom, even got the day right to do it on. She'd ridden blue chip stocks up on a slow rise over the following nine months, only to sell again just before a new series of moves to drive up interest rates.

That was the background to me sitting by the phone in the Paris apartment, bidding for a Gauguin.

That, I believed, was why I was to be killed.

Mr Rich man, they were going to swap me for parcels of money, weren't they? Hand in the corpse for the exchange.

The van came along. It passed us, we passed it. Some kind of a signal, I guessed. My mind sharp enough for that sort of connection by then.

We swung off the made surface, up a side road. I got the impression that the van had kept right on going straight ahead. For us it was a steep climb, maybe a kilometre, perhaps more. Then we pulled up beside a battered ex-army jeep with two men standing beside it. They looked to be more like the kind of friends you'd expect my mate in the back might have. Italians, I would have thought, at home in their own mountains. It was getting more and more bizarre, what with all these people.

When I'd worked out that I'd received a shot of penicillin to keep the blood from getting infected from the amputation, I'd decided I was among professionals. I hadn't been able to establish if I should welcome the conclusion or not. Now, looking at these two lounging against the dust-covered jeep, counting up the squad involved in the operation to do whatever it was that they had planned, I was starting to wonder. My notion was that professionals don't spread it around so much.

But, if amateurs . . . then what? Could I expect to end my days in the middle of a total fuck-up?

Suddenly I had it!
Behind the glass back there in the Sixteenth Arrondissement, it was two heads that I'd seen, one looking at me and the other turned away. The one turned away had been Pietro. Jodie was staring, her face a blank. A beautiful oval on which time had yet to write its message.

We waited. Christ only knows what we waited for. The two men with the jeep took turns to saunter about, each time returning to their position leaning against the vehicle's side as though it was ordained that they should be there thus. We three stayed in the Audi, the driver drumming his fingers on the steering wheel, and once adjusting the rear-vision mirror so that he could examine himself, run spread fingers through his hair, work his facial muscles.

One of the men outside our car reached in through the rear gate of the jeep and drew out a rifle with telescopic sights. That triggered a spasm in my stomach muscles. I stretched out my legs to relieve the tension, received a grin from the man at my side. But not one of reassurance, not by any means. There was a certain amount of showy aiming of the weapon, the barrel waving about, pointing at things at random. The clip was removed, checked. As a rifle it looked something more serious than the kind of thing you take out after rabbits, but I had no idea of the actual calibre, or the make. What does it matter anyway? You're dead, you're dead.

Shit!

The driver's fingers continued drumming on the wheel. He flicked on the radio, a few bars of electric music; the man next to me coughed, the radio was switched off.

That was when the van came up the track and joined us. Tony leaping out, all smiles, lots of hand slapping. His eye alighting on the rifle, he was reaching and one of the men handing it across. There was more aiming, laughter. Next Tony lighting a cigarette, offering the Camel packet around, then in through the window to my companion who took up the offer.

Our driver sighed, pressed in the lighter, passed it over when it popped. Smoke inhaled, exhaled. Tony, more animated than I'd seen him before, louder too. I hadn't had the pleasure of observing him at his social play, had I? Not going full bore like he was then.

It struck me how he avoided my eye. In a way, clutching at straws, I took heart from that, there were doubts in the southern Africa mind — beneath the bumptious front, perhaps even misgivings?

Curious how, with death coming, even to know that someone will end up uneasy is a source of satisfaction.

'Your turn, but keep it cool, casual.' Tony addressed the man with the built-up shoe. Then some Italian spoken.

The men who'd been leaning against the jeep walked across to the rear door on my side, yanked it open, pulled me out. I wasn't so much standing as suspended between the pair of them, both big men. They needed to be.

They made jokes which I presumed were at my expense, and laughed, laughed out loud. Next there'd be thigh slapping like ham actors on a music hall stage. One, who was balding on top and sporting a pigtail made out of what grew at the sides and back of his head, held out a finger, whipped it across my throat as you might a knife. Jesus Christ, they found that hilarious . . . except the Audi driver, who was already backing to turn his car around and head off down the track.

Tony was lighting a cigarette off the stub of the first. I was close enough to get a look at his eyes, the pupils, they were like pinheads. There was something more powerful than nicotine trolling through his system, that was for sure.

I tried to keep my thoughts off the subject of death.

My mind picture returned to the glass panel in the security door of that block in the Sixteenth, seeing there the back of Pietro's head, the wispy dark hair growing on it, forming ringlets at the nape of his neck. I was trying to make something out of the expression in Jodie's eyes.

I got it! She was retreating. She'd been approaching the door with the child in her arms, and I was walking across from the far side of the street where a taxi had dropped me. As I'd headed for the entrance there she was, Jodie holding the baby. Him facing me then. Jodie had been saying something, pointing. I assumed it was a greeting, even surprise that we had chanced to bump into each other at that moment, either side of the security door.

Then her expression changed, she was moving away and Pietro was watching me, his head over her shoulder.

That final look Jodie wore, what had it meant? Had she spotted the danger?

Because it was at that point I got a total blank. After it not so much as the hint of an image on which to attempt a reconstruction of the action.

Chapter 8

I could see a black sedan parked on the grass maybe four hundred metres away. Was there a man standing beside the driver's door?

I don't know why but most of my mind was occupied with the incongruity of the sky, with its clarity, the quality of blue up there. You can't mix that colour with pigments, it's to do with light.

There were even a pair of puffy white clouds hovering, like in a story-book illustration; they were stationary and dissolving back into the blue.

I was thinking in overdrive. And, funnily, a lot of happy thoughts. Was it just a mind trying to get away, out of death's firing line? Not so much thinking really, as registering things like the deep purple–brown markings on clover leaves outside the car window.

Tony wasn't there with us.

The others had been playing let's-not-talk-to-Essington.

After all I was only going to die.

There was the man with the built-up shoe, the Italian bandit type with the butchered ear, and me. It was just the three of us. Where had the rest of them gone to in the end? Well, I'd asked that question, and got no satisfaction.

The black sedan sat across those four hundred metres, its headlight reflectors throwing out twin disks of silver light. The sun was catching on its windscreen, reflecting off it as if off a mirror.

We had driven for less than half an hour after leaving the place where we'd met up with the jeep. Most of that journey had been on a made surface. Then we'd swung off down a side track, across a river and up to a ridge on the far side. There we'd turned in at a gate and driven on to low fertility pasture land, rocky with yellow-white stones showing through the dirt.

The black sedan — I couldn't think of it any way than as a hearse.

My companions were chatting in Italian while we sat in the car, the one with the built-up shoe had his hands busy. I couldn't see because of the seat, but I suspected he was playing with his pistol.

Or maybe with his dick. You read about people getting killing and fucking confused.

We'd had quite a display of weaponry before setting out on the last leg of the trip to that field. They'd been pulled out of the back of the jeep: two more high-powered rifles which seemed to belong to the Italian types; and some handguns, short-barrelled jobs, looking black and mechanical, altogether different from your standard mind picture of a pistol. Less romantic too. Tony and my driver had fiddled about with these, filling and ramming a clip home into the butt, working the safety catch, squinting along the rudimentary sights. They stowed them away for future use.

On our drive to the rocky pasture my companion in the rear seat had kept a rifle between his knees, barrel pointing upwards. He had both hands wrapped around it, as though in the attitude of prayer.

The door on my side of the Audi was opened by the Italian. It was as if he was being polite, having alighted first, come around; even a hint of a bow. Then he stood back and pointed the gun at my head.

'I expect he'd like you to get out,' said our driver. The toff's voice with the rough memory of something less desirable still hanging in behind.

I swung my roped ankles out to the side, stood on the sparse pasture, straightened up.

Blood circulated.

The barrel of that gun seemed to be trying to tell me something so I turned around, faced away from it, not wanting to know. Next it was pressing into the back of my head. I went where it pushed me, which was bending over the bonnet of the car. I had my eyes shut and was waiting for the sound of the discharge. Instead, the rope between my ankles was cut and my legs came free.

A car door slammed.

'Good,' said that affected voice.

I straightened up, all too aware of how you want to keep on living even knowing you're about to die, even understanding the certainty of it. You'd think there'd be a point where you'd simply throw in the towel, say it had been fun, goodbye all. I couldn't do that.

Again I registered the blue up there in the sky, and wanted to stay in its world, feeding off sensation, getting with the brilliance and the warmth of life.

'This is where you do it right or you do it wrong, Holt.'

I turned to the man. He seemed smaller than before. It made me mad, just for an instant, him being short like that. And not much meat either. Take away the advantage of the guns, of there being the pair of them, armed, and I would have been able to pull him apart with my bare hands, like he was a roast chicken.

Yet that burst of anger and resentment was so short lived. My mind had made the decision: think positive. Positive just then was three birds hopping across the ground a few metres away, and cheeping; it was the breeze I felt on my face; it was the sky's colour being a metaphor, standing for infinity.

Built-up shoe had the pistol in his hand, pointing at me. Did he look nervous, at last? I reckoned probably he did. And to the degree in which I could see that in him I felt more confident of my chances, whatever they were.

'You're being exchanged. Kind friends are waiting for you over there.' He waved the gun in the direction of the black car.

I wasn't so sure I believed in the idea of kind friends; I don't know but maybe I'd got paranoiac tied up in the shed, perhaps I'd lost all notion of the possibility of their existence.

I repeated the word he'd used. 'Exchanged?' I said.

'That's correct. Think of it as redistribution of wealth. Sometimes extreme measures must be taken to exact justice.'

Oh, funny bugger! With his fruity vowels.

I shut his voice out, listened instead to the natural sounds: the water running in the river we'd crossed not so far before entering the field, and the general background noise of small birds calling to each other. I watched the last traces of the twin clouds vanish from the sky. Or were they new ones, appearing only to vanish again? There was the sun's heat on my back, I savoured it, calculating I was going to be cold a long time.

Not to mention worm eaten.

Suddenly Built-up shoe pointed his nasty-looking pistol at the sky I loved. And he fired.

'Walk,' he commanded.

I walked.

My hands were crossed and tied at the front. I moved awkwardly, unnaturally, with them like that. I knew the Italian would have me in the crossed hairs of his sights. And every muscle in my body was waiting for the crack, the thump of the first bullet finding its target. I guess I walked slowly.

The figure that had been standing beside the black car was coming towards me. Nothing familiar that I could make out. Only that it was a he, dressed in sports jacket, slacks, a tie.

Something caught my attention out at the corner of my vision, a rabbit at the end of the field; it had propped stiff on its back legs, head up, sniffing the air — maybe wondering about the shot it had heard. It stayed like that for an amazingly long time then dropped forward and hopped cautiously into the cover of the undergrowth.

We met in the middle, this man and I.

And he started talking at me very quickly, English with a strong French accent: 'Follow your instructions, trust me Essington Holt. Do what they tell you to do. Now you must walk back.'

I couldn't think of a response. I didn't know this man from a bar of soap. Yet, I was so screwed up in my perceptions that I'd done a mind-about-face: suddenly I wanted to believe again, wanted some connection with the human race. And longed for Karen to be there, anywhere, gently mocking; yet present, and loving me at the same time.

My mind, filled with static! Confusion. Then I knew tears were welling in my eyes. I turned, started out on the long walk back.

'They know now that you are the genuine article . . . you have been identified.' God, he was a chilly bastard this little guy with the bad complexion. And I was hanging on his every word. Because I was seeing how it was possible I could live. All I needed to do was be good, to obey instructions.

Oh, I would be good.

'This time it's the exchange. We walk together.' Hell, he *was* nervous now. I could see it written over his face like a rash. Beads of sweat as well, lips quivering as he talked. Yet that tutored voice staying steady, as though he'd swallowed a tape recorder.

Off I went again. With a gun a few inches away from my shoulder blades.

The Frenchman in the sports coat, he must have returned to his car, for he was now carrying a suitcase in one hand, and there was a large rectangular parcel held awkwardly in the other.

I heard the man with the built-up shoe, his breath, coming sharp, loud, like he'd been running. Wheezy, maybe he was an asthmatic? It registered because my mind was getting clearer by the minute now we were close to the moment. To my moment. And inside me a rediscovered alertness, nerves tensing, eager to respond to action.

Then there were the three of us, together, my kidnapper standing off a couple of steps, the pistol aimed level in his clasped hands.

'Open it up,' he insisted.

The man from the black sedan knelt down, unlocked the catch with a key, opened the bag wide, began pulling out bundles of bank notes and tossing them so they piled up around the built-up shoe itself.

'Perhaps,' he asked, 'you would like to count these?' Almost a sneer in the voice. Cool, Jesus!

He was a neat-looking man, average height, average all over I guess. Short-cut hair. But wasn't he in control of himself? Not fazed.

And the breath was coming through the kidnapper's throat with more difficulty, he was sucking after it. Well fuck him, I remembered the trip in the van, that gag, the fear of choking.

'Are you trying to be funny?' This was a new, a wild anger in my handler. He was cracking up. So was the accent.

The French voice: 'I am simply telling you that you may count them, three million American dollars, as requested.'

The tone, you'd have thought it was a legitimate business transaction.

It was clear there was a problem with the money, that Built-up shoe wanted to count it, yet he didn't want to waste time. Not with being so close to the fulfilment of his plan.

'And here is the painting.' That man might use a tone like that in a boardroom.

'Let me see.' The wild excited note still there. Next thing sucking for air again.

The Frenchman ripped paper from the Gauguin's surface. I saw the back view of the Polynesian woman.

I didn't think anything.

Believing myself about to die, as I had, those material things seemed to be of no account.

Suddenly there was a void. We were standing in the middle of nothing. What was to be done? Details were not quite as they should be. My captor felt it. How many hands did he have? He turned the pistol on the Frenchman, checked with a thumb that the safety catch was off.

'I don't think you should dishonour this agreement.' That was the response his action received from my saviour. 'If you pull that trigger you will be dead at the same instant, you are covered you see. Good plan, friend, but not perfect. Now, take your money, we do not want people to be killed . . . and it's my job to return this gentleman alive, no matter what. So, take what you have and leave. Otherwise, I promise you a blood bath.'

'You're bluffing, we've checked the area . . . you couldn't have known where the meeting was to be.'

Falling apart.

The Frenchman, relaxed: 'You can believe that I am not a fool. How could I come here to die? Ask yourself that. I would not. Now take your money, the painting. Put the revolver away. There is your friend by the blue car, he is still looking through his sights; I think that's enough to protect you. But, remember, a blood bath, I promise.' Now, assisting my kidnapper, he picked up the painting and handed it to him. In the same gesture snatching the pistol from his hand.

In Italian, a command, screamed.

The Frenchman: 'That's wise, tell them not to shoot. And now I must explain to you how you're our safe passage: you will come with me back to the car.' The pistol was pressed into the back of the small man's head.

'Move quickly,' the Frenchman said, 'drop the painting and that bag.'

A thousand years of silence, stillness, uncertainty.

There was a burst of fire followed by another.

I spun around just in time to see the Italian slide down the front of the Audi, then fold. He was still for most of a minute before a hand flapped out as though waving farewell to this vale of tears.

At the black car — it was a big Citroën estate — there was the proof of what had been said at the exchange. A man with an assault rifle was scanning the hills with binoculars. He didn't stop doing that but said: 'I was watching, he was about to shoot.'

'Others?' the Frenchman asked.

'They're out there, waiting.' That exchange in French.

The next question was put to my recent kidnapper: 'You are making the plans, my friend, what do we do now?' Keeping the pistol on him.

No answer. He was almost choking by then, his face changing colour.

Christ! It was hair-raising getting out of there: driving across the field, expecting the bullets to start raining down at any minute. Me talking ten to the dozen, supplying these guys with what information I had, like the number of my kidnappers, their weapons.

These two blow-ins, they didn't care about the money, or about the painting. I was told that getting me out was the priority. So they'd let the kidnapper limp back across the grass, gather up his spoils, make it to his car.

We watched the Audi turn and head for the gate, then our Citroën had been gunned across the grass to catch up. We followed through as though we were the last guests to leave a country picnic. But keeping close enough to kill the other driver.

Looking back, as on to a jousting field, I could see what looked like a bundle of old clothes lying on the grass where the Audi had been parked. That was my friend with the sliced ear. Gone to meet his maker.

Lucky boy.

Chapter 9

We stuck with the Audi, keeping pace, both cars running along the road side by side.

Not only did we have some chance of safe passage because of our man in the rear seat pointing a military assault rifle at the Audi driver's head, but also, if those two from the jeep were hiding among the trees on the high ground, then that car running at our side was a protective screen.

Nobody chanced a shot. It had hardly registered on my fear-frozen mind but I suppose the other riflemen were under the thumb of the one we'd left dead in the paddock. It could have been that seeing him fall, and more or less everything else failing to go as planned, the young bloods had cut and run.

Still, Tony was around someplace. And God only knew how many other heavies they could have hired to back up their strategy.

Neither car was going all that fast.

'Why don't I just hit him?'

They weren't the first words I'd heard from the man in the back, but they were the first which registered properly on my mind. They dredged me up from a nether world of salvation dreams to the reality of our position. I thought along with him, aloud: 'Yeah, why not? We'd get the painting, the money as well. It would be easy.'

You see: one minute trying to adjust to death as a fact, the next wanting possessions returned. Small wonder the spirits in the sky find us difficult to love.

As though enemies in the wider world had been reading our thoughts a gunshot sounded from somewhere. Our driver's side window shattered. At the same instant the Citroën flattened on its suspension and leapt away from the Audi. There was another shot, a burst of them. I looked around. The man behind me had been hit; he'd fallen sideways, his shoulder oozing blood.

We took a long bend in the road drifting into the gravel on the wrong side, the tail swung out but the front wheels kept their grip, dragged us back on to the tarmac. A tray truck with a stock crate on behind came from nowhere. To miss it we were back into the gravel, then the grass, sliding. The Frenchman was fighting with the wheel, keeping the power on, bringing the car back under control. Our tail swung out to the other side, we swiped a fence post, bounced, got some grip and made it with a bone-crushing thump over a drainage ditch. That brought us back in line again on the road's surface and we were off, heading for God knows where.

'The man in the back . . . ' I said.

'There's nothing to be done. The job is to get you out of here. We'll get him out too . . . sure.'

Did the Citroën have a top speed? It just seemed to keep on winding up! 'Get the gun if you can. In case. Though they have what they came for. And so have I. Only fools would . . . '

' . . . Try a shot, but that's what they just did.'

He passed me a packet of Gauloise, indicating for me to light one for him. I guessed it must be nicotine for nerves—medicinal. I did as instructed.

He smiled. 'Well, Mr Holt?' Then a mouthful of exhaled smoke scenting the air.

We were flying, close to two hundred kilometres an hour. There had to be something special about the car. It was only later that I discovered how special.

The rifle was a French military FA-MAS, one of the bull-pup designs with which the industrial nations have equipped every murderous dictator of the Third World, a short weapon with the breech right at the back of the configuration. They hit you more or less anywhere with one of their heavy bullets and the shock kills.

I was turning it over in my hands, trying to work out if you had to do anything more sophisticated than pull the trigger. And hoping that I wouldn't be called on to find out.

The man in the back had brought his knees up, he was on his side now, his jaw locked, biting down against pain. The gun had still been in his hand when I'd reached over; he let it go, half gave it to me. Yet there was life in his eyes, and even an attempt at a smile. I didn't say anything, what was there to talk about with the man who'd only saved your life? Either nothing or everything I reckoned, electing for the former.

Which was fine. I knew from the finger amputation that words weren't what you wanted to combat pain. Indeed the mind hunts after some absolute silence of its own in which the endorphins can get about their work undisturbed.

This wasn't a road we'd come up on in the Audi. I say 'come up' because at that time I'd had the sensation, as though the field on which I'd been exchanged was on the roof of Europe. Somewhere in the Savoie region. I knew that part of the world a bit, thought I recognized the vegetation, the colour of the soil. The unknown in geographical speculation was that initial trip of mine trussed and rolling about in the back of the van. Since I still had no precise remembrance of the start of it, nothing other than the glimpse of Jodie and Pietro behind the security door, I couldn't tell if it had lasted hours, or days.

Suddenly it struck me: I could ask questions of this man behind the wheel; he was on my side, wasn't he?

And so I started into that, turning into the Incredible Machine Mouth, like when we'd first been heading out of the field. I guess I went over the same stuff again and again; but he was patient, told me what I wanted to know, and needed to understand. The first satisfaction was that my geographical instincts were right. Pretty soon we'd be in Briancon where, he said, there was a hospital.

'And the police?' I asked.

'No police, that is how you are now alive.'

'No police! How can you say that? Anyhow, a bullet wound . . .'

'It has been a hunting accident.'

'Quite a hunt,' I replied.

It seems that somewhere on our side of Briançon I fell to pieces. I couldn't be precise about how or why but after that I have a blank. Another one in a mind starting to feel like a holed bucket.

Chapter 10

I woke up with the dog, Desdemona, up on the bed, her head resting on my leg, eyes just gazing, checking the boss for signs of life.

I was only semi-awake, one eye open, just enough to register her presence.

'Come,' I said. She manoeuvred herself across the covers, brought the adoring head up close, a cold nose against my cheek. I wrapped my arms about her great shoulders and began to weep.

I fell asleep again.

Another time there was the smell of Pietro in the atmosphere, I was sure of that, even though on opening my eyes I found myself alone. Infants have their own aroma, different from that of a dog. But unique and quite unlike the acrid scent put about by us adults of the species.

The air was warm, deliciously so. I was comfortable. Sometimes I would talk. I seem to remember doing that, and voices responding: 'Yes Ess . . . no, you rest, why don't you?' The tone, indulgent.

And there must have been visits by medical practitioners, specialists, every kind of quack. Karen believed in the medical profession, particularly since the arrival of Pietro. We used them a lot, checking him out, making sure that he hadn't suffered too much from the obscure but guaranteed as sordid circumstances of his Neapolitan birth.

Now it was me, Essington, who required the thermometer, the stethoscope.

I guess I stayed out of it for so long partly as a result of the tablets I was fed: little magic bombs to send me off to sleep, to keep me calm, maybe some for the pain as well.

I remember psychic pain, like a total ache, only you couldn't put your finger on the spot. They discuss the falsity of the mind–body dichotomy — that's what Dawn went on about one night over dinner . . . before I owned Gauguins, got snatched, lost how many million US dollars? Well, I can assure her everything that constitutes me is all in one lump, inseparable. The soul is in there as well, and it can be feeling pretty bruised sometimes.

Thank God nobody seemed in a hurry to know anything. There were no questions, only me trying to tell what had happened, going on about this character, Tony, how he'd looked after me. He'd meant no harm, it was just that things had got out of his control.

I was told later how I had become the leader of a Tony cheer squad.

Then I was out in the garden with Desdemona. But not alone. I noticed my house had become like a military camp. There was this man on the gate; he was in espadrilles, jeans, a pink shirt with too many buttons undone. He was holding a gun in his hand, not unlike the one I'd handled in the Citroën with the man.

But what man?

All of a sudden I wanted to know.

I headed up to the front door of the house, past the Yellow Bentley Continental — well, this was the Continent, why not? — past Renardo who was sitting beside the door, reading *Le Figaro*, a gun across his knees. He was on relaxed guard.

I was almost through the door and there she was, Jodie, holding Pietro, his head facing away from me, hers full on, the eyes uncertain. An expression not so different from the one I'd registered before entering the big void.

She smiled. She said: 'Hi.' It was the way with Jodie, her 'hi'. And carried the baby past me through the door.

Some time earlier Desdemona had deserted me to amble down to the chain wire fence we have around the grounds, for a chat to the poodle that lives next door.

The chain wire fence!

I kept on having things leap out at me, making their separate point, punching me in the mind.

Just inside the front door I turned, watched Jodie as she walked on across the grass. She was so relaxed, and elegant, the blond hair tied with a yellow ribbon at the nape of her neck.

But I wasn't so sure.

Suddenly there was a feeling somewhere that made me worry, not just about Jodie — what could be wrong with a girl out of the Midwest? Except perhaps that she could set the aged pulse going too rapidly. I was uncertain of everything. The household itself was threatening me. What was that guy doing down at my gate? Lounging, the loose way he had three fingers hooked in the handle of the rifle. And was it a walkie-talkie he was using . . . ? Had to be.

For what purpose?

This — I believed I understood — wasn't my house! Then where was I? Where was Karen, for instance? I'd bet nobody would have been able to tell me the answer to that.

I passed Rebecca, she's the housekeeper — Renardo and Rebecca are a team, husband and wife. She nodded, muttered '*monsieur*', continued on her way. She was carrying a duster in one hand, letting it dangle. More than anything else she looked like someone with too little to do.

Was I certain it was Rebecca?

They were drifting, the lot of them, nobody under control. Who is running things round here?

Well, screw the lot of them, let them drift. Me, I was going to live my life with purpose.

And they weren't going to keep me there either. I quickened my pace up the stairs. By the time I was at the top where there is a gallery with a marble balustrade from which you can look down on the entrance foyer's polished tiles, I saw Desdemona come running in, tongue out, chasing after her master.

My dog was real.

I got changed. Hunted through the drawers of an Empire dresser for a set of car keys memory told me should be there. Memory proved reliable. It was useful to know it could do that. Then, dog at heel, I headed for the back of the building. I descended stairs to a rear court dividing the house from garages and the quarters occupied by Renardo and Rebecca, the Pincis.

The last garage in line was closed, I entered through the door set in big double doors. There it was, my battered Maserati coupé, dull silver, waiting to take me away from all this. I was climbing in the driver's side when suddenly it hit me: the cement floor! Oil stains! Light I could see pushing in from outside! I stepped back, pressed myself against the wall. Slowly I slid down, head in hands, and weeping.

Piss pouring down my leg.

There was a nurse sitting on a chair over by the window. I was watching her, taking good care that she wasn't conscious of this fact. A woman of perhaps forty, maybe forty-five. Short, her legs only just hit the floor. She was holding a book up in both hands like a child does when asked to read to the class. Most of her face was covered by the book. I could make out the title, *The House of Stairs*; the nurse's thumb was over the author's name.

An English book, an English nurse, perhaps. They are available in the south of France where expatriates from the Land of Hope and Glory trust the almost constant sunshine but not the local doctors.

I rolled over.

Then there was a hand on my shoulder, a voice: 'Mr Holt?'

I shifted on to my back, eyes closed. Opening them I saw a red, round and concerned face. Pink nose. What must have been blond hair, a lot of it done up into a roll at the back, wispy strands falling forward. Green eyes. The voice was richly coloured with the accent of the Scots.

We Holts were once Scots ourselves. Well, so they kept on telling me through my childhood in Australia.

'Och aye,' I responded. And apprehension drained from her features.

Karen came in next. I couldn't be sure how much time we'd spent together since they'd brought me home, nor bother myself to find out. The inquisitive element in me was pretty much drowned in the waters of lethargy that had risen to just below my chin.

Maybe that was the effect of the uppers and downers I was being fed.

Karen looked drawn, aged I would have thought. The skin of her face which had always glowed with health, was bloodless, white. There were bags under her eyes. Fine lines either side of her mouth. Elsewhere a certain pudginess, even under the chin. Yet it was Karen sure enough. I examined her the way I guess scientists examine suspect tissue beneath their microscopes.

There was something missing in what I felt towards my wife. I kept her distant, even with her approaching as she was, concern written on every feature.

Jodie was standing in the doorway, Pietro in her arms. Their heads side by side, and watching.

Well, bully for them.

Which of us had been chained to a wall? Who'd had a finger hacked off? I would see oceans pass under the bridge before I could relate to these people again, to my household; before I could begin to trust them, to trust Karen. Maybe the problem was particularly with Karen.

Someone wrote this book on the selfish gene. I don't know a thing about it, just the title stuck in my head. Most likely I've got the theory all wrong. But I did have my own notion of there being something strong that drives us finally against everybody and anybody so that we can achieve our own ends.

I felt that was what had happened within the walls of the Villa du Phare. There'd been instincts urging Karen on to motherhood, the demands of which the pair of us couldn't naturally fulfil. Thus the adoption. Yet the silk business had still charged ahead. So we took Jodie on board, a girl who was simply too beautiful to have around, with those eyes of hers so innocent you couldn't tell what they were saying. So innocent that they looked corrupt in some crazy inverted fashion.

What of all that had I wanted? How about my genes, their demands on life?

Did I get Karen as part of a slow and stable domestic life, tea and toast by the fire? No, of course I didn't.

If I was lucky I walked this Jodie creature down to the Villefranche beach so baby could play in the sand. Perhaps, once in a working week, I'd get Karen to come along too. But not just Karen, not Karen, baby and old Essington, hell no. Always Jodie as well, those eyes. What is it they say about the Mona Lisa? Enigmatic. Beyond enigmatic the resemblance to the painting ends. Jodie looked as though she had a lot more go in her than Mona; more juices.

Lying there I hated the whole bunch of them.

At the head of the list, Karen. She was hanging back, looking a touch confused. I would have liked to imagine, even sorry.

She could stay sorry.

'How's it going, Ess?'

'Going where?'

'Oh, I don't know . . . you seem . . . '

'In hell, and not coming out.'

'Ess, don't say things like that . . . Why? It's more than what happened to you, isn't it?'

'Depends on what happened.'

Karen gestured for Jodie to cart the baby off to the nursery we'd set up, the sort of thing that used to make Peter Pan feel like an outsider, every shade of blue you can imagine and all the half-tones in between.

Suddenly I hated the nursery.

Well, it wasn't my child, was it? It was a waif, picked up someplace. What if it too had this selfish gene, on a mega scale?

The selfish gene! How can you cope with something like that?

I'd read about Aristotle in a *Reader's Digest* when I was in hospital once getting my head stitched up. Aristotle had devised this code of how to behave, and of how to go for the jugular of thine enemy. I reckoned I had found a kindred spirit in Aristotle.

In my eyes, at least, Karen had been selfish. And I'd paid the price.

We were watching each other.

But I was seeing something else, seeing that door set in one of the big shed doors, the daylight coming in through there.

Then I was sensing the pain of the amputated finger shooting up my arm.

Trying amateur psychology and going over things wasn't my idea of what was needed. Right then I required nothing more complex than pure sensation.

Or vengeance.

There is a pair of glass doors opening on to a balcony off our bedroom. That was where I'd been put, in 'our' bedroom. And the other half of that 'our' was cooling her heels sleeping in some room down along the gallery.

Dreaming what thoughts?

The nursery was between us.

Propped up on my pillows I could hear quite a bit of the comings and goings. I guess that Jodie had been shoved one further down again with Karen suddenly wanting to sleep next to Pietro —

they'd snatched me and she looked to the safety of the baby! But Karen still went off to the shop, more or less every day. I don't know why she did it, I guess I never will. The same with the money, her feeling this urge to watch it grow. As far as I was concerned the whole lot, all inherited, it was as if it had fallen out of the sky.

So, why not dedicate your life to the celebration of that fact?

The next day when Karen asked if there was something she could do for me before heading off to Nice, to the shop — not the shop so much any more, but an office and design workshop they'd established upstairs after I'd shelled out what it took to buy the building — I said yes there was. Just to be a right bastard.

I let her ask what.

'When you get there,' I said, 'call a cab, send Farah over in it. I'd like to have a talk with her.'

Karen swallowed back on that. In better times we'd joked about this thing I had for looking at Farah. Me claiming it was the same as with art: to appreciate it doesn't mean you have to scratch the paint. Now though, you could see it hurt. What could Essington possibly want with Farah?

They'd surrounded me with women, it was their choice. So I'd talk to Farah. For one reason or another I'd decided I wanted her with me for a while.

Karen said: 'If she'll come.'

'Make sure she does.'

And then there was Farah.

She arrived mid-morning, was brought to the bedroom by Rebecca who wore an expression which was supposed to convey something to me, though exactly what was difficult to determine. For her part, Farah was composed, as always.

She sat, I grinned — I hadn't done so much of that since being kidnapped.

Farah was one of the odalisques in a Delacroix, viewed in profile, her dark, almond-shaped eyes seemed to be on the side of her head like those of a bird.

'Essington?' At least a hint of the question in those eyes.

'Did you see my nurse, Farah? She's what you would call a brick.'

'A brick?'

Farah and I spoke French together, though she would have preferred a shift into the English she wanted to improve. I wasn't up to the pauses, the explanations. My French was a hell of a lot better than what she could manage the other way round.

'It's what you say, "brick". She can be relied upon.'

'To do what?' Farah asked.

'That is yet to be discovered.'

I was beginning to feel more like my old self. I enjoyed Farah's company for more than her exotic beauty. She was a thinker: liberal, a political radical. If it hadn't been for unemployment in the south, and perhaps Dawn's tastes, it seemed to me such a woman would never have drifted into anything as decadent as the silk trade. Now, after a couple of years she was more or less part of my extended, if synthetic, family.

That was when she wasn't attending meetings of the organization, SOS Racism, designed to protest against attacks on North African-born French residents.

I asked: 'Farah, have you the least idea of what's been going on?'

'Going on?'

But I was sure she was acting then.

'Dawn's told you?'

A stiff face, then a shrug: 'Something, Essington, yes.'

'What, for instance?'

'That you have been a hostage.'

'And you thought: so what?'

She leaned forward, narrowed her eyes. 'Why do you say that? This isn't like you, I think.'

'Not like . . . what is like me?'

'To joke.'

'Farah . . . what if I'm past joking? So far past I don't even know where I am?'

'I should say that it will pass. A fat man who diets always returns to his former weight. A personality is the same.'

'What about Lucia di Lammermoor?'

'You see, you joke, as always.'

Would she like coffee?

I rang a bell by the bed. My aunt, the one from whom I'd inherited the wealth, had been an autocratic woman. Bells and servants, the two going together like camel hair and head scarves.

The nurse entered, thinking the bell was for her. She was holding a book in one hand, a finger between the pages.

'*The House of Stairs*?' I asked.

'Finished, another fine writer.' A jolly smile.

I introduced Farah to Nurse Findlay who stepped forward and shook her by the hand, pretty much like one bloke to another. And then Rebecca appeared at the door. I asked for coffee, off she went. You see how it is with one man in a house full of women. Little wonder I'd become so bloody paranoiac. Maybe it wasn't being chained up that did it after all.

Nurse Findlay was harder to get rid of than she was to summons. Eventually she went, but only after I'd explained that Farah and I had personal matters to discuss. Then explained it a second time. And still it was as though she believed I was lying, that the instant she disappeared I'd be wrapping this exquisite Moroccan in my arms, sucking her ear lobe.

Would that I could, perhaps. But no, we were what you call friends. Right at that moment I trusted Farah more than anyone I knew.

I got Farah to explain exactly what Dawn had said to her about my disappearance. She told me, it wasn't much. I brought up the subject of the man in the black Citroën who'd come up into the mountains to do the bargaining.

Farah shook her head: 'Essington, it could be anyone, how should I know?'

'There was a second man, I would have thought Algerian, or Moroccan, he was shot.'

'Dead?' Not so much expression in that though, as if nothing would surprise Farah, she'd seen it all. And maybe she had. The sad truth is I'd never bothered to ask. For me she was part of the present, the person sitting across a table, or out on a terrace in the Mediterranean sun.

Perhaps that was why I trusted her — no history, see?

'Not dead, Farah. I believe he was taken to the hospital at Briançon, a hunting accident . . . so they pretended.'

'But why?'

'Because what happened to me has never been reported to the police.'

'This man?'

'Farah, I want to see him, to thank him.'
'Then why not simply do what you want.'
'Because nobody should know, and anyway, right now I'm not up to it.'

She regarded me for a long moment. 'What do you want with this man?'

'As I said, to thank him.'
'Essington?'
'He is tough, Farah . . . you have no idea. The man is . . .'
'You are planning something secret. Why?'
'I'm planning nothing. But if I was everybody else would try and stop me, that's why.'
'Stop you from what?'
'From recovering my princely wits.'

'Are you mad, my Lord? Are you out of your princely wits?' That had got into my mind from somewhere. Funny, isn't it, the stuff packed away with the marbles.

Chapter 11

Who was it came home, drew his bow, threw everybody out of the house, re-established his mastery? Was it Ulysses?

The thought hit me.

I'd been tucked up in bed long enough, being mollycoddled, stuffed full of pills, my brow stroked. There'd been a bit of frigging around with the decapitated finger as well: getting it to drain. I was informed that the doctor wondered about gangrene for a while. Gangrene!

I rang my bell.

Nurse Findlay came, book in hand, a finger holding the place. Her spectacles had gold rims, the glass was thick; light which reflected off it obscured the clear green-hazel of her eyes.

'I'm getting up.'

A squawk. 'That's not possible, Mr Holt!'

'Then watch.' I got up. 'A lesson for you, Nurse, on the art of the possible.'

'It's not right,' she said. Her face had coloured, she was holding herself like a ramrod. Discipline, the nurse's physical presence demanded, must be maintained.

'Nurse, I am now going to get dressed. I understand that in your profession a naked man is of no more interest than a sack of wheat. Still, I warn you, my beauty hath no bounds.'

Prim, but acting the part, a smile in her somewhere: 'Mr Holt, you'd cause a maiden to blush.'

'And you?'

Blush! She was red enough already, with indignation.

'I expect I'll leave you to it.'

Which she did.

Dressed in a shirt and white cotton slacks, tennis shoes on my feet, I was hunting through my drawers for a pullover.

The nurse reappeared. 'Mr Holt, I have to tell you I've rung Mrs Holt, as I was instructed to do.'

'How long have you been here?' I asked.

'My second day.'

'I thought as much. Nurse, during the last week or so time hasn't been defined so clearly. And, before you, who was there?' Funny thing, I was picking up her Scots accent, it's infectious.

'I believe they had a man.'

'Because . . . ? You can tell me, Nurse.'

'All right then, Mr Holt, I believe you had these turns, you'd thrash about a bit, see things that troubled you.'

I grinned: 'That, Nurse, is called reality.'

'Not in my book, it isn't.'

'With respect, your book is about butlers and corpses in country houses, hardly reliable.'

'You know what I mean, Mr Holt.'

We were standing there, facing each other, me towering above her.

'How are you with children?' I asked.

'Children?' She seemed surprised. 'I like them well enough.'

'Good,' I said. Then I asked. 'What did Mrs Holt tell you to do when you rang?'

'What I could. She said she'd get home as soon as possible.'

'Nurse Findlay, would you mind watching Pietro for a while and asking Jodie — that's the girl who minds the baby, if the rude buggers haven't bothered to introduce you yet — to come to the balcony up here? I want to talk with her about something.'

You could see the nurse thinking, trying to work me out. Was I off my head, or recovered? That was the question she had to be deliberating upon.

'As you wish,' she said.

Farah had been gone most of an hour by the time Jodie came out through the glass doors — not of the room where I'd been sleeping but of the nursery: the blue play paradise. If they kept that sort of decorator's indulgence up Pietro would grow into a wimp.

Waiting, I'd watched Desdemona patrolling the fence, her nose down, muttering dog secrets to the neighbour's poodle who yapped in sharp response. I noticed that the man on the gate still wore a pink shirt, I wondered if it was the same one. I also wondered who'd put him there.

Renardo wouldn't be sitting by the front door reading his daily paper any longer. For he, and the yellow Bentley were on the road to Briançon with Farah sitting up in the back as though she was the Queen of Morocco.

Of course I still had drugs in me, maybe there were some antibiotics working away there as well — the finger wasn't the only open and suppurating wound I'd carried home: there were sores, plenty of them, and cuts on my scalp, in my hair, the result of blows. I had a weal right across my face from being struck with the end of my chain.

I looked a worse mess than I actually felt now I'd taken things into my own hands; inspired by the Greek hero and his bow.

Jodie got me every time, simply looking at her. Gold sparkling off her hair. She was smiling, that wide Scandinavian mouth, the teeth, neat wedge of a nose. She took a seat in a high-backed cane chair on the other side of the marble-top table. Fingers woven together she placed two hands demurely on her lap.

Clear nail polish with just a hint of pink. Once, in Monte Carlo, I'd seen this losing gambler turn to a smart young guy who'd been spooking him. He'd put one hand in through the front of his double-breasted suit as though reaching for a gun. 'What you want,' the gambler asked, 'I fuck you or I shoot you?'

Well, the gambler's question was what I ought to have put to Jodie.

Instead I just examined her.

'Mr Holt?'

I was seeing not her face at that moment, but the face in the door, seen through the glass, the face that had been watching me cross the Parisian street. And with the baby turned away.

It had meant something, hadn't it?

'Jodie, that day . . .'

She stiffened, the fingers tightened on each other, the long painted nails dug into her palms. To relax herself, she took a deep breath.

'Why did you have Pietro with you in the entrance foyer?'

Jodie's brows knitted, she put on a puzzled face.

Funny thing, the way you have a hunch, then follow it through, get to feel more and more right as you progress.

Jodie didn't respond to my question. She set about playing muscle games with her face.

'Jodie,' I coaxed. 'I need to find out what happened to me. And you saw, didn't you?'

'I rushed back upstairs . . .' She bit back on that.

'And told Mrs Holt I was in trouble? Is that how things went? As it happens I haven't spoken to anybody about this. You see, I think they feel I'm still too crook, too befuddled in my mind to handle going over what happened. So we've all been playing happy talk. Now, suddenly, I want to know what happened, you understand? I want to put the pieces together. So far the one piece I have is you, me seeing you there, and on the point of coming out through the door.

'Why would you want to do that? Why would you be carrying Pietro out into the street? It wouldn't have been to play, would it? Because as I remember you didn't have anything with you, no pram, no bag of toys. Jodie, what were you doing?'

'I . . .' She gagged on the reply.

'I remember your eyes, Jodie.'

She blinked.

Hell, even blinking she looked like an invention of the gods; certainly not one of us poor flawed mortals. She was dressed in dark blue slacks and one of those sailor tops they wear in musicals and films about the south of France: blue and white horizontal stripes, a slit neck. Her nipples were standing out. Curiously, grilling her, I was getting randy. Dawn must have been right about us males and our sex drives: the instinct to rape.

So much of me hated Jodie as she sat there acting out confusion, concern, as she became fidgety under my gaze.

Then I thought: Nice tits!

Nice eyes too, the whites of them clear. Even faking concern as they were.

'You don't have an answer?'

How long had we sat silent? She seemed to jump when I put the question.

'An answer?'

'You were at the door, remember, with Pietro. And when I arrived, firstly you were surprised, then indecisive. You were looking out at me, but also at something beyond me. What was it? People? I want you to tell me what happened.'

'I saw nothing.'

'That's what you decided, isn't it? You went upstairs and kept that pretty little mouth of yours shut, didn't you? Yet, you'd seen. And there's more. Lots, and some of it to do with you.'

Her head shaking from side to side. She was acting as if she couldn't believe what she was hearing.

'You've been ill, very ill, Mr Holt, I don't think you know what you're saying.'

'I know what I'm saying. And not ill, Jodie, injured. Bashed, dismembered, imprisoned . . . I have this feeling you know why.'

She was on her feet then. Standing, leaning forward, tips of spread fingers on the marble surface of the table, taking her weight. Her voice had gone up a couple of decibels: 'You can't say anything, prove anything. Anyhow, you don't have credit, you're out of it. Except you can't see that, can you? Not while stuffed full of medication. Who's going to listen? Maybe you suffered some rough handling, I wouldn't know. I wouldn't have a clue. Only what I hear, what I pick up around this house. But you don't have a thing on me.'

She bolted for the nearest exit.

And me after her, racing in through the nursery doors. I caught her just before she made it out on to the gallery. A tackle which brought her screaming to the floor, to the pale blue carpet with its pattern of pairs of dark blue birds, their wings entwined.

Jodie was squirming, kicking. I had her around the waist, she reached back to grab a stool, something to bash me with while keeping on screaming blue murder.

The blue and white sailor's top had edged up, one breast was showing by the time I was sitting astride her, my hands pinning her arms.

The screams were howls, and language like you wouldn't believe from a baby minder.

Karen came running into the room.

The look on my wife's face!

Any other time it might have made me laugh.

Chapter 12

There were discussions. I was told to keep out of them.

Nurse Findlay was walking about the house, holding the baby, humming 'Lord of the Isles' like she was a set of bagpipes on legs.

I tried thinking, and nursing the hand with the missing finger — there were phantom pain signals shooting up my arm.

Karen suggested I take a tranquillizer.

I refused. I was past tranquillizers. This was the new me . . .

'Raping the help?'

'Have her checked out, if you like . . . if you want to know the truth. Check her for semen, isn't that what they do?

'Essington, you were on the way. For heaven's sake, I saw you at it!'

Karen was part angry, but most of her — and this made me madder — was playing at being saddened. And she was understanding as well, going on about what I'd been through.

I'd give them 'saddened', the whole fucking lot of them! I went downstairs, found the whisky, half filled a tumbler, went out on to the lawn to talk to the dog.

A bright afternoon. Did nature ever realize how we cloud its effects with our bloody-mindedness?

An hour later a taxi arrived at the front grill gate. The man in the pink shirt was still there, again talking into his walkie-talkie. I thought I might have a word, I wasn't sure I wanted armed strangers hanging about. Was he keeping people out, or me in?

Most likely the latter.

The cab drove up to the front door. Oh, hell! Jodie coming out followed by Rebecca carrying half the luggage. They were piling it into the boot. Jodie making sure she didn't look in my direction.

I headed for the gate and was half-way down the drive when the taxi came slowly past.

I saw her eyes again, through glass. This time they looked defiant, the whole expression saying: Up you, Essington.

Well, we'd see, wouldn't we Jodie?

Karen was in the front reception room, on the *chaise-longue* under a Sisley of a river with poplars growing along the bank. I guess the Gauguin might also have hung in there somewhere. Or upstairs in the bedroom — naked ladies, that's where us, the bourgeoisie, hang them. They are our bedroom trophies. And deer antlers, swords and spears of conquered tribes, portraits of race horses, hang in the billiard room.

Karen was at her absolute worst. Her eyes were red-rimmed, from fatigue, I guess, and perhaps from tears she'd fought back.

The wounded look didn't have an effect on me, if anything I felt angry at the idea that she could presume to confront me while wearing the appearance of someone who was having a rough time.

As far as I reckoned the rest of the twentieth century, the ten years still to go, ought to be devoted to making life easy for Essington Holt. Or they wouldn't be devoted at all.

'Essington,' falteringly.

'You let the bitch go!'

'Don't you even know right from . . . ? Oh, Essington, I know you've been through hell, you don't feel . . . '

'I don't feel what?'

'But, that girl, you were on top of her. You can't . . . '

'Say I wasn't on the point of putting it into her! Yes I can, and I do.'

'You don't have to say anything, to pretend. I know, you know. What if she went to the police?'

'She won't.'

'How can you be so certain?'

'Because there's more to it than you see. Since when have you become Mrs Morality, anyhow? God! You work all day with Dawn who can scarcely keep her hands from going up girls' dresses. That mob in Paris at the parades, crack, ecstasy, snow . . . you name it, they're into it. High on the sex kicks as well. You lot thinking it's a great joke. Meanwhile, back at home, Karen, we go Presbyterian, is that it? Would you believe I was trying to get Jodie to talk, to explain a few of the puzzles I carry around in my head?'

'You could ask me, Essington. Do you realize that since you were brought home you haven't uttered a word about what happened? Not a hint of curiosity! You haven't even wanted to know about how we organized your release.'

'That Gauguin you badgered me into buying, the cash. You understand why I don't want to know? Because I don't care. I don't fucking care! They can take the lot . . . only next time ask them to leave the fingers, will you?'

I got up, stormed to the door, paused.

'When you let Jodie piss off like that you kissed goodbye to the only chance I may have of finding out what happened in that street when they . . . what did they do? Since you're so in touch, you tell me, then. Explain to your rapist husband who it was waiting outside the apartment block, what they did to make me lose all memory of it. And maybe you know — since you were off watching Chantal Thomass, Sonia Rykiel or some fag march his tin soldier ladies up and down the cat-walk — maybe you can tell me why Jodie what's-her-name was waiting just inside the security door.

'Me walking towards her, I saw it, I was about as welcome as a cold sore on a bride.

'Only she didn't tell you that, did she? Claimed instead to be upstairs with the baby, pretended she didn't know, isn't that right? By doing so she ensured my kidnappers had a couple of hours start . . . at least. Well, Jodie knows I know. She's off in a taxi, and unless we put police on at the airport I'd say the chances of ever finding out are zero.

'So, Karen, you and your fucking misreading of more or less everything in the past Christ-knows-how-long, you've blown it.'

She was sitting there, part shocked, part not believing.

That was her problem. I kept on moving, heading out to the big wide cage we call the garden.

I was watching that man on the gate. There was something about the way he held himself which offended me, the stance of a man who'd swagger when he walked, if he walked. Maybe, I thought, he ought to walk. So I responded to the body language invitation in the only way I know how.

He watched me approach, no change of expression, a man acting tough the way they do when they're piss weak. I'd seen politicians with that same look in the eye, and letting their arms hang just so.

In fact I'd never seen a politician without it.

'G'day!' My greeting.

He shrugged. The bugger shrugged!

'Tell me something,' I asked. Oh Christ, I was having fun. 'Why are you standing here, at the gate?'

I hope I sounded reticent, timid. Two people can act at the one time. But it's best if they choose complementary roles.

He half turned away from me.

I switched to English: 'Arsehole, I asked you a question.'

His head flicked around, checking me out a second time. He said, in French: 'I work for the lady.'

'Doing what?'

'Guarding, of course, what else?' And then such a nonchalant tilt of the head.

Ho, ho, ho.

'That's what I wanted to know.' I assured him.

He held the walkie-talkie up in front of his face as though it was of some religious significance to do that. His thumb was close to the talk button. There was no sound coming out.

'You were here yesterday,' I said.

'I was.'

'Tell me: the man, Renardo, the one who drives the yellow Bentley, you know him perhaps?'

The bastard spat. He spat on my fucking gravel! Then puffed air out between his lips. The French call that 'making a mouth'. You couldn't see this twit's eyes on account of mirror sunglasses. Mirror sunglasses which I regard as ideologically unsound!

'You mean you don't know him?'

'Mister, what is it that you want?'

The assault rifle was leaning against a gatepost, just out of arm's reach. I guess he'd got tired of holding the damn thing. Why hold four kilograms of gun just because somebody who wouldn't know the difference is paying you to do it?

From this guy's general attitude, I didn't get the sense of a man doing his job properly. I hadn't got that sense the previous day either.

'I want you off the place,' I said, 'quick.'

A shrug but no action.

'You know who I am?'

'Yeah,' he replied, 'I think you are the lady's old man.'

They're so cocksure these guys who reckon they're in their prime.

'And,' he went on, 'I work for the lady.'

'Well, I'd say you're wrong there,' I said. 'There's only one person controls what happens inside this gate and that's me. So from now you work for no one.'

He grinned, as though he thought he was guarding the gate of a loony bin, and I was an inmate. I wasn't worth taking seriously.

Did I really look that bad? Well, maybe yes.

Then he pressed the button and started to speak into his walkie-talkie. I'd become invisible.

Walkie-talkie! There must have been another of them doing the rounds outside, checking the streets.

'Why the guard, Karen?'

We were sitting out on the side balcony, upstairs. Nurse Findlay was giving Pietro a ride on Desdemona's back, holding his little arms out to maintain balance. 'Ooh!' she was exclaiming. 'Gee up horsey.'

'It's a fucking dog,' I said.

'Mr Holt, I'm sure there's no need for talk like that.' A mischievous look towards the infant head. 'Tiny ears,' the nurse added.

I couldn't hold down a smile in return. There was something about the woman, something I liked.

Which couldn't have been said for Karen at the moment when she repeated: 'The guard?' — as though he might not have existed at all.

'Where does he come from?' I asked.

'I hired him.'

'But, there's Renardo!' Which was true enough. Renardo could look after the gate. Renardo was the dark horse of the Villa du Phare. He and his wife, Rebecca, they had been with the house since before my aunt bought it. It seemed to suit them to remain. Yet Renardo had standing among a native population which was more Italian than French. Almost as though he moonlighted as a mob boss. On more than one occasion while walking with him through the old market area of Nice, I'd witnessed the respect in which he was held.

Renardo made the Godfather, as played by Marlon Brando, appear *arriviste*.

'There's another of them, isn't there? He's out somewhere, round the block. Thus the walkie-talkie caper.'

'Must you sound so aggressive?'

'Because, Karen, I feel that way. Silk you know, perhaps. But all of this that's happened to me . . . my guess is that you're out of your depth.'

'You are here, Essington.'

'Thanks to . . . what was that man's name? Him . . . I wouldn't mind meeting up with him again.'

'I was beginning to wonder if you'd ever ask.'

You could tell from her tone change she thought we'd suddenly taken a little leap, relationship-wise, the two of us. Maybe it was the pleasure she appeared to take from that realization which made me turn totally nasty.

'I'm not asking you anything, not now, probably not ever.'

'You look so tired, Essington.'

I felt it too, overdoing life on my first day up. I said: 'Nor are you going to keep me as an invalid, like some kind of a pet.'

It was her turn to walk out on the conversation, as I had done earlier in the day. She was on her feet. 'For God's sake!' she said.

I shouted: 'The man on the gate, he goes!' Then I repeated it, full voice. Bedouins, they would have heard me from over in North Africa.

They wouldn't understand, see. It was my place, and essentially my money too that they were playing about with. As I saw things, they were doing it wrong.

I was going to have a go at doing it right. But first I had to wait till Farah returned from Briançon.

Perhaps I should have talked the lot over with Karen. Specific points like how the ransom and the exchange had been arranged. And where she'd found the man who'd pulled it off. I wanted to see him again. As far as a house guard was concerned, that seemed to me like too much too late. The exchange deal had been made, no doubt about that, me being there was the proof. And it would take a really stupid bunch of hoons to come back for another bite at the cherry, even if they were pissed off with me being alive and one of their lot dead. *C'est la guerre.* So why waste money, what was left of it, on some mirror-eyes shit lounging at the gate and talking at a piece of plastic to while away the time? Paid time! If somebody wanted to eliminate him all they had to do was drive up, shoot the bastard straight through the head.

I wouldn't have minded the job myself. It might have made me feel good.

The truth was that I had a lot of rebuilding to get on with. There was too much Essington left up there in that cement block shed. I'd grovelled, I'd deluded myself, sought friendship from people intent on exchanging me for money then wiping me off the slate. I hated those memories of the gratitude I'd felt when afforded what seemed at the moment like kindness. Not to forget there was the woman as well, the one who'd brought the food. Surely she had some learning in store for her.

I didn't trust these people — it was primarily Karen, wasn't it? — who'd paid up the cash, and now carried on as though all that was required was for me to get back on my feet. Well, bugger that, life isn't so simple.

Nurse Findlay brought me my meal in bed. She dumped it on the table beside me and propped there, arms crossed, watching.

I said nothing, nor did I bother about what was on the tray. Food is one of the nice aspects of life I'd somehow learned to do without.

Either that or my stomach had shrunk.

I rolled over so I was looking away from the formidable figure standing in attendance.

'You've had quite a day, from what I understand.'

Why should I respond to that sort of shit?

'We are sulking, are we?'

'Nurse, go and screw yourself . . . take the rest of them with you.'

'Which rest of them would you be referring to?'

I let that ride.

'Apart from the driver's wife and your wee son, we are the only souls in this house.'

'You call yourself a soul? And on the gate?'

'There's nobody there, either.'

'She did it then, she got rid of him . . . learning.'
'I hope we all are, Mr Holt.'
'Some more slowly than others.'
'Kindly tell me what is that supposed to mean?'
'Why don't you shove off too?'
'With pleasure.'

And when I turned around she was gone.

I sat on the edge of the bed, my head in my hands. This business of people, of the human race, it was difficult. Maybe I should start to try.

That was one voice.

Another warned me against the lot of them, it showed me the details of their conspiracy, to achieve what? No way of telling. Yet what was I to make of Karen getting Jodie out of my way, cutting off the only path back to the precise moment of the kidnap?

When I went down Nurse Findlay was sitting outside the front door. I guess she had been trying to work out how to push buttons to get the front grill gate to open. It was an electronic contraption, you had to know the magic word to get through. Findlay didn't have the magic word. Not that it upset her; she was perched on a suitcase, reading by the outside light.

She didn't lift her head as I approached.

'I'm sorry,' I said.

'So you should be. You know, Mr Holt, I don't want ever to see myself behave in the way you've been going on.'

'Maybe you don't want to have your finger lopped off either.'

'Nobody invited us on board. We must learn to accept life as it is. Weakness is always weakness, no matter how you try to dress it up.'

Like I thought: beauty is beauty. A world of absolutes.

There was always the old belief: vengeance is vengeance. Still, it seemed to me that I could get along with this woman, maybe try once more with them all. And even then manage to get back what was mine.

But not, no never, the finger . . . alas.

Chapter 13

The encounter at the front door between Nurse Findlay and myself was interrupted by a wail coming from the direction of the nursery. It was a sound which I knew from past experience might be heard only once, diminish to a whimper and then silence would fall again upon the house. Yet, in better times when we were in bed together, not so much as a sniffle could come from that room next to ours without Karen sitting bolt upright, shaking me by the shoulder, insisting that we listen together. Any increase in volume and it was lights on, up and at it. That I guess is the thing with adopted children: your responses are too considered, the relationship is like a cross between that which you might have with a natural child and with some expensive, delicate toy.

The nurse looked towards the staircase: Pietro's plaintive noise offering a chance for her to change her mind.

As though his subconscious connected him to the rest of us, even while he slept, the noise he had just made was repeated, volume up a fraction. Then louder again. Next came the howl, sudden, as though there was an element of rage in behind it.

The pair of us hurried up the stairs leaving the suitcases where they were.

We were standing on the balcony; stars in the sky, and a new moon holding the old one in its arms. Was the baby seeing these things up there, wondering, its mind drawing lines between the points of light? Nurse was humming some pentatonic and repetitious Scots melody, soothing Pietro and myself with her music.

Automobile lights turned in at the gate. Desdemona was barking, letting us know she had our best interests at heart. I could make out enough of the body shape to know that it wasn't the Bentley come back from Briançon. The gate slid open. It was Karen in the Citroën, what in Australia we'd call the 'family wagon', returned to try the atmosphere of the house again. To see if she could take some more of my malevolence.

I picked up the clip clop of Karen's shoes as she mounted the stairs.

There were resolutions in my brain, very recent ones. I was going to try and repair the damage, stitch the relationship back together. I could feel the intention within myself, like something existing in the physical world, and me even experiencing that warm inner glow of the contrite which is just one more phoney emotion.

I could hear drawers being opened, slammed shut. The action repeated several times over. Then there was the flare of yellow light in the bedroom, our bedroom. Karen had found one of her packets of cigarettes, she was lighting up.

That was a sign of something. Karen smoked when she needed to, usually when she was at the end of her emotional tether.

I was still at the end of mine, I reckoned probably I always would be.

I thought to tell Nurse Findlay to shove off, and to take the kid with her. Then I thought: Why bother?

At the moment Karen stepped out on to the balcony I hit on the real basis of the problem between us. It wasn't just that I'd been snatched, chained, made to play the coward for the entertainment of a bunch of thugs, that wasn't why we couldn't talk, why I was filled with this unwillingness even to try. It was because of Pietro. Poor innocent kid that he was, having nothing to contribute to the tension, he remained the cause of it, simply by the fact of his existence in the house.

It had been 'baby' this, 'baby' that, for most of a year. Yet baby was regarded as some kind of *thing*, as separate, an object! Not part of this mishmash, this continuum to which we are collectively doomed to belong.

Of course the worst had been Dawn's obsession with the astrological portents of the child's birth, with what the fates held in store, the kinds of preferences it would grow up to have, its skills, abilities.

None of it felt right. If and when I'd bothered to object to the mumbo-jumbo, Karen had gently deflected me with the argument that the signs of the zodiac, cusps, houses, they were nothing more than systems we have dug up for toying with the great unknowables.

It could be that she had a point. The only thing was that with me, it was in my blood to want to look over the edge into the pit. I reckoned I didn't need games.

And I'd gone completely off glitter — once you've lived in your own shit a villa out on Cap Ferrat can feel less significant than meaningless; even an affront to nature, to necessity, to everything that's real.

Karen stood there, a dark shape behind the glow of the cigarette.

I said: 'I'm sorry . . . I can't say how sorry I am. Please, Karen, forgive me. Could we pick up the needle, put it back at the start, try the record from the beginning again. The love duet.'

'Fuck me drunk,' she said.

'And that too.'

'Ess, it's compact discs, laser, there aren't needles any more.'

Nurse Findlay discreetly headed into the house through the nursery.

Karen and I had developed a ritual — sometimes rituals are useful, they help to build bridges. That wasn't the first time we had stood out on the balcony, contrasting our troubled relationship with the movie-style harmony of the night world surrounding us. Maybe it's just suggestion, I don't know, but to stand where once Romans, and before them the Greeks, had stood, it does something to a boy reared in the antipodes.

'Wine?' It was Karen who made the suggestion, the grin on her face not entirely bitter.

Step one with us was to get into the booze.

I toddled off downstairs to check over the selection of what was cold. It would be a gamble, drinking. The couple of whiskies I'd tried since weaning myself off the medicines had more than likely contributed towards the worst extremes of my day of manic hate behaviour.

I picked up a bottle of Chablis, two glasses, carted them back to the battleground.

Karen had a fresh cigarette shoved in between her lips; she was on her feet, leaning against the railing, the moon a crescent over her head.

I put the bottle down on the marble-top table, poured, sat, and waited.

'Dawn said . . .'

'Let's not start with Dawn.'

'There are rules, are there? Tell me who drew them up, Essington.'

'Are we going to try, or aren't we?'

'Dawn said she thought you must have developed a Diogenes complex.'

'Karen, where in God's name does she pick up all this shit? I mean . . .'

'She said a person can get to be like that . . . looking for some kind of moral truth and hoping to find it by living in squalor. As though it's purifying.'

'You call this squalor?' I took a gulp of wine.

'No use trying to drink your way out of it. The time will come when you have to open your eyes, see what's out there for you, in the future.'

'You can't seriously believe that I'm like this — what was his name again?'

'Like Diogenes. Dawn said he was called The Cynic. Well, Essington, you hate it all anyway, don't you? A part of you does at any rate. I know it. You'd be just as happy to go off and live with the dog. Cynic: she tells me it comes from the word for dog, in Greek or something.'

'Karen, that's not quite fair. Still, if you want to believe it, well and good. Meanwhile, go on, what else do I want to do?'

'Oh, you know Dawn, she's got her theories.'

'The middle-aged man, the young wife . . . is that one of them?'

'If you're intending to buck like that at even the hint of criticism, I don't want to continue.'

'With what? Continue with what?'

'Aren't we trying to negotiate a truce?'

'Karen . . . Oh hell! I don't know what we're trying to do. I really couldn't say. You just don't have any idea of what it was like, of what happened. I don't mean to my body . . . I mean what happened to me inside my head, the things I went through.'

'Dawn and I discussed that as well.'

'Was it some kind of a group therapy session only with the sick uninvited? The two of you, I can see it, oh yes, of course . . . working it out . . . the universe, solving the riddle of beginnings and of endings. Is that what it was? Infinity and after. Where we all come from. How do we get Essington back on his feet, keep the poor bastard smiling?'

'Essington . . .'

'Gauguin let himself get screwed up that way: "*D'où venons -nous? Que sommes-nous? Où allons-nous?*" And look what happened to him?'

She'd caught the tone, me trying to build up a head of joke steam. Karen just managed to bring herself to ask: 'What happened to Gauguin?'

'He died.'

She lit another smoke. 'You came back a mess. It was an ordeal, I know. I'd been through enough by then anyway — little thought you've bothered to give to that, I'll bet. I mean, Essington, you were missing for days before we even got another word. At the beginning . . . just that they had you, and that we were to tell nobody, or else . . .'

'Kaput.'

'Exactly, kaput. I couldn't bear the not knowing. Nobody having a fact. Then you come back . . . Essington, you were thrashing about in bed, lashing out if I came near you. And calling out stuff that didn't make sense. This was all hard to digest, to adjust to . . . and how should I feel? I mean, I just didn't know what was real, of what you'd say, what was rats inside your head. Suddenly you are out of it, recovered . . . except it's a different you now, Essington.'

'Karen . . .'

'Shut up and let me tell you my side of the story. For instance your finger . . . what about your finger?' She stalked across to the furthest corner of the balcony; she turned around, faced me, a big final draw on the cigarette, then I saw its glowing point fly off through the air in an arc. 'What in God's name do you think it did to me to open up a packet, and find a finger there? I understand, you went through a tough time . . . I did as well . . . we all did. You had the pain, experienced the direct physical abuse, I accept that. But, I mean, what do you reckon I was up to while those bastards were holding you? You think it was business as usual, don't you? Me at breakfast, sucking away at the *café-crème*, dipping a croissant, thinking it's a nice day. Well, that isn't how it was. It was as if they'd plugged me into the mains current, that's how it was. Full voltage pain every minute. Then I have to confront you in your sorrows. Well, it concerns me, I want you to get well, to come back into the world, into our world — the two of us, and Pietro. But I'm not going to hang about being treated as though I've been sleeping with the enemy. I mean, what do you think you're up to? Essington, with you, ever since you first opened your eyes, I feel as though I'm one of those women who had their heads shaved after the war, were forced to parade their shame. That was all shit — you know it, I know it. And I don't feel like putting up with shit. You've had a rough time, I understand that. But every minute of each and every day that passed, I was praying for your survival; part of me was out there, wherever, with you, hoping, just hoping. There were moments when I'd think that even to close my eyes was some kind of act of betrayal.

'And then you get out of bed and start behaving as though you are the only victim in the world! There's love . . . did you bother to consider that? Love! The effect of the finger on me . . . and the rest. Time itself, like a series of walls you can't break through. Time . . . hours, minutes, seconds even. I grew to hate time, Ess. Because of you.'

She hadn't moved, not a muscle, she stood there, her feet apart, hands hanging limp at her sides, the words coming straight out, not needing acting to back them up.

If it wasn't truth I was hearing, what is?

'If it hadn't been for Dawn I don't know what I would have done.'

'I'm sorry, I said I was sorry, I'm . . . hell, I don't know, I can't think straight. When I got out of that bed the main thing on my mind, Karen, was Jodie; I'd had her eyes on me the whole time I was locked up.'

'Tell me about it then, for pity's sake tell me everything that happened.'

'Your turn first, Blue. Tell me how things were from your end.' I refilled the glasses.

Chapter 14

As Karen told it, on the day I was kidnapped they'd returned to the apartment after the Angelo Tarlazzi parade at the Jardin des Tuileries. Makihei was due later that evening, no doubt with his convoy of Rolls-Royces, to take them, and me, across town to dine at the Tour d'Argent.

I asked: 'And Jodie?'

'She was there with Pietro, having a bit of trouble I seem to remember, him screaming and her less capable than normal. Not that I took a great deal of notice, why should I?'

Disappointingly perhaps, it seems the question of where I was didn't arise till Makihei turned up, and then it was resolved by the arrangement of leaving instructions for Jodie to direct me on to the restaurant.

The fact that I never went AWOL — well, very seldom — didn't loom large in anybody's thoughts. As the poet says: a good time is a good time is a good time. And that was what Karen and Dawn reckoned they were having just then.

Which, it appears, was the way things were up to when Jodie telephoned through to the restaurant with the relayed phone message that Karen should ring a certain number, that Mr Holt wanted to speak to her.

'You did that?'

'And was told that they had you, to watch the mail.'

'Nothing else, Karen?'

'They told me to keep the call to myself.'

'Why would you do that, on a stranger's say so? It wouldn't make sense!'

'Directly after that I called through to Nice, to Chevet, for advice. Because I was confused, I didn't even know what it could mean. Till in the morning, when I got . . .'

'The first note.'

'Exactly.'

'The voice, what kind of a voice was it?'

'A man . . . I wasn't concentrating. I got the message . . . it was so quick, next thing the line went dead. I got the message and *then* it hit me that something was wrong.'

'Jodie, how did she sound at this point?'

'Rather matter of fact, if I remember. I'm sorry, Essington, but there was no reason then to suspect anything. Why would I? Why be noting how people sounded?'

'The little bitch.'

'Dawn thought you fancied her. Even advised me to take care.'

'Projection — does Dawn's mind ever lift its sights above the human navel?'

Talking, Karen was relaxing a little. Maybe the wine was helping. But she was still going through the cigarettes. Unusual, normally one is enough for a confrontation. She laughed, semi-spontaneous: 'Unfair — I would have thought you were two of a kind.'

Where do ideas come from? How a couple of people can be sitting trying to remake a marriage, and suddenly there it is, the thought . . . or is it a feeling?

Eros, what does he carry? A wand? No, it's a bloody bow and arrow, isn't it? Like the man who came home to claim his wife, Ulysses!

Only Eros has wings to fly.

'Above *your* navel, that, Blue, suddenly I find hard.'

'What's this, seduction time?'

Perhaps we dozed off, I couldn't say for sure. Waking, entwined: pillows, heads and arms and legs and sheets this way and that way, the scent of our bodies and of our love. It was still dark, the moon had gone down leaving the stars more brilliant than before. The Egyptians over there across the water — turn right at Tunisia — they'd once believed there was a woman who was the sky bent over the globe, her body twinkling with stars; she gave birth to the sun in the morning, swallowed it at night.

To make love is to plunge out of the world of language into another, a more fundamental world. I guess that's why puritans, in all their guises, try and argue us out of the activity.

To my regret, the instant we got into talking again some tensions returned. Karen was intent on proving the degree to which she'd suffered during my disappearance, and it became like a competition. She lit up yet another cigarette.

There'd been a couple more notes delivered before the finger arrived — words cut from the daily papers, stuck down, formed into sentences.

'And still Jodie said nothing?'

'We didn't tell her, Ess. That was the decision. As I said I'd spoken by phone to Monsieur Chevet, it was his advice not to tell anyone.'

Chevet was the foxy lawyer I'd picked up since moving to *la belle* France. He was a gift from the gods. All mind and an endlessly flexible morality. It's amazing how often I've required his services. That's the thing with lawyers, land yourself a good one and you wonder how you lived without him; get a dud and you start doing it yourself. Chevet had been one of Renardo's recommendations, an expensive one too, but worth every franc if you happened to be in a fix. I sometimes suspected that he had the police on his payroll.

'Chevet didn't trace the number?'

'He did, it was an apartment in the Marais. Vacated two weeks earlier by an American couple . . . on sabbatical or something.'

'The phone would have been cut off!'

'A serviced short-stay apartment.'

'The owner, Karen?'

'A company, they believed the place was empty. We are talking about Paris! How many phones could you get at if you knew your way around? They only had to be there, at the number, for half an hour, maybe less. Would that be so hard?

'As instructed, we packed our bags, headed for home. It was in the initial note to do that. And Chevet was advising that we follow instructions. He said we had to be seen to be one hundred per cent co-operative because we would be being watched.'

'Watched? By whom, Karen?'

'No way of telling.'

'Jodie, as if nothing was going on, she collected up Pietro's stuff, packed it in the car?'

'She never said a word, Ess, not as I remember.'

Karen was perched up one end of the bed, kneeling. I could see her as a silhouette against the light from the balcony, one bent arm raised, the cigarette held out from her lips.

'Anyway,' she continued, 'I was on happy pills by then.' She hopped off the bed, walked across, flicked the glowing butt out the window. 'More wine?'

'Women,' I responded, 'and whatever happened to song?'

'Woman — one at a time, Ess.'

'Depends on what you've been brought up to.'

What time would it have been? Three o'clock, maybe four? I didn't ask.

I thought I caught the sound of wheels on gravel.

Karen had been out there draining the bottle into our glasses. And watching the car come up to the door.

Farah, returning with Renardo. Strange her turning up like that, just when we'd been playing the woman–women word game. If I'd been asked to choose a third person to mix her body up with ours it would have been Farah every choice down the list.

'Hell, I forgot.'

'Essington . . . oh, why?'

'Why?'

'Don't you see, we were getting somewhere, you and I. Now . . . it's Farah, isn't it, back from wherever you sent her?'

'You like her, remember.'

'But not at this moment. There's still so much more to discuss. You . . . you know what? You avoid it. That's what you do. You don't want to learn what happened; about the ransom for instance, how we arranged it. Why not Essington? We were saving your life — doesn't that interest you?'

'Sure,' I said. But I was up, slipping into a cotton kimono dressing-gown with MAKIHEI printed all over it — black on gold — a gift from our designer friend.

Renardo and Farah were being cautious, ringing the bell. I flicked on the light. Renardo looked drawn, a long day for him, he wasn't any chicken. There were three of them. In front of Farah there stood the wiry figure of a man, one arm in a sling, his hair a helmet of tight curls.

Of course I'd seen him before, he'd only saved my life.

Farah did the introductions. His name was Moulay Yusuf. He said that they called him Mou. In French *'mou'* means 'soft'. You couldn't see the softness in his eyes though. Nor had I noticed it in a previous life when I'd reached over into the back seat of that black Citroën to take the rifle out of his hands.

Mou: its true meaning must have been 'indestructible'.

It was this man who later told me of a Sanskrit poem which said that we can't know the name for a thing till it has completed its purpose on earth.

Chapter 15

Pietro was sitting on his little bed, legs crossed, hands folded in his lap. A relaxed baby, his thoughts at home within the dome of his head. Large brown eyes penetrating beyond the confines of the room, reading the script of dreams written on the ether.

He was awake, surely, yet as though in a trance.

I had made no noise; that's a habit I've developed where baby is concerned, to tread quiet. I stood just inside the nursery door, taking in the scene: Nurse Findlay slumped in an armchair, her head tilted to one side, glasses askew, book — what title was it this time? — fallen to the floor. She looked innocent, almost herself a child. Her lips were set in a smile, enigmatic — shades of the ubiquitous Mona Lisa.

I was tempted to leave Pietro to his contemplation. Instead, stepping into his line of vision, throwing a shadow across his thoughts, I reached down, lifted him into my arms and together we strode outside to welcome another new-born day.

I couldn't say for sure, but I had the feeling then of holding Pietro for the first time: suddenly understanding the fact of his existence, of his separate consciousness. I was cradling a spiritual entity in my arms, something that would grow, become its own confused self, confront the questions I confronted: wonder about desire, about truth, how we all came to be. And in those thoughts, Neapolitan as he might be, there'd be some Essington influence, a grain of crazy me in crazy him. Perhaps Pietro'd come to hate me for it, and yet, with a touch of luck, mightn't he see me for what I'd been to him? A link with time past, a push in the back propelling him into the future.

Me, the surrogate father.

Yet, even as I entertained those thoughts, I knew the moment to adopt that role was still some distance off. I had other things to do, because the record had to be set straight. Not just for the sake of revenge, nor for justice, either — aren't revenge and justice the same things anyway? I had to do something about what had happened to me because if I didn't I'd blow a fuse, permanently perhaps, or just from time to time. When least expecting it the power would surge, lights would shine too brightly, wheels accelerate, then boomph, black-out. I knew how it could go, because, in some mysterious way I understood that about myself: the dicey circuitry.

No bastard can make you shit in a corner, and cower, can cut off your finger, steal so much of your cash, not to mention a Gauguin . . . no bastard can do all that and get away with it. Funny thing, it was holding Pietro that made me absolutely certain of what I had to do.

If Pietro was growing up into this world then I knew of two people at least who, if I had my way, weren't going to be out there to welcome him to maturity.

Nurse Findlay was the only member of the household to get a good night's sleep. The rest of us had been too busy — there'd been copulation, hadn't there? May it thrive. And exchanges of information, filling in gaps in the story of my kidnapping and deliverance hence. There had been eating, drinking, tobacco burning. Beauty prowling the rooms, emitting its disturbing scent. Karen, glowing again, her face relaxed, her soul swimming within the pools of her eyes. Farah, remote, self-possessed, jet black hair cut short, like a boy's. Tapering fingers. It was the first time it had registered, her habit of tapping a forefinger, a slow regular beat. I'd watched it, wondering what the hand was trying to say that the head wouldn't permit.

Well, in the sleeping department I guess there was Renardo too, he'd hit the sack on returning from Briançon with Moulay Yusuf and Farah. Rebecca, on the other hand kept herself busy doling out food and drink.

As the night had passed, the first light finally invading the sky over to the east beyond the ridge of the Cap in some never-never land even further away than Italy, we had drifted from room to room, out on to a terrace, back in again; the dog, Desdemona, following, perplexed to find life's rhythms so disrupted.

We'd talked, Karen mostly, very occasionally Moulay. Farah

simply hung about, sometimes close to nodding off, or sitting up too straight, her head high, alert, as though to be any other way would mean collapsing with fatigue.

And the finger beating out its code, unstoppable.

I don't know why I kept on drifting back to Farah. Sure, I was interested in what was being said, in the details of my story — that's what it was after all, it was my story! Moulay had a walk-on part at the end, didn't he? Yet despite my registering the facts, the details, still I couldn't get the image of Farah out of my mind: the olive surface of her belly turning into the triangle of pubic hair, the swell of her breasts, and that scented skin covered with a thousand million glittering stars.

Farah was in jeans, a loose blouse of emerald green silk, over that a suede jacket.

I wondered what the Arabic is for Milky Way?

And once when I had rested my hand on Desdemona's back, Farah reached across, scratched the dog between the ears, slid her fingers down between the great shoulder blades, and on until they touched mine. Hadn't they lingered there for a fraction longer than might be expected?

There had been the earlier notes, then the piece of paper on which I'd scrawled my name, that came with the finger. The final negotiations had been carried out over the phone.

Chevet had been involved all along, but it must be Karen who talked, they'd insisted on that. A sign of the police; of Karen, of Chevet, of anyone associated with our household going to the police and I would be killed. That had been the first assurance. And the principal condition of negotiating an exchange.

I asked about the voice, what sort of a voice?

The man had spoken French, with an English accent, but acceptable French.

He had said that the villa and the silk shop were being watched.

So, there were no police. Chevet had been of that mind all along and they'd stuck to it. Call in the police, the wily lawyer believed, and you'd certainly finish up with a corpse on your hands.

Instead Chevet called in a private investigator.

The rue Berlioz runs down from Nice railway station to the sea and the famous Promenade des Anglais. The *quartier* is called

Musiciens, mostly apartment buildings with shops or more usually small businesses occupying the ground floor.

Not such a bad address. Even with the fumes from a panel beating and repainting workshop at the end of an alley running back along one side of the building. The kind of toxic smell that makes the mind run to cancer.

I took the steps to the third floor. I like steps, I believe that climbing them is good for me. What's life for but to keep the meat off your girth — and to wonder.

Everything was spick and span, a smell of lavender wax in the air, its polish on the parquet floor. I pressed the brass bell beside a door which it had pleased some craftsman in times past to construct with the kind of care that will never come again.

It swung open. I was confronted by a woman, perhaps forty years of age: chic, made-up, perfumed, a businesslike pleated skirt of dark blue, white blouse, grey cardigan hanging open. It was summer but the day was cold, winds blowing down from the hills at our back, cloud keeping the sun away.

'Mr Holt?' She had those intelligent eyes of the French bourgeoisie, the female of the species, like they see the joke but don't want to let their spouses know.

I said: 'That's right Miss . . . ?'

She laughed: 'Mrs — gallant! *Alors* — Tournier.'

'Like the author?' I'd practised that, pronouncing the name, to give myself some class. You know how it is. I needed to masticate on French names, even after the time I'd spent living there. I guess my ear wasn't finely tuned enough to work out quite how those nasal vowels were spelt and, vice versa, how the spelling should sound. Anyway, I reckoned you were safe referring to culture; they like culture in France, it pleases them to believe it exists.

'Tournier?' she repeated, puzzled.

Except this time I'd missed. My author, Tournier, was a discovery of our Dawn's: a famous novelist, rather controversial I gathered.

The woman who answered the door had stabbed a finger's perfectly manicured, painted nail into her cheek. She was pondering,

Who isn't?

This was my man's wife then?

'Ah . . . *alors*, you mean Tournier!' Which was what I'd said!

It happens all the time like that and still I couldn't have picked the difference between the two pronunciations, hers and mine.

'*L'Ogre*,' she said.

'Not me,' I said.

'Of course not . . . or so we hope.' Laughter.

'You never know . . . I could try.' Joining in the spirit of this unexpected exchange.

'Oh do, Mr Holt. Yes, please do.' Rubbing her hands together now, as though nothing in the world could be more fun.

'An ogre . . . you don't think your husband might track me down?'

'He is good, but against an ogre . . . who can say? Here, follow me, he is expecting you.'

Not like in *The Maltese Falcon* where there's a shabby office, a woman with breasts like footballs knocks on the door, pretends to be upset at the death of an aged husband, pulls a hundred-dollar bill out of her handbag.

Not with Monsieur Tournier it wasn't like that. He was rising from a two-seater couch. Beyond where he stood there were bay windows, and a view of buildings with the odd stroke of aquamarine between them, representing sea. Not too bad. The room was large, very large, a grand piano standing at one end, music in place.

'Mr Holt!' We shook hands.

'You play?' I asked Madame Tournier as she stood there, long fingers pressed together cathedral style.

'No, it is my husband who is the musician.'

'Well, he didn't tell me.'

'I did not have the chance, I don't think.'

'We were pretty rushed,' I explained to the polished floor.

I was steered into an armchair. Mr Tournier sat back in his two-seater; the book he'd been reading was resting open where some second person might be. His wife had positioned herself on a third chair, one with a tapestry of flowers and birds covering the padding.

Maybe I looked bewildered.

'You are not at ease, I think, Mr Holt?'

This Tournier had a smile on his face. As though it amused him to play his little joke of being the unlikely character, and to watch it work time and again.

'It's so . . .' I tried. 'It's . . .'

'Respectable.' Madame Tournier helped me out. 'I think you've seen too many films . . . Jean Gabin, Alain Delon?'

'Of course I've been expecting you, Mr Holt. And I understand that now you have caught the disease, you have kidnapped my employee.'

'It had been there, in my mind, since I got it back . . . the mind I mean. I'd thought of him a lot; of me considering only my own salvation . . . and of him getting hit.'

'So you have rushed up to Briançon, a knight on a white horse.'

'Not me, a friend.'

'But your automobile, the yellow one, not so very discreet.'

I caught on. Slow, admittedly, but I caught on. 'You mean you left him there because . . .'

'Precisely. Certainly he needed treatment, and the sooner he had that the better. But also, Mr Holt, people have long memories. After such an operation — it's not too dramatic, the word "operation"? I think it's best that there should be no connection between us. There are people who can get angry because a father dies. Or they have a code of conduct, perhaps, and might regard avenging a death as the only honorable course of action.'

'Up there in Briançon, surely he was a sitting duck!'

'If they knew he had been injured, perhaps. And if they happened to find him. Even then, Mr Holt, I did not leave my employee unprotected, I have a friend in the police, he was keeping an eye on our Moulay.'

'I was told the police were right out of this, that they had been from the start, and because of being out then it had to stay that way. Or their feelings would be hurt.'

'And you have been told the truth. Still, there were other plausible explanations for the law.'

'None that haven't got to have a villain at the end of them.'

'Mr Holt, for the hospital I told them . . . perhaps you can't remember us even arriving there, you were worn out, and then you had been unconscious for a long time as well. I have said it is a hunting accident. Because I need them to look after Moulay, and because I am dealing with people I can trust, I have told the police . . . well, not the truth of course, but that it is my business, for the moment at least. I've asked them just to watch, to make sure Moulay is safe. If there is an attempt made on him, then they will know everything. I've given my word. If not, it will be best if they wait. This is what I've said.'

'Tea, Mr Holt?' Madame Tournier interrupted; she was back on her feet. Her black hair gleamed like a starling's wing and she pushed it back from her brow with spread fingers. Curiously, once I'd been released and regained a few of my marbles, I'd begun to get excited by women, by a lot of them. It's true. To some extent this has always been the case . . . well, there's the birds and the bees, aren't there? Yet there I was looking at Madame Tournier's hair, observing the way the cut emphasized the form of her cheeks, the modelling of her long neck, and I was getting horny. I needed bromide, or maybe even castration! Which would have been Dawn's solution. So she could have the field to herself.

Did Madame Tournier notice?

'Tea,' I said.

She left the room.

The way the pleats made the cloth shift with each step, that together with a certain movement of the heels in her medium height sling-backs . . . the effect was unhinging.

'It's done.'

'What?' I asked him.

'You have shown all the cards with your act of . . . I expect it was kindness. And,' he continued, 'as far as I can ascertain no great harm will come of it. We don't believe it was noticed in the wrong quarters that a man with a bullet in his shoulder had been in the Briançon hospital. There was considerable physical damage, you understand.'

'So Moulay told me.'

'And when your unique automobile arrived for our Moulay I was contacted straightaway. So my official friends knew what to do. I told them the cat was out of the bag! But they weren't sure which bag.

'Still, you have not come to see me on account of that. And of course, had I thought these people were still watching, I would not have permitted this meeting today. I believe they have their money now, their dead as well. Possibly they are thinking more of their necks.'

'Chevet,' I said, 'I talked to him. He said I should see you. Of course I was going to anyway, to say thanks.'

'There is no need. I am employed to do a job. I have done it. Successfully, thank God.'

'Well, now there's another one to do.'

'Another job? I'm not so sure about this one, even though you have not yet explained what it involves.'

'First, Mr Tournier, perhaps you could tell me a couple of things about that day — just for the record, and to settle the brain cells.'

Tea was something fancy, delicate, the same with the cups and saucers. There were little cakes as well: madeleines to coax the memory. That's what they say: you dip them in the tea, take a bite, and the past sweeps in like a flood.

After pouring the faintly tinted aromatic water Madame Tournier left us to our own devices and retreated from whence she came.

My host filled me in on the operation to which I owed my life. It seems he'd been called in before the arrival of the signed sheet of paper and the finger. Of course, as he observed, the finger could have belonged to anyone, unless there was a set of prints to compare it with.

I made some weak joke about a blameless life, its disadvantages.

Tournier ploughed on: 'I sensed the action was soon to start. The finger was to let us know who we were dealing with. Already it was decided that we were not to gamble, nor to try a bluff. I had one instruction from Monsieur Chevet, that was to get you back alive. The cost was not important. I was to do nothing to try and save the picture or the cash. Our one object was to effect the exchange.

'My reading of events had already informed me there was only a slim chance of success. For, it would be one thing to deliver the ransom where and how they demanded, and another altogether not only to bring *you* back, but *myself* as well. I had to consider that.'

It was strange, sitting there sipping at the rim of the bone-china cup, nibbling on delicately flavoured cakes, talking to this man in a room the walls of which were papered with pale mustard fleurs-de-lis over which hung matched pairs of nineteenth-century hunting prints. If Tournier had appeared unsuitably dressed on the day of the exchange, in his slacks and sports coat, now he appeared even more removed from the role of man of action: corduroy trousers, Bordeaux red, soft leather slip-ons, open-neck shirt, stretched maroon cardigan patched with leather at the elbows. Quite the homebody; could be an academic, or a music teacher.

He was packing a pipe, slowly, deliberately. So it was only cigarettes out on the job, in the field as they say.

'What to do? It was a puzzle, Mr Holt. Yet, in my business one likes to — how should I say? — appear competent. Otherwise why would I set up in the profession at all?'

I shrugged my shoulders to show I was with him.

'Moulay Yusuf . . . actually a dangerous man and not completely reliable. But, so good. He'd been fighting in the Saharan War when King Hassan, Commander of the Faithful, was battling against the Polisario, nationalists for the Saharan Arab Democratic Republic. Sometimes I think Moulay fought for one side, sometimes for another. His stories are of that quality. What does it matter? He survived. And he came to France where he has residency and, I believe, somewhere a wife . . . probably to guarantee his status in our country.

'Whatever might be said of him, for the man, or against him, he is the tops. It's rumoured he had some connection with the road pirate gangs which rob automobiles heading south in the summer. Then it's also said he works with the anti-racism people, as a guard outside their meetings, and protecting targeted immigrant families against attack from the new fascists. This I do believe but I think he is in it for the money, a mercenary. Our Moulay is not an idealist. This way, or that way, he makes a living, most of which, in my own opinion, comes from the prostitutes in west Nice.'

I had seen them waving their cans around out along the rue de France after it crossed Boulevard Gambetta. Trading on the dusty streets as briskly in the daylight hours as at night.

Tournier had his pipe lit up; he was sucking contentedly, a fog of smoke enveloping his neat head. 'I am not here to pass judgement on such people as Moulay. I employ him when I require his talents, that's where it begins and where it ends.'

Good on you Tournier, because that was exactly what I'd

decided to do with Moulay Yusuf. Whether or not I could get Tournier's co-operation.

'So, the problem, Mr Holt, was for me to arrive at the exchange in the mountains, but with — how should I say? — some back-up. This was not easy.

'I would have to drive to the nominated spot, then receive instructions as to where to go next. Of course I was certain I would be watched through the stages of the drive. And that there would be other vehicles keeping an eye on side roads, on tracks and so on. I would only know where I was heading once I arrived . . . in other words, too late. So, only at the last minute would I be in a position to judge whether or not it would be possible to carry out the exchange. I resolved to leave my mind a blank. I carried no weapon on my person though I had the one pistol in a clip up under the dashboard of my automobile . . . something to fall back on if I should be provided with the chance for action.

'It's a fast Citroën, the model with the Maserati motor, as fast as effectively you can be fast. Also I have made some other . . . let me say, adjustments. Some minor ones, made a long time ago. Now I had more done at a small panel-beating shop quite close by. The rear section was reconstructed so there was a gap below a false floor, just enough space for one man to lie with his head cushioned in foam rubber against the vibration.

'Now it's true I had not a great deal to bargain with. But these kidnappers don't want to go to so much trouble for nothing. They must get the money. The one power I have is the money. They must suspect that if I feel something is not right I do not deal. For them it would be goodbye to all those crisp American dollars. Also they will be on edge, whoever they are.

'My trump card: if I can have Moulay get out from where he is under the false floor.

'We drove up there. Initially I had thought to take one more automobile as well, another of my associates driving that. Actually the man I had in my mind for that has followed you here today, for safety. But then I could see no purpose in two cars. The best thing was for these people to build up their confidence, and to believe they had the deal in the bag.

'I was stopped as I had been told to expect when instructed on procedure. My Citroën was searched. They have even felt in behind the dashboard. And there they have discovered the pistol in its clips.

'One man screamed at me, called me dishonest! Imagine, he called *me* dishonest! And he is a kidnapper!'

'What man?' I asked, butting in. I felt excited waiting for the answer. It was as though I wanted Tournier to describe Tony. The way a lover may bait a conversation so the name of his beloved surfaces.

'How should I know what man?'

'It's important. For Christ's sake, I was held there by them! You get to develop an interest. Believe me, Tournier, you do.'

'So, he is . . .'

And there it was, the description I'd been fishing for. Tony!

Then Tournier continued: 'The important thing was that they find the handgun. They were so pleased with themselves about this . . . to have discovered it. I think: I lose the pistol, yet perhaps I gain something else.'

I was talking to a brave man, in his cardigan, smoking his pipe. And an unusual man. I interrupted, asked him why he should bother to risk his life like this. Me being a stranger! He explained that in any profession there are a lot of people, most of them average at what they do. He thought it proper for it to be like that. After all what else was an average? Then you had to have the man who was the tops.

Smiling modestly Tournier held out his hands as though to indicate that there had never been a choice. 'I get the difficult jobs. I'm paid to do them. Because I am lazy. I do not like to work. Better one or two jobs a year, but get them right, and to be paid well for my work.'

I didn't ask how much, I didn't dare. Nor had Karen and I broached the subject. The money and the Gauguin were left for another day.

'Then, Mr Holt, the difficult part was when I drove into that field and waited. I stopped where I was told to stop. Such careful preparation, they had even placed a marker on the ground!

'I was feeling like the target on an army range. And Moulay was already moving his body forward, wriggling out of his hiding place and into the interior of the automobile. He had his rifle with him: it's short, seventy, seventy-five centimetres, and twenty-five rounds in the magazine. He had a spare magazine with him as well.

These weapons will fire at a rate of eight hundred rounds a minute. The trigger is set to deliver a three-round burst so with the kick of the gun there is some spread. I think if Moulay is with me we are safe. I've been in the forces, special operations, I know you only need one man, if it's the right man. Then you're winning. Moulay Yusuf is the right man. Perhaps he has the wrong mind, his life is not as it should be, but he is so sure in what he does, so exact . . . and no fear, none at all.'

'He got hit,' I said.

'He did, but if we'd stopped, and rolled him out on to the road, even dying, he'd have killed every one of those people.'

Me: 'Then why didn't you let him?'

'Because, I was asked to bring you back alive. That was the job: to pay the money and bring you back. Didn't I do that?'

What can you answer? Talk about a rhetorical question!

I couldn't say anything.

'More tea?' He was reaching across to the occasional table on which his wife had placed the pot, the milk, a plate with the madeleines. 'Or perhaps, you'd like something a little stronger. Although the sun is not yet over the yard-arm.'

'The sun's not where?'

'That's what your British yachtsmen say, when the alcohol level in their blood falls too low.'

'We don't put it like that in Australia, but yes, I would.'

'Wine?'

The wine was elsewhere in the apartment. Tournier left me and went off to fetch it. I was standing by the piano when Madame Tournier came back in. I was looking at the music; it was Bach, not my kind of stuff — counterpoint deranges the mind, too many things going on at the one time.

'He will play, if you ask,' Madame Tournier said, smiling.

Chapter 16

For the three months of summer I was concerned about the family's lost fortunes. According to what Karen and the accountants initially estimated we were still so far above the breadline that it didn't matter. And there were always pictures to be sold to keep the *Vin de Pays* flowing at table. Not to mention the market value of my hoards of silver, furniture, cars, real estate, and God knows what else.

That was the way Karen and her cohorts first made the calculations. Maybe we were still playing at keeping Essington happy. Not getting far, though, with me brooding, sometimes settling down in a chair and staring at the sea through the trees for hours at a spell. Sure, there was laughter, there were smiles; but the whole thing between the two of us was brittle. We were playing at a relationship. I had the feeling it was Pietro who kept us at it. Nobody wanting to be the one to cut and run.

There was a lot of watching him grow while exchanging looks between us, wondering what lay behind them.

It was towards the end of the first of those three months that Karen calculated the fortunes a second time without the optimistic distortions.

We weren't in debt, that was the new conclusion.

That is unless you regarded what would have to be forked out in tax as a debt. To my mind money owed is money owed, even to the taxman. That was why I'd been so poor before I became so rich, I wouldn't get into debt. If you don't borrow the stuff there usually isn't so much with which to start doing the multiplications.

So we were in the red! What's the expression? 'Asset rich, cash poor.'

I wheedled how much we were down out of Karen. And then I

sat again and stared at the sea, establishing an all-time record for doing so. Desdemona crouched at my side, sensing something wrong.

'Karen . . . we've blown it.'

It was meal time. The pair of us sitting either end of the dining table, wine glasses reflected in its polished surface. Rebecca in her kitchen, poaching the fish. People reckon servants are the first to know when a household is collapsing. That's their selfish gene, keeping its nose to the wind, sniffing, alert for changing circumstances.

'Hyperbole — you'll do that every time.'

'Do it, for Christ's sake! Facing reality, that's some kind of crazy reaction, is it?'

'We have not blown it, that's all I'm saying, Essington.'

Rebecca entered, a plate in each hand, the fish. It was red mullet, white wine, a touch of fennel. I stared at it, sitting there on my plate, a symbol of that life we could no longer sustain.

'Essington, we have . . . For heaven's sake, we own everything!'

'Not true.'

'There are payments with the shop building, granted, but the silk's growing all the time.'

'Not quick enough, it's subsidized, you have to face facts. All this' — gesturing around where I sat — 'keeps the silk protected till . . .'

' . . . It's got there. Understood, but Essington . . .'

'And it hasn't got there yet, has it, Blue?'

'You have to account for intrinsic value; there's so much potential. Anybody would loan against it, be mad not to.'

'To a bunch of foreigners, liable to skip the country at a moment's notice? Australians what's more! What I'm saying, Karen . . . it isn't hyperbole, it's the situation.'

Rebecca had returned with plates of vegetables. She was used to us screaming at each other in English. Maybe she just wrote it down to the fact that we were hot-blooded souls from the Pacific rim.

Sitting there, each hand a fist, I hadn't touched my knife and fork. In fact my soup spoon was still clasped in one hand. My eyes were fixed on a lump of bread.

*

Four days later there was the announcement of Makihei's rescue bid. He was going to buy forty-nine per cent of the silk business with a management contract allocating design and marketing control to the Karen–Dawn partnership for a period of ten years. Effectively that meant they could sell off more of the business if need be, and still remain in the box seat.

The building was to be purchased lock, stock and barrel by Makihei's organization.

The price of all that would be the brand name: 'Makihei' was to be it from then on.

Karen: '"Makihei" — people pay millions for the right to use a label like that. We get it for free.'

'You paid for it with your sovereignty.'

'Essington, you're medieval, you know that?'

I asked: 'When does this dream solution become reality?'

'There's paperwork, lawyers . . .'

'Chevet?'

'This is corporation work.'

'Then who?'

'Chevet mentioned a firm in London with Paris links. Anyhow, I can't believe a nice man like Makihei is going to try to put one over us.'

'It's not Makihei, Karen, he's just a pretty face, and the design touch. There're rooms full of inscrutable men in suits; they'll be wearing steel-rimmed glasses and trying every trick in the book. You know that.'

'People do these things! Dawn and I are doing it now. All you need to know is that the money isn't a big problem, not any more. We are not bust; not technically, not in fact.'

As it finished up, the deal was handled by a London firm that had a man who specialized in business involving France. He was called Howard Fischmann. I got to speak to him once when Dawn and Karen were gadding about and he'd tried the house number. I took a message.

I still felt bad.

I continued to sit, to brood, to gaze at the sea. There is a French poem that starts: '*Homme libre, toujours tu chériras la mer.*'

The trouble being I wasn't feeling all that free. There were the financial problems, but even I knew it was more than that, it went deeper. I still needed to execute an act of revenge.

It was true, the pictures could be sold.

But I couldn't bring myself to do that. Since the death of my aunt I'd kept everything pretty much as it had been, adding but never subtracting. Villa du Phare went with the Pincis, Rebecca and Renardo, with the yellow Bentley, the paintings: it was all one piece. I could still remember the first time I'd met those people, and those objects. That had been my magic moment. I couldn't take what a doting aunt had put together and pull it apart like some late-phase money hoon might do, plundering the fruits of imagination and hard work.

If I was going to sell a picture, I decided it would be a fake one. That was it: I was going to pop the Gauguin back into the system.

The system: in my mind that was part of 'they', of the mob that had nabbed me and done me down.

Morality does not apply as far as the art market is concerned, nor is there a problem with quality — I guess there never has been. It's all fads. The rich throwing money about, the clever among them nobbling the market.

The one central fact is that none of them — not the corporate buyers nor the new generation public art administrators — are interested in art. It is the art–money nexus that fascinates them, and which hauls awe-struck crowds in through the gallery doors.

So, I was making a Gauguin, a replica of the picture taken out of my hands. I believed it would be a long time before the original found its way back on to the open market. And we'd been put in a position where the police couldn't be alerted to the fact that it was out there, on the loose. That was Chevet's and Danny Tournier's rule at the start: no cops. Now I was safe and poorer they reckoned that to show and tell would only bring the wrath of the law down upon our heads.

Forgery is my form of creativity. It's the meeting point of science and art: you can't get away with it if you miss on the art aspect; and in modern times the science side is getting pretty tricky, with new methods of studying pigments, their age, composition, and of photographing layers of paint hidden beneath the final surface. You won't pass off a forgery if it arouses sufficient curiosity to be subjected to detailed expert examination.

So you have to avoid that. The way is through the provenance: that list of authentic owners through whose hands the work has passed. You have to make that look right.

My Gauguin had an impeccable pedigree. The Renouard family had owned the work since Gauguin sent it to Paris all those years ago. Nobody outside the family and the Renouards' circle of friends had seen it. I was next on the list of owners, and between us there was a reproduction in the auction catalogue. Not much chance of a challenge arising out of that.

I'd sinned against everything in which I believe when I'd allowed myself to be persuaded to buy art as an act of financial speculation. The young wife pushing the old boy along the paths of evil.

Eve feeding apples to Adam.

Now I was going to give that world back what it deserved and, at the same time, expiate my guilt. Laugh as they read the documents, tucked the picture under their arm, headed off into the wild blue yonder.

Since forging is my *métier* I was already stocked up with most of the materials required. For several years I'd combed Paris and Nice for old canvas stretchers, paper, glues, raw pigments; ancient stocks of paint going hard and discoloured by lead oxide from inside the tube, their labels eaten away by silverfish.

I love the stuff. Aged stretcher arms bearing the marks of borer attack like an old soldier's battle scars. There is a smell to it all, distinctive, pungent, aromatic, yet musty at the same time.

I had stores of commercial canvas, as old as I was able to procure, some already coated with ground, awaiting the act of painting, the rest raw, just the woven flax fibres.

Stage one in any piece of forgery is the research. On a quick trip to Paris I managed to work through the Gauguin source material at several libraries, mostly concentrating on letters sent by the artist to his friends, Emile Bernard and the supportive Georges-Daniel de Monfreid as well as to his estranged and bitter wife, Mette. But the greater part of what I required was already available in an old copy of Maurice Malingue's *Lettres de Gauguin a sa femme et a ses amis* turned up by a book dealer in behind the Boulevard Jean Jaurès at Nice. From this reading I put together a fairly clear idea of the kinds of paint and canvas Gauguin had taken with him to Papeete on his first voyage. Most of his paints had been standard commercial decorator's colours manufactured by Lefranc & Co. As well he had casein, white fillers, and glues to make up into grounds for the two rolls of canvas, one coarse the other fine, he'd brought from France. The Gauguin I had spent so much money on had been painted on a coarse canvas. There is a possibility that the ground under it was the result of one of the unsound experiments he had undertaken in the Pacific, making use of juices extracted from local fruits. Most of Gauguin's materials were replenished from San Francisco, Sydney, or France itself when there was money to back up the order, though often he had to wait months for essentials and adapt his technique in the meantime.

In the Renouard Gauguin, painted on the coarse canvas, there was evidence of a poor-quality ground with perhaps some of the paint's binding oils soaked into it and right through to the fibre of the canvas itself. Where it was turned over the edges of the stretcher it had been reinforced with paper. At some earlier date an inexpert job of backing the canvas had been carried out — in this case the backing canvas on to which the old coarse one, rotted at the edges, had been stuck was of extremely fine weave.

Searching out appropriately coarse canvas was the first of my problems. Eventually, with the help of a disapproving old friend in London, I was sent several metres of the stuff through the post. It was in fact new canvas, made in Belgium. The fine, whitish coloured fabric for the backing was picked up by one of the Nice art supply shops who sent away to a Paris wholesaler for it. In Nice nearly all of the canvas available is already stretched and coated with ground. We are a bunch of hobby painters down here these days: no more Matisse or Dufy pushing the boundaries of the pictorially possible.

The glues I already had.

First to paint my picture. I had an excellent photograph from which to work. This had been taken for insurance identification purposes the day after the sale. I had been delivered a copy. The photographic image was large with just sufficient sidelight to emphasize a sense of brush stroke. The detail of colour change was pretty accurately recorded, and anything I lacked in that department could be picked up from fine-quality reproductions of similar compositions in art books.

I worked in secret, not daring to tell Karen what I was up to. At first hardly even possessing the courage to admit it to myself. After all, success would mean that I had recovered some of my financial position together with considerable self-respect. Failure, being detected, would mark the end of everything: I'd be cooling my heels in a French prison.

After already finding out the hard way that I didn't lock up well.

The fact is forging was a crazy course to follow, particularly since it was pride driving me, as much as necessity.

The trick with faking is to produce something good enough to get the bidding going at an auction. Once these works go into a private collection the last thing the speculator wants is for some little prick of an expert to come along and knock his masterpiece off the list of the tried and true. There are no refunds for fakes though maybe you could have a go at the auction house, sue them. Such an action might succeed, or at least get a settlement out of court. And if my buyer did that, because of the perfect provenance, I could move into line, sue in my turn, if I could think of some kind of loss to claim. There is always loss of face, isn't there?

And providing such a scandal didn't cause the picture I'd originally purchased to surface and make everybody's face turn red.

In my dreams there were recurring fears, set pieces repeated, so that on nights after days which had been worse than usual I had to fill my depressive self with enough whisky to ensure, if not sleep, then something close to unconsciousness.

I'd developed some other me. A hidden, furtive Essington. Keeping from Karen not just the fact that I was working up a fake Gauguin but also that I hadn't forgotten revenge. Tony, the South African, had caused me to feel grateful to him . . . for what? And in the end I'd make him pay for that response of mine.

Moulay Yusuf accepted a position in the household, at least, he said, until his shoulder got back in working order. Karen had tried to fight this, perhaps suspecting that I had my plans. A previous history of excessive anger, of hate rendered tangible, made it more than likely that I'd eventually set out after my one-time captors.

'We have Pietro, Essington. We are alive, the two of us.'
'You're stealing my lines.'
'Your lines?'
'Sure, contentment, the simple life: live off your good luck; leave the rest for the rest. But you wanted pictures that could print money while we slept, didn't you? Too much! It was you, Karen, who didn't have enough!'
'You twist things around.'
'Do I? Like twisting what, for example?'
'Words, Essington. The thing is, that man always hanging about gives me the creeps. He's like a cat. Never even speaking. Do we need him?'
'Think of him as Mou, it'll make it so much easier.'
'But what is he? I feel like we belong to the Mafia or something.'
'Mafia is Sicilian. Tell me then, did we need that arsehole you put on the gate with the walkie-talkie? Or do you want me to answer for you? No we didn't need him. But if there's the idea of a dead man shot up in the hills, and not yet avenged, then yes, maybe we do need Moulay. We owe him as well. He saved my life, remember?'
'Employed to do it, as a professional.'
I asked: 'What in God's name can be wrong with using a professional?'
'Playing with words again.'
We agreed to differ.

When I wasn't doing Gauguins, or off hunting the roads, trying to put together the memories I had of that drive to the field where the exchange had been made, Nurse Findlay and I spent time with Pietro.

Or I'd be watching the sea, making sure it didn't vanish some time when my back was turned.

I discovered that Nurse Findlay was a writer: twenty-six romantic novels to her credit! While with us she was working on number twenty-seven.

I'd said: 'Babies, Nurse . . . initially you were to look after me. Is it possible you're over-qualified?'

'It's all the same, Mr Holt. The one thing is I only do what I enjoy.'

'You enjoy writing, sitting at your . . . is it longhand?'

'Good lord no! On Ollie, he's the typewriter, faithful he is too. Twenty-three years we've been together, Ollie and I — Ollie for Olivetti you see.'

I did see — well, sort of. 'And this one is about a young wife living in a big house with a sort of Frankenstein's monster for a husband.'

'You've been reading my notes, Mr Holt!' she exclaimed.

'Not at all, I'm living it. Tell me, Nurse, the end, have you plotted that out yet?'

'Never, Mr Holt, it isn't my method of working. But the solution always crops up.'

'How about a knight on a white horse?'

'A knight, most probably, yes.'

Chapter 17

I'd got my hands on a bundle of army ordnance maps showing contours, rivers, pondages, small black rectangles where there were buildings; every road and track marked. These related to a master map grid drawn over the north-west corner of Italy, right down to the sea. I'd ruled out Switzerland.

I had the equivalent maps for the French side, too.

Working on these in my studio, I was running a pencil along anything that could be navigated by car, checking out the detail. Those with promise I overscored with highlighter. So I was developing my personal picture of the roads to hell, watching it build like the web of a spider, only there was no design to it, no symmetry, just wiggly lines heading for anywhere: a diagram of the nervous system.

I knew I had to use another car for the search, something unobtrusive, certainly not a yellow Bentley, nor a dated silver Maserati. I even rejected the idea of commandeering the Citroën Estate Karen and Dawn used most of the time as an extension of the business.

I went to a car lot out near the airport, picked myself up a Renault with rust breaking through the white paint at the bottom of the doors.

While on those reconnaissance drives I left Moulay at home to watch over things.

Karen disliked the idea of Moulay. Renardo positively resented his presence. The idea of an Arab who wandered about with a bull-pup rifle in his hand offended Renardo's proprietorial instincts. I tried to talk to him about it, to say it was only for a while, because we were worried about Pietro . . . that somehow the idea of a kidnapping had made us excessively protective.

Renardo wouldn't listen.

Karen felt protective towards Pietro, and believed we ought to be ready for some follow up to the kidnap. It was just that she'd developed this thing about Moulay, because he'd killed a man!

I'd object: 'Karen, you'd rather it had been me left bleeding up there?'

'That's not what I'm saying.'

'Then what are you saying? Moulay, he's killed a man. I'd put money on it he's exterminated whole tribes of them. That's what he does! Like Placido Domingo plays the piano.'

'He sings.'

'What?'

'Placido Domingo sings.'

Doing my trips into the mountains, following routes I'd inscribed on the ordnance maps, I got to know the region. I could eventually have applied for a position as travel guide. There were times though when my internal system would seize up as I thought I recognized something of what I'd made it my business to memorize on that trip in the Audi. And then, the next turn in the road would introduce a landscape totally foreign to me.

How could I have brought so little mind to the task of remembering details of that trip? Sure, my co-passenger had made a point of shoving my head down from time to time so that I wouldn't pick up something too precise, but still you'd think even in the state I was in my powers of retention would have been a fraction better. You'd think in vain.

Danny Tournier almost became a friend. So he should have after the payment Karen told me we'd shelled out. But he was insistent that snooping about the country, checking documents in public registries, taking photographs of people in bed . . . none of that was his cup of tea. If he had to collect that sort of data he used someone else for the purpose.

'Who?'

We were at a restaurant down by the flower market in the old part of Nice, not so far from the opera house.

'I spread the work around a number of people. There are benefits in sustaining a range of contacts.'

It sounded like a demarcation trick to me. As with the unions: subdivide the labour and you extract more money from the employer.

I said: 'If you won't do it I reckon I need somebody.'

'It's best this way, Essington. When the moment is ripe, that might be when I can be of use. Anyhow, work is not how I intend to waste my life.'

That evening a retired policeman by the name of Jean Dolent answered my call. His name means what it sounds like, doleful, plaintive. And that's what he'd spent sixty years growing into as I discovered when I visited him the next day. He was a lean man of average height, with a stoop, almost a hump on his back. His hair was thick, curly, black; he looked like the sculptor Giacometti, dressed like him as well: shabby sports coat, trousers gone baggy at the knees and the cuffs frayed where they hung down too low, dragging on the ground.

Jean Dolent lived in the town of Villefranche, on the third floor of a Thirties block of apartments gone drab. There were two rooms joined by folding doors which were open, tall windows gave on to a Sixties block of apartments of several more floors which shut off the view of the bay. Instead of sparkling sea we got a detailed layout of water and electrical couplings, not to mention drainage.

The balcony was just wide enough for a chair to fit, sideways.

I could smell food, cooked, or in preparation. Maybe the place always smelt like that. And there was a picture of a young man in military uniform who looked as though he was Jean himself, in his prime.

A bachelor, I deduced.

Yes, Monsieur Tournier had already rung him, explained that I would call, and had indicated something of the kind of assistance I'd be wanting. Instead of telling me his fee Dolent slid a card across the plastic-coated floral table-cloth. The name was on one side, followed by letters which I took to signify decorations. No mention of police rank. Turning the card over I discovered the charges written there.

Would I like some tea?

Unusual stuff, the French with their reputation for guarding the interior of their dwellings, and there I was, the second occasion that I'd been invited into, not some office, but the inner sanctum. Private investigators, it seemed, break all the rules.

Tea would do fine.

Monsieur Dolent hoped I didn't mind but there was no milk.

No milk, that would be fine too.

He was off into the kitchen. I could hear water running, cups plonked down on saucers: tea-making noises. The electric jug must have been on the same plug as the radio because suddenly we were blessed with Sacha Distel getting the facts straight about the back streets of Naples. How was Pietro going to react to 'Where Do You Go To, My Lovely?' when he was cruising the bars of the Côte d'Azur in dad's Maserati? Poor little bugger.

Standing at the windows I found I could glimpse water at an oblique angle, and the edge of the town's Sardinian fortress which the locals called the Citadel.

When the tea arrived I was watching an old woman talking to a dachshund in a garden below, catching her in plain view among flowering standard roses. Without saying a word Dolent took a cup from the tray and slid it in my direction. He poured.

'You like it weak?'

'How it comes.'

Jesus! How long was this ritual going to last?

He sat, I sat.

'I like a nice cup of tea,' he explained. Probably thinking he was being terribly English in that.

If he was telling the truth then he had nothing to whinge about. He had the cup of tea.

He took a sip. 'Ah . . . ' A smile spread across his unsmiling and grey-toned features. 'Mr Holt, isn't it? What can I do for you?'

There were lots of things he could do. I checked them off as I worked down the list. Like he could try and find out what the hell had happened to Jodie Winton. She was from the United States of America, had worked for us, her passport had been sighted by Dawn who, stirred up as she might have been by the girl's glow, had made a note of the details. I could give the retired policeman the name of an American town, Mount Vernon, in the state of Ohio.

'And this woman arrived in France at what date?'

'Sorry.'

He shrugged, took another sip of his cup. 'I have no biscuits,' he explained.

'I don't even know if she's still in France.'

He shrugged again.

'Just find out what you can, flight lists, that sort of thing . . . I don't know, this isn't my area.'

'What is your area, Mr Holt.'

What is my area? I could see then the intelligence behind the expression. Dolent was no twit. You get people like that in life, who settle for less rather than for more. Maybe electing for that is an indication of a superior mind. Certainly I never saw a rich man who looked as though he had brains, and I'd looked, made quite a study of it. Even myself, in fact I was the proof.

Was that what Jean Dolent was thinking? Thinking: Essington Holt, custard where his brain should be.

Dolent would do what he could with Jodie, there were certain avenues of enquiry possible, but he couldn't promise anything.

Then I gave him a date, asked for funerals that had occurred right across the country to the north in the couple of weeks after that date. Italy too, was Italy possible?

'Yes, Italy, why not?'

'That's terrific,' I said.

He shrugged again; keep that shrug up and the lining would drop out of his stained sports coat.

I'd counted off two of my requests. Before I could start on the third he interrupted: 'You have seen my fees?'

I took out a cheque-book: 'How much do you want as a starting shot?'

He blew air into his cheeks, made a sound like 'booph'.

I said: 'Five thousand francs?'

A bushy eyebrow went up. Then the other one followed. He was screwed if he was going to smile though.

I wrote out the cheque. 'One thing, Monsieur Dolent, could you ring me each day, tell me what you've got, even if it's nothing? But don't tell anyone else who answers . . . just say you're a friend. And, you find you have to travel, please don't hesitate. I'll cover costs.'

Say you are my friend! That was a laugh. Who did the old Essington have as a friend, for Christ's sake?

*

There was Molena, we owned some apartments together. Legal complications in that quarter denied me the possibility of selling my share. But Molena was in New Caledonia trying to muscle into some real estate business while people were too worried about the island's internal politics to invest. New Caledonia was going to be Molena's big success. So, knowing Molena, was everything going to be, probably since he'd been a kid in Naples.

He was also godfather to Pietro, a role he took seriously. Molena was due back any day. I couldn't wait, I needed a shoulder to cry on, and someone to talk with who might feel the same way as I did about what the world doled out to a man.

I suspected Moulay could have played the part of friend. Except he didn't drink, nor for that matter did he talk. Moulay was Moulay, good at pulling triggers, other than that he kept the shutters down.

Earlier I'd asked Farah about her trip back from Briançon with Moulay, what they'd discussed.

'Politics.'

That had surprised me.

'I had not expected to be sent off to fetch a man I already knew.'

'Knew?'

'Yes, Essington.'

'He's on our side, Farah.'

'Our side? Your side? I think most likely, Essington, he is always on his own side.'

'You said politics . . . what politics did you talk about?'

'We did not converse in French, of course, not with your driver, Renardo. No, and I am not so sure he would have liked what we were saying.'

'So, it was your anti-racism thing. It's funny that, you object, you get liberal thinkers on your side, and then what? Then you get to be racist yourselves . . . holy men following bigot obsessions, knives flashing.'

'We have our liberals too, we are liberals that come to the meetings. Islam is not one thing, any more than Christianity can be thought to be. Our true tradition is one of enlightenment. At the same time there are fundamentalists who catch the headlines.'

'Moulay, he's liberal?'

'Perhaps not Moulay, but he is brave.'

That was one conversation with Farah.

I hadn't been in on the other one when she resigned. That, it seemed, was to do with racism as well.

There'd been two Japanese gentlemen checking out what Makihei's gesture of buying into the silk business meant in terms of cash, bricks and mortar, expansion. Figures were checked, questions asked.

The Japanese had been determined not to impose on our hospitality; they stayed at the Negresco on the Promenade des Anglais. Not just because it was the best place in town but because it was the closest you could get to the shop.

And yet something about these two gentlemen got Farah's back up, she started into generalizations about the Japanese, then she resigned.

Farah had resigned!

I was appalled.

And that was only a couple of weeks after she'd taken the unexpected step of moving into one of the refurbished apartments three doors up from the Negresco.

Big changes in a girl's life, both of them.

Dawn said stuff her, called her an ungrateful bitch. But you could tell it was a shock in that quarter as well.

As far as my investigations were concerned, I had the ball rolling, and was getting nowhere. Meanwhile the Gauguin had progressed. Paint was going on by then. Gauguin applied the colour in sequences of parallel strokes, usually vertical, working along in lines. And he kept it thin — probably because he couldn't afford to do otherwise. On the rough canvas supports you can't see the strokes so clearly because there was also the problem of filling the surface with pigment.

With no impasto and the brush strokes ordered like that the job of imitation proved fairly easy. The thin paint was quick to dry, that was an advantage as well. There is a logic to Gauguin's work, to the way it's made. It's interesting — I'd found the same thing studying other paintings from the end of the nineteenth century. You can see that he was rational about how to relate the colour areas within the figure–ground jigsaw he produced — say the relationship between leaf forms and the shape of areas of sky left in behind them.

I'd always liked Gauguin partly because he included kangaroos in decorative friezes of at least one major painting — that's the nationalistic Holt rearing its head — but mostly because he was so wild about beauty. His life was a quest for it, for beauty and for what it might mean if he found it.

Poor bugger: big ideas, a big temper as well, and he was only five-foot-four tall.

Paul Gauguin was shorter than Karen!

Chapter 18

Built-up shoes were being searched for in snaps of the Paris fashion parades and associated events. Dawn had been in contact with Makihei on that one.

He'd promised to have a check made of the strips of colour transparency film. There would have been miles of the stuff: you never saw so many cameras lined up, motor drives full speed ahead, as at the Paris parades.

Of course, he assured Dawn, he wouldn't be able to recover most of the film, it had gone to the far corners of the globe. But, what he could do, he would do. And they had a great deal of visual material themselves, video as well: his own parade right from the moment when they had brought the scarlet Rolls-Royces to my apartment to carry us away.

I took a chance on using Dawn for something connected with the kidnap. She might have had weird views on all sorts of matters but my reading was that Dawn Grogan was reliable.

I'd been at her apartment. She lived in the Port area of Nice, very smart too: views out over moored fishing boats and the big Corsica ferry.

'Thanks for that,' I said as reward for the troubles she'd taken on my behalf with Makihei.

'But why these built-up shoes? Is it some new fetish? There's no stopping you men. The mind boggles.'

'Whose doesn't?'

Generally Dawn saw the joke . . . well, in most things. But maybe not where Farah resigning was concerned. That had broken her up. Even a full month later she'd lose some of her shine at the sound of the name. And then could turn nasty.

'Japanese, I mean, Essington, a nice little man like Maki! Who could be more perfect? Yet she hated them. Why?' Dawn always shortened Makihei's name like that, and he liked it.

On her wall a big blow-up photograph of Tony Curtis as he was in *Some Like it Hot*.

She continued: 'If you ask me it wasn't the Japanese at all. What would that make of all her SOS Racism stuff? Mince meat. No, and let's not forget she'd bought that apartment on the seafront.'

It wasn't just a cup of tea, not with Dawn, she was doing the whole bit, even a silver art deco pot with a black insulated handle. God, what would that have cost?

'I have to say it, at first I thought it was you.'

'Me! Why, Dawn?'

'The abrupt change with Farah. She moves out of here. One minute perfectly happy, the next she's out. And never offering an explanation.'

'Maybe she got sick of . . .'

'Me doing it to her . . . that's what you were going to say, wasn't it? Do you know, you are *so* coarse, Essington?'

'I thought we were talking about you, about Farah . . . being coarse, if that's how you want to refer to whatever it is you girls do to each other to stay happy.'

Dawn was on her feet. She'd be quite a bit smaller than Gauguin. Dressed in black, always black. And the hair, a red gleam to the blackness of it. Her face was powdered back to white.

Me sitting there, suddenly feeling uncomfortable because I'd upset her. But no, she was on her feet to be serious, to make a point. She'd opened a door off the living room where we were sitting. I could see through to a bed and beyond it a narrow balcony, the shutters half open. Otherwise no furniture, nothing. It struck me how narrow the bed was.

She closed the door.

'There was no fucking, Essington, nothing. That I promise you.'

Dawn and I talked about a lot that afternoon. Dawn smoked, I didn't. She was rolling them, spitting out the loose ends. We talked about the changes the deal with Makihei might mean, about her plans for the next season's designs, and I got it across that I didn't want Karen to know what I was on about.

That was the difficult bit.

Dawn objected, yet you could see that the idea of me going after the bastards made more sense to her than it would have to Karen.

'How much do you know?' I asked.

'What Karen said, she couldn't hide that there was . . . that the sky had fallen in.'

'And you asked her for the details?'

'Wouldn't you? Karen and I are . . . well it sounds teenybopper doesn't it, but we are *best* friends. Truly we are.'

'You don't have to tell me.'

'When you're in pain, that's what friends are for. Karen was in a lot of pain.'

'But that would be in the stars, writ.'

'Crap it would. You're so bloody-minded. Karen, she's a saint, you know that?'

'I know you're not.'

Dawn refilled the cups, the brew getting stronger, more like my mother used to make.

'If you're so close, why won't you tell her about this as well?'

'You might not like it, Essington, but you are also my friend.'

'And Farah?'

'I'm over that. And do you know, the apartment she bought, she wasn't even living there at the start. Our beautiful Farah'd vanished. Now she's back, we had coffee. But cool, you know.'

As I was leaving Dawn asked: 'You're friends with Maki, why not ask him yourself?'

'That man called Tournier, Dawn . . .'

'*L'Ogre?*' That was Dawn all over, the closet intellectual who'd burst out of the closet. And the elephant that never forgets connections.

'He told me to keep everything as indirect as possible. Tournier even suggested thinking more about Makihei, if he had some role. He said there were coincidences . . . and whoever it was masterminded the kidnap had a lot of inside information. He has this theory about the Japanese obsession with French art. I think he got it from his wife. Mrs Tournier is a considerable woman, Dawn.'

'I'm not certain I like your tone.'

'Mrs Tournier's theory is that there's a cycle involved. First, in the late nineteenth century, the Impressionists pick up ideas from Japanese art, they collect it too. In fact the whole of Paris goes mad for the Orient. For the music as well, like with Debussy. Her theory is that now it's the other way round. Japan is the dominant economic power but it wants our art.'

'It's an idea,' Dawn said. 'But real inside information . . . that fits our Jodie to a tee, doesn't it?' Dawn let smoke drift out with the observation.

In the photography quarter we were looking for shots of people waving cameras and for something to trigger a memory, even a fragment of visual information that may have stuck in the mind of another photographer. I was still convinced there had been someone taking pictures of me. The notion felt right, inside my head.

Dolent was doing as much as he could with descriptions of Tony and the other man as well. At any rate that's what he told me, daily as instructed. But what hope was there? Three hundred million people live in Europe, and most of that number again in the United States!

Two needles in a gigantic haystack, that was what I was searching for.

Chapter 19

I'd been back to the place where the exchange was made; after recovery that was my first trip north in the battered Renault. Nothing could have stopped me going there. And what did I find? A field, much like any other. No corpse rotting down beneath tattered clothes, neither was there the atmosphere of dread. I walked about crushing clovers beneath my shoes, backwards and forwards, checking the ground, hunting for signs, for a spent cartridge, even for the stain or scent of blood. That was how crazy I'd got, down on my hands and knees, sniffing. Getting Desdemona to do the same.

The dog couldn't give a damn. She hunted after rabbits, scared the daylights out of a flock of neglected sheep.

Yet the day was much the same as it had been for the swap. Cerulean sky, a clarity of atmosphere and of colour. The clouds, as though they'd been waiting to repeat the trick, the pair of them appeared out of nowhere then vanished.

The landscape of that corner could forgive anything, or so it seemed. It's true of the whole of the south of France, along the coast; I had often thought when visiting the places where allied forces made their landings how strange it was to see happy families bathing, to look at couples drinking coffee, eating ice-cream topped with a jaunty miniature tricolour, and above them the ancient buildings pock-marked from the bullets of that terrible string of battles.

My field appeared as happy as any other, framed where the ground rose around it with larches, firs and pines filled in with furze and kermes oak.

It was hot. Stupid Essington sweating, going over the action in his head. Not realizing that the more I hunted after what had happened the more I set my mind to work like a loop tape, coming up with the start, with the end, over and over, always the same. And making it seem that there couldn't be a true end to anything, not ever.

It turned out that the field was at the western point of a straight line running horizontally across the map. The east was marked by the words 'Valle del Chisone', a geographical feature which runs approximately half-way between Turin and the French–Italian border. Jean Dolent had searched through the funeral records of the municipalities on both sides of the border from Haute Savoie down to Ventimiglia. A process of elimination. He had the date of the death up there at the time of my exchange, he had our educated guess as to the dead man's age. So he'd compiled lists from public records, cross checked, excluded the possibles one by one. He may not have been a lot of fun, Dolent, but he was thorough. Most of the dead for the period were old; souls that had given up the ghost in a familiar bed or while attached to tubes in the local hospital. Well, most of the young had pissed off to the cities at the first opportunity. Then there had been the road accidents. Not so many of those, and the victims for the week in question were all in their teens — they'd been eliminated anyway by checking on the nature of the injuries sustained.

In the end Dolent had three likely candidates. Two on the Italian side of the line, the other from a farm twenty kilometres outside Digne. This last had been a shooting accident. But investigation had shown that the dead man had been a member of a party after quail. He had stepped into the line of fire of some half-wit who had dropped back behind the rest of the group and then got carried away. Shotgun pellets had taken away most of the victim's face.

Dolent, in his perfected pedantic manner, emphasized the complexities of investigating these things without stirring the interest of local police. Or, in making the process seem so difficult, was he simply softening me up for the bill when it was presented? I couldn't tell. Are private investigators as rapacious as plumbers, for instance? Or as pathologists? We shall see, Essington, we shall see.

Of the two dead Italians left for him to find out about both, it seemed, had been planted with indecent haste after 'accidental deaths.' In neither case had there been an autopsy or a medical report — well, not that Dolent was able to turn up.

He reckoned that was strange indeed.

And then Dolent got a feeling about the Falcone clan.

'Because of the name?'

'No, it was more than that. On everyone's part there was a general reluctance to comment . . . almost I sensed that these people were afraid. How can I tell you? There is a manner in which the eye searches for escape when a question is put. Or a fingernail will pick at skin on the side of the thumb . . . perhaps a tightening of muscles around the mouth. And if you ask two people a question at the one time they cast glances at each other as though anxious that the intended reply is approved.'

You see, Dolent letting me know he was tops. The way a garage mechanic will lull you with chanted mantras of engine parts.

Dolent's conclusion was that the character we were after had been laid to rest in the town of Massello. Leaving nothing to chance he even brought back a polaroid snap of the grave: flowers in jam jars, not too many weeds seeded yet into the dirt. And a second shot locating it among weathered headstones; this, I guess, in case the plot vanished between visits.

'Are you sure? How can you be?' I quizzed him.

'A body must be buried. And with the rites of the church. Who would risk it otherwise? You may not be able to trace the living, but the dead, Mr Holt, the dead are always present at roll call.'

And he'd asked questions around the town; discreetly, he assured me. But of course.

Nobody, it seemed, would elaborate on how the man had died. It had been an agricultural accident surely. Head shaking, muttering about how steep country should be worked with horses, with oxen; tractors slip, roll over. Wheels are for flat country. That was the old people. Only the old people would respond to Dolent's enquiries. The few young to be found let their features relax into a mask of stupidity, learnt from TV perhaps, then turned and walked away. A hunch to the shoulders, fists thrust into the pockets of toil-stained trousers.

One or two people, however, caught out in the open and on their own, ventured the opinion that Signor Falcone deserved what he got.

The family story built on itself. These brothers, and the father — the Falcones — they were not loved by the community. They were . . . was bandits too strong a word? Living out in their hills, a law unto themselves. It was a pity, for a couple of generations earlier it had been a respectable family which had moved there from over near Casale Monferrato. The great-grandfather had been much respected in the region. He had his farming land in the high country and, as well, built a large house with a walled garden on the outskirts of the town. For a period he had been mayor.

How that made him respectable, I couldn't say.

And then, Dolent had been informed, in the period of *Il Duce*, the Falcones had devolved into staunch fascists.

It wasn't hard to imagine the rest of the story: finger pointing, recriminations, the family going outside the society, huddling together up in the hills; their men roaring like the lions they would like to be, dreaming of better days that had passed, days when they had been really something.

Longing to be something again.

If Dolent proved long-winded in supplying me with the information, at least he had dug up what I was looking for — a part of it anyway. I had a starting point.

I had the Falcones — the name. And I reckoned it suited the mountains. I'd seen a bird of prey circling there, in the blue sky. I'd watched it, wondered. Would these Falcones prove to be birds of a similar feather?

I drove the rust bucket of a Renault along the coast to Ventimiglia, then headed north. Moulay sat beside me, saying nothing — it seemed he could do that for days on end. Occasionally he'd rub his shoulder, as though it was a habit; maybe he needed to do it, as well, to ease pain from the wound. There simply wasn't a way of telling with Moulay, part bionic man, part mystic.

He had the assault rifle stowed under his seat, strapped against the wire springs. That was a precaution against the chance we'd be stopped at the border. It had been my idea, because I'm the worrier.

In fact I was conscious of Moulay watching my face as we approached the checkpoint, as I screwed up a gear change slowing down. Hell, the tension! Yet never had I been pulled up there. I imagined that guilt was written all over me, splattered like blood down my shirt-front; even that they must be able to smell my intention.

I don't think the guard noticed us.

But Moulay had made a mental note of my nerves, registering what he was teamed up with. That's the way it goes: the professionals, they calculate the risks, adjust their responses to fit the reality of a situation, check the variables. I was only too aware of myself as a variable.

I didn't even know what I had in mind. We were sailing for some unknown shore. What would happen? Would I knock on this weathered door, recognize a peasant woman's face, ask it for information about a man with a built-up shoe?

Moulay and I had set off early that day. We didn't get far fast, the Renault made fairly slow going in the mountains, and I had to watch the oil — we were blowing smoke out the back. A typical Essington Holt buy, a stuffed motor. They ought to keep me at home in mothballs, air me in the spring, pass cheques to sign when the larder runs down. That's as long as there's sufficient money in the bank for the cheques to be honoured.

Hell, it takes some adjusting to, the threat of poverty, after you've been living high. Sure, poverty was too strong a word. They reckon these things are relative: what's riches for one is the breadline for somebody else.

What the hell was Moulay thinking? With me almost wetting myself at the border; and the car having worn cylinders. I bought a can of oil at our first stop. He'd sat there watching me as I pulled up a couple of hours later, lifted the dip-stick, wiped it off, topped up. His dark eyes were telling me nobody did that any more, not in France anyhow.

In Morocco, perhaps.

You see, I'd economized, hadn't I? All that money down the drain, I was going to put things right by buying the cheapest automobile on the lot.

What if we needed reliability to get out of where we were going? Well, at that stage I hadn't put the question to myself. To Moulay I'd put nothing. Neither did he seem to need anything. The rifle was out from under the seat now, he rested the barrel against the window so that it rattled on the glass. It got to me, that sound was working on my nerves. I suppressed the desire to tell him to stop it — he had enough crosses inscribed against the name of Holt already.

Enough crosses! There were cement saints, some older ones in marble, there were tombs of every description, family vaults, and strange sculptural creations of the monumental mason's art. The theme was death. Lichen, that did well; God must have had it in mind when he conceived the idea of cemeteries. As with so much else, we seemed to be slipping in the late twentieth century, not doing it so well. Recent graves tended to be less various in the style of decoration they boasted, and the scale of things had been reduced, no doubt to save money for the refrigerator, the TV, the motor car. What had taken off was the black-and-white photo stencil of the beloved, baked on to a ceramic surface, so that the bereaved could remember what had once been a technicolour existence. Those images, they also served as a *memento mori*: the reminder that we too must die.

The most recently arrived just had the pile of dirt, a more permanent marker yet to come. There were lots of flowers; in fact the cemetery had a certain gaiety about it with those flashes of red, of yellow, purple and orange all over the place.

As Dolent had said, Pietro (wasn't that a coincidence?) Falcone had his flowers in jam jars.

It was early afternoon. We went to a bar for coffee; I had a ham sandwich as well. I asked where the Falcones lived. I'd used up all my Italian on ordering the snack and the waiter didn't understand what I was attempting to say. I tried English — no go with that either. I had another attempt, more slowly this time, in French. That went better — the languages have got a lot in common, French and Italian, it's just that the Italians pronounce the letters.

I couldn't return the favour of comprehension. So the waiter, a friendly type, took to drawing me a map, repeating the name, 'Falcone, Falcone,' as he meandered the tip of a ball-point across a torn sheet of paper he'd dredged up from under the espresso machine.

He chanted distances as he progressed with the map, and he indicated a point of the compass by writing 'Paris' on the paper's left-hand edge.

All that was good. I'd concentrated, trying to remember it right. Moulay didn't appear to give a stuff. He just sat as was his habit, his lined brown face expressing nothing. Maybe he was missing the rifle that was nestling snug again under the seat away from inquisitive eyes.

We were heading up into the hills, poor farming country mostly, rising to scrubby trees surviving in thin, leached top soil. Moulay had the window wound down; he was squinting into his telescopic sight, lining up passing targets, making a 'phit' sound under his breath. At least he was keen. And if we ran into trouble we'd need to be keen.

Trouble! The thing was that until we were right up there I'd hardly given it a thought, other than trouble with the authorities. And, having my confident companion, taciturn at my side, I still couldn't find too much to worry about.

Not now we were so close.

Suddenly I felt a pull, as if from a magnet. I knew where we were, I just sort of knew! Next there was a turn-off, direction Paris by the waiter's map. It was the dirt road we'd followed that morning when I'd been taken from my shed to be exchanged for — how is it with the Bard? — 'Thus much monies.'

I didn't go down that road, not now I didn't. Instead I headed straight up the hill. And there was the wire enclosure with, set back quite a distance, the shed constructed out of cement blocks. I brought the Renault to a stop at one of the gates. They were closed, padlocked. And there, facing me across an expanse of dirt, was the door, the small door that was built into the big double ones, the door I'd been shoved through. The one whose rectangle of light, when open, had symbolized freedom. I stared at it, thinking of the black square that it was when shut.

But it was open.

My mind trying to hold itself together. I flashed a look at Moulay. Like I'd thought, he was watching me, checking on my reaction.

He spoke! 'It was here?' he asked, unnecessarily.

I said: 'Yes.'

He said: 'Never forget, not anything.'

Moulay's was a mysterious mind. Next he asked: 'Do you want to see inside?' Suddenly Chester Chatterbox! Well, hardly that, but communicative at least. Or had it been that till then he'd presumed we were on a wild-goose chase?

'Let me think, Moulay . . . they fed me . . . the woman would bring me food on a tray. Just enough to stay alive. And water, she brought me water.'

'She drove?'

'I'd have heard, any motor would cut through the silence, even from way off below in the valley.'

It was exactly as I'd remembered: the sense of the place being on the crest of a hill, built at the end of a ridge leading away in one direction.

That was a thought: the road must have done a loop of some sort. Because I was sure the Audi had headed off along that ridge when they'd taken me away. The man with the cut ear had opened the gate so we could get through. Yet, when I'd driven there just then, it had been directly up the side of the hill. It had to be a loop because I'd known I was close when we'd hit that junction half a kilometre, less, away from where we now stood.

Moulay: 'She is bringing it on a tray, there is a house close by.'

There had to be.

In which direction? A house — the Falcone's farm perhaps? I checked the map the waiter had drawn. It was difficult to tell, there were squiggly lines heading off in so many directions. That man had been more a Paul Klee than a cartographer.

We were both out of the car. Moulay was looking about, but more up at the sky than through the trees trying to pick up signs of nearby habitation.

He said: 'Why don't we find out and, at the same time, Mr Holt, you see inside your palace?'

Moulay shot away the padlock on the gate with a burst from his beloved rifle. 'If people live near here that will bring them,' he predicted. Then, urging me to follow, he jogged across to the shed.

We slipped in through the door.

Inside, I said: 'There's a gate behind us as well, a track leading up along the ridge.' But even as I was saying that, my eyes were adjusting to the low light level in there, my gaze panned the walls, the floor. There was the ring up there, I saw it. The rest was expressive of nothing, just a strongly built shed with oil stains on the cement floor. And a work bench. It struck me then how it must have had some government function, a search and rescue base, or perhaps it was connected with military exercises. I'd seen dumps like my ex-prison before, all over the world.

The idea of the second gate worried Moulay. He reached inside the cotton jacket he was wearing and pulled out another gun. My facial expression had him laughing. 'Ali Baba . . . I rub the lamp and, presto . . .'

He passed it to me as together we moved back towards the shed door. 'You are able to use this?'

Before I could answer he'd slipped the safety catch off. 'You pull the trigger, that is all. Hold it in two hands, I think that's best. You can fire this thing, Mr Holt?'

I said I could. But he was off without waiting to register the confirmation.

And I was alone in the half-light.

I didn't like the feeling of being in there again. My mind began to slip, into paranoia and into fear. Sweat was oozing from every pore in body, I could sense it drenching my shirt.

I was scared out of my brain.

Anyway, what was I doing up there in the first place? It was madness . . . the total madness of an abstract desire for revenge. Now I was faced with the reality of what I'd let myself in for. A revival of that psychotic collapse brought on by the prism of darkness in which I was now standing. Suddenly I couldn't believe it. And of my own free will!

I had to escape!

I bolted through the door like a rabbit out of a sack.

There was the crack of a rifle shot. Three quick rounds responded at a different pitch, and louder. I dropped to the ground, lay still, then, lifting myself to a crouching position, belted back into the shed.

From the inside looking out I could see where the wood of the door jamb had splintered. And I knew it to be an imperfection that had not been there before. After all, this was my home, I belonged in it, with it. Even though it filled me with horror to be there, at that instant the dark space felt more mine than anything else in the entire world.

Silence out there.

I was standing facing the rectangle of light which was made brighter by contrast with the gloom of the interior. I held the revolver in both hands, one finger on the trigger; I held it rigid at head height so that I could sight along the barrel.

It enveloped me, the smell of my urine, of my shit, the sourness of the atmosphere inside those walls. And to imagine I'd endured a lifetime of it! Had come to need it! That was what I realized, suddenly I required the excrement, the pain, the degradation, pools of my own fluid. Those things had become elements collectively representative of some higher truth.

It was right what Dawn had said to Karen: the Diogenes syndrome. Maybe I'd been like that from birth, just waiting for the discovery.

I was created for squalor, for living in my own filth! And Tony had shown me this truth.

It could be that I'd stood propped like I was for five minutes, ten minutes. Or for an hour. A hundred years. I'd go away in my mind then return again to the white rectangle of light, to the sweat that was soaking my body, to the fact of the gun held out at arm's length, its trigger a hair's breadth off firing.

A silhouette appeared at the door. Next there was the barrel of Moulay's assault rifle pressed against the side of the visitor's head. And it wasn't Moulay who was in trouble, the hair told me that, I wasn't looking at his fuzzy mop.

Then they were in there with me.

And I came out the other side of hell.

Moulay said: 'There's another out there . . . you know this man?'

Of course I did, it was one of the pair who'd been with the jeep when we'd stopped on the way to that field where the third — of course, it would have been the father — had been shot.

And on that day those other two had been covering the action from somewhere. But, with their father dead, they'd frozen, hadn't they? Perhaps not knowing what to do next.

Except somebody had had the presence of mind to take a shot at our Citroën, and to score a hit. Could this be the man who'd pulled the trigger on that occasion, this creature who was now cowering before Moulay's gun?

There was some justice in it.

Moulay wasn't even excited. The captive sensed this. I could see it scared him half to death.

The problem was how to converse. We couldn't even put

the question to find out how many other people were out there.

'We have to take a prize.' Moulay was looking at me, smiling. 'We'll stick it up on one of your big walls. How do they do it? On a piece of polished wood I think. Except we need him to have horns. For this, Mr Holt, we can kill a goat on the way home.'

Funny really, isn't it? There *is* a common means of human communication, it's called violence. With it we *can* abandon our Tower of Babel! It was working between Moulay and this young Italian. You could see. I would have laid a bet our captive knew that to make one move meant to die. Moulay had that about him, an animal presence, the air of one who's careless of the fact of death.

Like a tiger, burning bright . . . transcending the need for the spoken word.

Taking total control of the operation, as no doubt he'd always known he'd have to, Moulay, after forcing the man to undress, got me to tie his hands together behind his back, using as ropes strips torn from the clothes that lay in a pile on the floor. Next came the blindfold. The belt that had held up his corduroy trousers was buckled around one ankle, to function as a lead rope.

We came out through the door together, Moulay, laughing out loud, the muzzle of the rifle shoved into our captive's mouth. Under instructions I held the loose end of the belt in one hand and the pistol in the other, pointing at the naked chest.

Nothing in all that wild world moved. Connected in that way, we shuffled to the Renault which whoever was out there backing up hadn't even had the sense to shoot up.

'The first thing they must do . . . and they get it wrong. This is why you are still alive, Mr Holt, these are stupid men. It happens in the hills. Catholics, they fuck their sisters and each generation is less good at life. They are idiots who can't understand how we must follow the law of God.'

So, we'd caught a minnow, and I'd got myself a theologian for a guide.

Chapter 20

How can someone like me finish up pointing the remote-control jigger at the gate sensor in front of my own Villa du Phare, with a bound naked man in the back seat of a clapped-out Renault Five? It didn't cross my mind then, but it does now, that we were doing a scene from one of those gay rough-fuck movies they show in the small cinemas up the wrong end of the rue de France.

Moulay had gone to sleep, Islamic moral verities inhabiting his untroubled mind.

It was well after midnight. I was tired out from the long day of driving combined with the loss of mind control I'd experienced up there in the shed, in my shed. I took the car around the back, to where the garages are located. As well there are several rooms there, intended for tools, for storage, for God knows what. I checked out one next to an unused laundry. There were bars on the window and a door with two bolts, one at the top, one at the bottom: tailor made as a prison.

Leaving the door open, returning to the car, I found Moulay already dragging our passenger out, by the feet, to the tune of inarticulate and muffled objections sounding from the wrong side of a gag.

We stuffed the man into the room, fastened the bolts; I switched off the electricity to that block of buildings.

Moulay bid me an unconcerned goodnight as he wandered off to his room, the assault rifle in one hand, in the other that pistol I'd held earlier in the day. The man so casual, you would have thought we'd been mushrooming, that is if you didn't wonder about the armoury we'd taken along, and the lack of a bucket.

I needed a whisky.

I poured myself one.

I held out my mutilated hand, fingers spread, attempting to

sustain faith in the religion of vengeance. I couldn't keep the hand from shaking.

I didn't try to sleep. My mind was too full of the things I'd done wrong. And as though expecting a reprimand it would drift off to that time in which I'd first talked to Danny Tournier. What would he say if he knew I'd captured the son of the family Falcone?

Surely he'd explain what I already understood, that they would know where to come to fetch him back. If that's what they decided to do.

What was it Moulay had said to me after we'd headed for home? Something like: 'Every round thing is not an orange, and every long thing not a banana.'

What in God's name was I supposed to make of that?

I'd pondered the mysteries of the Islamic mind while working the Renault's gear-stick like I was stirring soup, keeping the revs up through the corners. There had to be more than a reasonable chance of us being pursued. It was one thing to get a Falcone brother across some bare patch of dirt and into the back of an underpowered heap, it was another to get clear of the country. Let alone of its inhabitants.

No map, a case of steer by the sinking sun.

That was as it had been when I'd come on to a made road surface God knows how many kilometres outside Sestriere where, in the dying light before us, suddenly there was a landscape of farms. Moulay turned in his seat, he spoke. Needing everything I had to keep the Renault on the road, and the needle up above the hundred kilometre per hour mark, I couldn't give him my full attention. We lost traction around a hairpin bend, slipped over into the dirt. I changed down, planted my foot, blew smoke, pulled out of it.

'Stop!' Moulay commanded, and as though trained by the military I did as I was told, stamped on the brakes, sensed the back swing through a hundred and eighty degrees.

Which brought Moulay into position; he had the gun ready as a yellow Fiat 1·5 came around on our tail. With an explosion of sound the rifle discharged its burst of three shots into the radiator of the approaching automobile. It was out of control, two wheels off the ground. The Fiat flew off the road's shoulder, bumped half-way down an embankment, flipped over. I let out the clutch and continued towards civilization, wondering if that was the enemy we'd just knocked out, or some poor innocent luck had put in our way.

Kismet. The word surfaced.

'Give what is in your pocket, and God will give you what is absent.'

A new-found verbosity of Moulay's!

I had asked how we were going to get into France with a naked man tied up in the back.

He laughed. 'They stop you if you do not have one.' That was a Moulay Yusuf joke. In time I'd get on to the wavelength. Or would I?

Out on the other side of Sestriere I planted my foot, wrestled a way around the bends and only eased up when I saw the border control.

'Moulay, the glove box . . . passports!' The glove box was where I'd shoved mine at the start of the journey.

'Passports!' He grinned. 'I don't have such a thing, not today. You must understand, Mr Holt, it is better sometimes to have no passport than one with Morocco written on it. Papers, yes, I have those . . . of dubious provenance perhaps, but they work.'

All the way up to and past the border checkpoint he was so cool, as if we were discussing the price of almond oil. The man had no nerves at all.

Me. The old body began to heat with the fear of being stopped as though somewhere deep in the heart of this Essington there was a nuclear meltdown taking place. And sweat running rivers.

Still, we got home, housed the captive, and Moulay sauntered off and slept while I stayed downstairs drinking, trying to get calm reclining on an Empire *chaise-longue*, gazing out of high windows at the sea, at the night, at Africa. I felt that often: how you could sense Africa across the water.

Desdemona was barking, one God almighty burst of vocal aggression. Had I dozed off? Pre-dawn light, me slowly realizing the dog sounds were coming from round the back. I belted out to investigate. There she was, at the double bolted door, the Great Dane showing teeth, legs stiff, hackles up. A lion on a Saturday afternoon at the Colosseum waiting for the next Christian.

And there too was Renardo, on the point of investigating the contents of that room.

I rushed at the pair of them, at the man and the dog . . .

Renardo, it would be fine, I explained . . . it was my business, something I had in hand.

Saying that was enough to satisfy Renardo Pinci. Since the boss was mad anyway. Hadn't Renardo already heard from his wife, Rebecca, of how a seldom-used lavatory in the rear section of the house was now converted into a smoke chamber, with fumes rising non-stop from a steel container of smouldering sawdust mixed together with tobacco? What was one more crazy experiment? A man like Renardo had to shrug his shoulders, wonder what it was these Australians had inside their heads where the brains should be.

No, with me about, the Pincis were prepared for anything. Even for gag-muffled groans sounding from behind some locked door. Renardo retreated, shuffling as he liked to do, acting the part of the aged patriarch.

You wake into a new day, you have doubts. That's how it is. I was kind of standing there, holding the dog, watching the door. At that moment I didn't need to know about the captive, about any of it. I wanted a total exemption from life, at least till its players were safely relocated.

Had Moulay witnessed my indecision? He took me by surprise, just his being there, some distance off, the rifle in his hand. He was pretending interest in the sky, a characteristic stance of his, head up, eyes gazing at that immeasurable depth. Perhaps that was what he believed in, actually taking the dimensionless dome to represent the presence of the one God.

Or maybe Moulay had a stiff neck from dozing squashed up in the Renault.

Not one to rush, he remained where he was.

That's how we were for some time. Then he came over. He was in fact such a small man, light-boned, so little flesh, you wouldn't have thought much muscle either. That densely curled hair was sitting on his skull like a cap of steel wool.

He said: 'There was a man who carried five eggs in his pocket. He told another man, a friend: "If you can guess what I have in my pocket and how many eggs there are I will give you all five." The other man responded: "Offer me another clue."'

I said: 'What's that supposed to mean?'

Moulay shrugged, whistled between his teeth. Then he laughed. It surprised me to recognize how he liked to laugh.

I told him that perhaps I should call a friend of mine, Molena, if he was back. 'He speaks Italian.'

Moulay suggested that first we should take a look inside the door. 'Or do you want, maybe, to be dumping a body?'

Dumping a body! Jesus Christ!

I did what I had been reluctant to do. I took the key out of my pocket, undid the padlocks, slipped the bolts, swung the door open.

It was like looking in on my own recent past: surely it was me there? Only no, it was this other creature, this naked man, his face swollen, and gone blue around staring eyes. He was lying on his back, his head propped against the wall, awkwardly, because of the tied hands. He tried getting to his feet: struggling for dignity.

'He is alive,' said Moulay, pointing with his rifle. And grinning!

Me, my mind was a blank. I saw around the prisoner's feet where he had pissed. I breathed in the stench of ammonia and of fear.

It is a curious thing what it means to be human. We talk about it — 'to be human' — and of what it is to have 'humanity'. They reckon it's important that we remain apart from the animals. Because, see, it's us who are the beloved of God.

Bullshit, we are.

This fettered thing on whom I'd opened the door was an animal. There was so little remaining about him that could be termed human. And just as with a captive animal, I feared him, feared what he might do if I was to let him free.

I said: 'Shut the door.' But could not do it myself.

'Perhaps he enjoys the light.'

Doubts surged about inside my head. The worst thing is not knowing what you want out of a situation.

It took a long time for me to grasp that with this guy we'd caught, whatever else happend to him, first he must write down a phone number. We had to deal. Moulay was that far in front.

What the hell would Molena think of the mess I'd created for myself by taking a prisoner? Talking on the phone, I hadn't been exactly straight about that. I'd glossed over the actual situation, saying that I needed to talk Italian to someone who might help find out who'd kidnapped me in the first place.

From Molena's end, during that conversation, I got satisfying sounds of shock, of sympathy and of horror.

How was I to demonstrate to Molena that from some twisted perspective there was a rightness in what I was doing? And of course he'd know straight off that if he joined in with me he too was outside the law. If you are a property developer, like Molena, you have to keep a respectable front even if the world knows you're having your enemies poured into the foundations of shopping malls.

How could I justify what was going on to someone if I had trouble convincing myself that it was right?

Moulay, he remained unperturbed.

Molena showed up looking sharp: silk sports jacket, cream trousers, the kind of shoes you wear on yachts sailing Long Island Sound. As a new affectation, a high crowned, soft felt hat on his head. Maybe he was getting conscious of hair loss.

Who isn't?

Or he was playing the Great Gatsby. Or both.

He was indignant: 'For ransom! It's not possible . . . there is no crime . . .'

' . . . that gets people's backs up like a . . .'

'Exactly, Essington . . . like a kidnapping.'

'It's justice. Anyway, since when have you been so righteous?'

'It's not righteous to object to taking hostages!'

'For a day, Molena! To get information. See it my way — I have to do something.'

He was unmoved, the bastard.

We went inside the house, me with a hold on his arm, steering. And leaving behind Moulay and Desdemona, neither of whom looked troubled listening to the groans coming through the closed door.

I stuffed the stub of my amputated finger up my nose. 'How's that for a trick?'

Molena batted his eyelashes. I'd offended his delicate Latin sensibility . . . again.

Nothing to lose, I kept on. Told him the rest of my tale, with warts and all. I finished with the question: 'Can revenge be that wrong?'

I'd had some effect with the story, even if the theology or whatever you might call it was like water off a duck's back.

'You can feel this way, my friend, but you can't set yourself up as a . . . as some kind of . . .'

'The police were out of it from the start, that was how it was played. Most probably Karen and Chevet could have elected to stay within the law, saved the cash, picked up the body. But the fact is they didn't — and I live. What's so bad about that as an outcome?'

'Consider yourself lucky then, Essington, and leave it alone.'

'Like hell I will!'

We were standing in the entrance foyer. From above, from the gallery, I could hear Nurse Findlay tending to Pietro, getting him comfortable. Molena could hear her as well.

'Molena, you're the godfather . . . then think about Pietro! Consider that it was him they were after, not me. Think of the chance he'd have had in their . . . well, care's not really the word, is it?'

'They would not have chained him, an infant! Anyhow, it's hypothetical.'

'Bullshit it is!'

Nurse Findlay leant over the balustrade, she had a finger to her lips: 'Shish!'

'Screw it!'

'Mr Holt!' A stage whisper.

Don't fool yourself, your house is never your castle. I led Molena back outside. I reminded him of a favour he owed me. He was on a promise. And this was it, I was calling the favour in.

'It's the way the world works,' I explained, forcing myself to smile.

'You twist things to your point of view, Essington. You were the one who benefited when we last did business. A favour? You must be joking.'

Not so long back I'd put up money for Molena's apartment block at Villefranche, and pulled some strings. For his part he'd lifted a child, Pietro, out of the Naples slums, together with a bogus set of birth papers. There'd been humanity in what he'd done, but business as well. And now I was pushing him, not just against his judgement, but against his nature.

Because I was off my head.

Molena regarded me, bemused. He touched his chin with a manicured finger. A thoughtful gesture.

Was I getting through to him?

Next, standing some way off, hands stuffed into his pockets, Molena was gazing out to sea, like he thought that he'd never see it the same again. Not after he'd done what I asked. Don't we all look to the sea for something? And never find it.

'Just do it, Molena, please. You can trust me. No matter what, I don't say a word, not one word about any involvement on your part.'

'I don't like it,' he said.

'I am not asking you to have fun, that can come afterwards. I'm asking you to do this one thing. I am begging you. For Pietro's sake, if you like.'

I dialled the number.

A babble of Italian, it was a woman's voice. I signalled to Molena who had been hovering, uneasy still. I passed him the receiver. 'What's she trying to say?'

'*Buon giorno* . . .' he began.

Molena's eyes watching me as he spoke to this woman, or as she spoke to him: his contribution to the conversation was mostly limited to monosyllables.

'*Un momento, signora* . . .'

He had his hand over the piece.

'It *is* them, isn't it?' I asked.

'Them . . . ? Yes, Essington. And this woman wants to make a bargain, she wants her brother. She says . . .'

I told him to ask what she thought she was talking about. To keep her rattled, confused, under the pressure of uncertainty.

Then I said: 'Tell her we'll ring back in ten minutes, we will talk with her then.'

He repeated the message.

The voice rose; I could hear the words, shrill.

'Hang up,' I told him.

Molena dropped the receiver.

'You are a bastard,' he said, 'You know that.'

Chapter 21

'This smoke,' she declared, grim faced, 'it is everywhere. Why are you setting fire to the house?' What must Rebecca have thought I was up to?

'A slow fire, Rebecca. Trust me, I value what's here. Believe it or not I value you as well. Nothing will burn down.'

Despite my reassurances Rebecca insisted I go with her and demonstrate that the house was not in danger.

Renardo was on guard outside the offending door, hands clasped behind his back as though working on an impersonation of the Duke of Edinburgh.

What choice was there but for me to open up?

Next thing that smoke, more than the hint of tobacco to it, was billowing into the corridor where the three of us were standing. Rebecca held a handkerchief to her face, acted through a coughing fit.

'See,' I said, 'no flame. Where there's smoke there's fire . . . it's just not true.'

'Why do you do this?' Rebecca seeking a reasonable explanation for the obviously irrational.

'It is for art. Think of it like that.'

And it was in fact for art. The Gauguin, my Gauguin, was in there getting time laid on to its surface. I would give it the treatment for a full week keeping the back of the picture protected, so that it aged as it would on a wall. This was going to finish up a work that had endured for most of a century in the hard winters of northern France, hanging above glowing fires. Gentlemen would have sat beneath it smoking their cigars, their pipes; talking of property, bonds, arguing local politics. Perhaps, from time to time, commenting on the prospects of bliss offered by the Polynesian nude's ample hips.

'Renardo,' I said, 'it could be you'd feel better if you go to Nice and buy a fire extinguisher, demonstrate to your wife how it's activated, place the damn thing outside this door. But you must promise, not a word to the *pompiers.*'

Maybe complaining about the smokehouse I'd created was the Pincis' way of letting me know they didn't mind me keeping prisoners.

His name was Giulio, at least that's what he said it was. For the sake of comfort we'd brought him around to a front reception room. Comfortable? Well, relatively speaking.

He wore his hair long; it was black and curled down his neck. There was something sullen about the eyes that I suspected would have been there even if he hadn't sucked off a gun barrel in the last twenty-four hours. Christ, didn't he look a sad-sack dressed in my clothes? The cuffs and sleeves rolled up — there would have been five inches difference between us. Maybe more.

Moulay watched the guy the way a cat watches a mouse. While Giulio observed nobody in particular, just sort of stared off into space. His hands and ankles were tied. His feet were bare. I saw tufts of hair growing from the toe joints, and the nails struck me as well, looking like those of some old man: yellow, curled.

Yet Giulio was young. He might not yet have reached twenty.

Molena, even more reluctant in the interpreter's role than before, told him about how we'd called the number, twice. He explained that there was a process of negotiation taking place. The difficulty, Molena went on, was money. A problem it seemed, at their end.

Giulio snarled something.

'What did he say?'

'He says the money's your problem.' You could see that Molena was half in agreement with the sentiment. Yet he knew once he'd gone along with me just a little way, by making the first call, that he was in. Exactly where he didn't want to be.

There was this strange stillness about the house that morning. Nurse Findlay had wanted to go out, to take Pietro with her. I'd decided they were confined to base.

There'd been objections to that. A confrontation in fact. It took place upstairs before we brought the prisoner inside.

I'd felt obliged to explain that the restriction on movement was for Pietro's safety.

'You're a writer, nurse, you'd have an imagination.'

'If I do it's my own. But if you want to tell me something more I'll not object. What's obvious is . . . well, I've said to myself: "There's something going on here, and you wouldn't know the good of it from the bad."'

I asked her: 'Tempted to hazard a guess?'

'This morning you, and I couldn't say who else — that frightful heathen with his rifle — it's my belief you've got some poor blighter here. And locked up.'

Nurse Findlay was sticking with Pietro. And I was downstairs watching Giulio, the stubble on his grey-white cheeks, tension now around the eyes. His mouth was kept shut, shielding the exposed nerves of broken teeth.

Moulay wanted to say something.

He told Molena to leave us alone for a few minutes. Molena shrugged, went out the door.

'Mr Holt.'

Giulio watching the pair of us, his eyes alert now, as though anticipating action.

Moulay continued: 'A business proposition.'

He was sitting, his back to the wall farthest from the bay window. Above his head there was a red crayon drawing by Modigliani, a study for a caryatid, the stylized head turned down.

Moulay had the rifle in his hand, the barrel resting across his knees.

Oh, very neat.

'Business?'

'You are paying me to do these things — but to do what? I sit here, it is comfortable, yet . . .'

'You want more?'

'Not more . . .'

Giulio trying to follow this foreign language.

'Moulay, the first reason I asked you to stay here was that, in my mind at least, I owed it to you. I was alive, see, and you were injured on my account.'

'An act of the greatest merit, to give people water.'

'I beg your pardon?'

'I understand, you have offered charity. You have paid me to do nothing.'

'Not quite nothing, Moulay . . . at least, not since yesterday.'

'This must finish. I don't want to be . . .'

'Kept?'

'Yes, kept, if you like. Indeed I would rather we had some proper business arrangement.'

Funny thing, when you have a discussion like that generally there's something to be learned from the way the other person looks at you. With Moulay though there were only these two dark eyes recording what was out there, no anxiety, nothing more showing.

Just fucking lenses!

Cold.

Moulay continued: 'These people in the mountains, the Falcones, I believe they have the money Monsieur Tournier delivered.'

'Some of it, maybe. I wouldn't know how much.'

'Still they must have some.'

Giulio's eyes bulging, his head swinging from one side to the other, forehead wrinkled, eyebrows raised in confusion. I guess he'd picked up Moulay's mention of the family name.

Moulay continued: 'So we must find out how much money that is.'

The upshot being that there was a kind of agreement reached between us. From now on Moulay was working on commission. He was going at it for ten per cent. It was his idea; the business brain in there somewhere, beneath the holy killer exterior.

'Mr Holt . . .'

'Moulay, at least change that. You say we have a business relationship, let's have it on first-name terms, for Christ's sake!'

He said: 'Jesus Christ was a prophet. Mohammed is *the* prophet. You must not use these holy names in such a fashion, Mr Holt.'

I was going to remain Mr Holt.

Giulio still watching.

Moulay: 'This one will know how much money there is, and by that knowledge what he himself will fetch on the market.'

Giulio picked up the specific nature of the comment, he rolled his eyes. He said: 'No.'

But to what?

'No.' As a sound, it's universal.

'The money, Moulay, how do we find out? We'd need Molena back in here, and I don't think . . . '

'We need only myself, that's sufficient. Translation, it is a luxury we don't require. Is this the United Nations?'

'OK, as you wish,' I said to Moulay.

Molena was sulking somewhere in the garden. He'd get over it. I guess I'd worked out my position long ago: if I had to be barbaric, if that was the necessary therapy, then I'd do it. And the thing was how it felt so right. There was a bit of Scots blood in me too, Nurse Findlay didn't have a monopoly on that.

I was going after the bastards like most of me had intended to do right from the start.

Number one just happened to be this Giulio.

I abandoned him to Moulay.

The instant I left the room I heard the prisoner cry out.

And from above me, red-faced Nurse Findlay screaming over the balustrade: 'I'm not staying an instant more, and neither is the wee babe.'

So angry she looked like a blood blister.

Next thing, highly excited, Desdemona was barking outside the closed door of the reception room.

Mayhem!

Hell, what to do?

Then Renardo was approaching from the front, coming in through the main entrance. Molena with him, both of them talking fast, going at it, hand gestures like a pair of priests on fast forward.

Renardo agitated, I could see that, even some colour in his face.

I opened the door to the reception room again.

Giulio was on the floor, half on, half off a worn Ersari Turkoman tent carpet. He was on his stomach, both hands out in front of him; there was a ball-point pen clasped in one of them with its tip resting against a piece of the house's addressed notepaper. I guess Moulay must have found that in a compartment of the walnut keyhole desk.

Nothing was written on the paper.

Encouraging something to happen, the much favoured rifle was being jabbed against the back of Giulio's head.

Yet, strangely now, it was quiet inside that room. The noise was all at my back: the dog, the nurse, Renardo and Molena. And on top of it all, Pietro had decided to have a real go, striving after high C.

I got some sense from one part of the cacophony: Renardo was on my side!

That was a big plus. Molena, through his contacts with that section of the local community which had been Italian up until the 1860s, had respect for Renardo who might have lost the language but not the bearing. In fact Molena and I had met through their connection.

Well, over the dog's barking, and the screaming of Pietro, I could hear Renardo loud and clear: he was talking of honour, of the respect in which the house must be regarded.

The house!

It was the way the man had of expressing himself.

Collectively, noisy, vulgar bunch that we were, still there was this thing, a building which contained us, and the honour attached to it.

If not to me, the picture smoker, the forger.

I didn't care. The important thing was for Molena to come around, to start seeing sense. We might require him for the next go at Italian speak. More importantly he was my friend: I *needed* him as my friend.

Molena stepped into the room, he closed the door behind him. Moulay hadn't responded to our arrival. He just kept on jabbing the rifle into the back of the prisoner's head.

Molena flinched to witness that.

I was back out of there and after Renardo who was already doing what I'd wanted him to, restraining Nurse Findlay. Holding her firmly by the arm and steering her in the direction of Rebecca's kitchen. Pietro's head was visible over the nurse's shoulder, his eyes on me.

I'd seen that look before!

How was the child going to grow up normal with these memories of a father who was always receding in his field of vision? And whenever that happened, there was the scent of something terrible on the air.

Not so much later Giulio was slumped in a chair. His features now composed. Maybe we had the truth, maybe we didn't. I wasn't so sure I cared any longer.

Molena was clearly relieved, welcoming anything that might stop Moulay raising the threshold of pain and fear.

Three hundred thousand dollars, that was the figure Giulio had quoted.

They were my dollars!

Three hundred thousand dollars, that was what the Falcone family had been paid for assisting with the exchange.

Tony, and the man with the built-up shoe as well, what about them? They had to have the rest of the cash, didn't they?

Giulio didn't seem to want to know how much they'd kept. Pushed, he calculated off the top of his head that maybe it was about the same again. It was his father who'd reached the agreement with those two Englishmen.

Now his father was dead.

'Molena, ask him where the Englishmen are now.'

'I did.'

'And . . .'

'He says he doesn't know. He brings a curse down on them.'

'Because they'll come back for him if he tells.'

Moulay smiled. 'In the end he'll tell me everything.'

'But you won't understand! You need Molena, Moulay, for translation, like I told you.'

'I only need this.' He held up his beloved rifle. 'Then he writes.'

But in the end he did need to fall back on Molena again, didn't he? Rather than rely on pen and paper. I guess there was always the question: could Giulio write?

And at least with my friend present there wasn't too much brutality, not on the spot anyway. Finally a script was worked out between myself and Molena, and the next phone call made.

Moulay only wanted to earn his percentage. He insisted that we leave the details to him. I would get my money.

Fool that I am I agreed.

Why?

Moral cowardice of course.

OK, Giulio was to be exchanged by Moulay. The money, I'd believe in that when I saw it.

*

After Molena had played his part he stared at me so hard I thought there'd be holes drilled through my forehead. Then he shrugged. He said: 'I need some sleep,' and took off. Funny, he never removed the hat, not the whole time he was with us.

That was Molena, for the minute.

Desdemona looked at me, I looked at her. They reckon dogs can feel things. Like, if you're sick they know because you smell differently. They stick with you then, hoping their presence might bring comfort.

My problems: I began counting them off on my fingers. Starting with the thumb, that was Nurse Findlay — how in God's name was I to deal with her? Whatever the procedure was going to be, I'd best get into it fast. The forefinger, that was Jodie — I still had this strong feeling that finding Jodie would produce the information and get me to Tony and to the man with the built-up shoe. The index finger, that was those two, the ones Jodie was going to point my way towards. Ring finger was . . . but with the forefinger of my right hand counting off on the left suddenly all I could see was the stump of the little finger, of pinky!

And all I could feel was hate.

Pietro was crying. Nurse Findlay said it was teeth. He had red cheeks, one red ear too. His eyes watched me, but without the concern displayed by Desdemona.

'Wee pet.' She called him 'wee pet'!

She had him sitting on her knee and was jiggling him up and down. 'I want someone to buy me a pony,' she sang. 'Not too fat and not too bony.'

Not such a bad old stick really; good psychological recovery rate.

Of course, it struck me then: the little finger, if it had been there to count on, it would have been Farah. The ring finger being Makihei and the photographs he'd promised to try and turn up.

But first to Nurse Findlay.

Renardo was standing in the kitchen, his back to the door leading out into the main body of the house.

'With a jig-jog, jig-jog, jig-jog, jig-jog, jig-jog, jigger-jog-jig,' Findlay sang, to Pietro's delight. That was the trick to stop his squawking.

Midst the domesticity the nurse flashed a nasty look at Renardo who stared back, baleful.

Rebecca was clattering utensils more noisily than usual. The kitchen was her domain, she didn't take well to invasions.

The household falling down around my ears. I said: 'Nurse...'

'Can there be anything to say, Mr Holt?'

I held up the mutilated hand, and observed the void a part of my anatomy should have filled.

'Not by you, Nurse . . . so shut up and listen while I tell you a *wee* story.'

She looked from me to Renardo, then back again.

'I demand you let me go.'

'Just listen. You write books?'

'True. What's that to do with it?'

'Well, Nurse Findlay, maybe you should just hang around, check it out. This might be the big one. Film rights: Meryl Streep, Clint Eastwood, a walk-on part for Marlon Brando if he can still walk. How you were held against your will by a criminal Australian . . . or is that a tautology? Anyway, a criminal Australian what? Somebody who's protecting the child you spend so much time clucking over, who's trying to get back what's his so that . . . well, in the end, so you continue to be paid. Do you judge these criminal acts?'

'The poor man you had here . . . you and that Arab.'

'Wait a minute, you talk about Moulay as "that Arab". No more "that Arab" than you're "that Scot".'

'I resent you suggesting I'm a racist.'

'I'm not suggesting a thing, Nurse. But I'll tell you what, if it wasn't for Moulay, for "that Arab", I wouldn't be able to stand here wasting my breath on an obstinate woman. The truth is that right now you can't go, I can't let you. And if you want I'll tell you why, in detail.'

I told her about the snapshot my mind held of Jodie through the glass of the security door in the Sixteenth Arrondissement. And the rest of it. A whole sequence of nightmarish reality.

She had to listen.

Renardo and Rebecca watched each other and the two of us — the Australian and the Scot who'd invaded their realm — while failing to follow my rapid and short-tempered account of recent history, delivered in a rough equivalent of the Queen's English.

Then I left the nurse and baby to mull it over.

She had some wisdom, Nurse Findlay, there wasn't any getting away from that. When minding me in my sickness we'd chatted. One thing she'd explained about was tears. In fact there'd been considerable urging for me to let them flow. But I couldn't, not then. Hadn't I cried enough chained to the wall, living in shit and pain and misery? Not to mention fear. What Nurse Findlay had said was that tears were a washing of the tissues of the brain. I guess she was speaking metaphorically.

Chapter 22

At least I'd established a truce with the nurse, if not a peace. Peace wasn't to be, not in any quarter. First thing next morning I was called by Danny Tournier who'd got up from his piano stool and thrust a finger into the tepid water of life.

Now he wanted to see me.

That was something. And a surprise.

We met at the Grand Café de Turin in the Place Garibaldi on the eastern side of Nice, where a stone effigy of the Italian revolutionary hero stands in the centre of a square of grass.

Danny Tournier had brought his wife along with him, to join in the fun, whatever that might turn out to be. He didn't smile. He sat very straight at the table, his hands neatly folded on his lap. If you didn't know the man you might have thought him tense.

I didn't know him, not really, so I did.

'Essington, I have this for you.' It was an envelope; he passed it across.

The flap wasn't sealed, but tucked in. 'You know what it contains?' I was catching on to Tournier's mood. As though immune, his wife was studying the menu and looking across to where a mountain of seafood had been built as a display.

'I do.'

'Then tell me: why should I bother to look?'

'There is no addressee as you can see. It is from Moulay Yusuf, from your friend.'

'My friend! Wait a minute. I don't know what's going to spring out the moment I lift the flap, but let's get things straight. Moulay, I like him well enough, but . . . it was you who dug him up. I want you to remember that, Danny. If for no other reason than that he's wild. I know how wild, so do you.'

'I don't believe you do know.'

Madame Tournier said: 'I'm not sure I'm up to shellfish.'

'What are you trying to say?'

'Open it,' Tournier replied.

'I might prefer fish of the day . . . Mr Holt?' She was passing the menu to me.

And I was slipping the note out of the envelope. A childish hand, the words misspelt, it read: 'A man went to the market to buy a sheep. It is well known you must feel the tail to see how fat the beast might be. His son asks him why he does this thing. The father answers that it is how you buy a sheep. Then, asks the son, does our neighbour want to buy my sister?

'The father returns home and kills his neighbour.

'And the son eats the sheep.'

I wondered what happened to the sister. I had her there in my imagination. A replica of Farah.

Tournier was going through the menu with his wife, both of them seemed to take the process of making a decision very seriously indeed.

'So?' I asked, interrupting.

He could see the sheet of paper I was holding. 'Oh, that is Moulay's joke. There is another, a more immediate communication as well.'

Which was true. A second message. I unfolded it and was informed that two hundred and seventy thousand dollars had been deposited in a safe deposit box; I was to get the key from Tournier.

He said: 'It doesn't take a great deal of intelligence to work out this money is some of that which I passed over to your kidnappers. It might even be they carry the serial numbers that I have recorded.'

'You got that part right,' I said. 'Well, at least I expect you did.'

'However, the money is not why I suggested we see each other today. There is something rather more serious.'

The waiter arrived, his white apron stained, accumulated change bulging in his pouch. And at a place like the Grand Café de Turin you don't muck about when the waiter arrives, you jump to it. I went for the *moules au citron*. Lazily, I suspect, Danny Tournier followed suit. Madame Tournier was attracted by the *bourride*, made, she was assured, with fresh *loup de mer*. She went into minor ecstasy anticipating the *beurre de Provence* on which the fish would be bedded in its serving dish.

Danny, unresponsive to all this, gazed across at Garibaldi's back.

His wife protested: 'Left to his own devices he'd eat hamburgers. How is it? Fast food?'

'Your reward for marrying beneath yourself, Maxine. The wine?' Danny went on to ask.

I always give way to the locals when it comes to wine. They are supposed to know about these things.

Danny asked for house white.

He didn't look happy. Neat, yes: collar and tie, seersucker jacket, dark blue cotton trousers. Happy, not a bit. Either that was because he was separated from his beloved piano, or on account of what he was about to announce.

Two bodies beside the railway line, between it and the road outside Embrun on the shores of the Lac de Serre Ponçon. What did it mean? Both had bullet holes in them. One, it had apparently been reported, was bound with twine at the wrists and there were signs of rope burns on the ankles as well.

That was the question Danny Tournier had put to me: 'What does it mean?'

'How the hell should I know what it means?'

Not entirely true, for as I was saying the words truth was dawning. Why else would a man like Tournier be asking?

He said: 'We don't know about the woman, not yet. But a man would be a fool —'

' — not to,' Madame Tournier cut in.

I turned to her, astonished.

She returned my surprised stare, a parody. She blew out her lips, gestured flamboyantly with both hands. 'Those people', she said, 'they have sown the wind.'

'And?'

'My wife has nothing inside her but rock. She was brought up a Protestant . . . you understand?'

Maxine laughed at that. 'He is always saying such terrible things. It gives him pleasure. But, mark my words, these people have intended to kill you. Myself, I was opposed to my husband accepting the job in the first place. For kidnappings are the worst crime, and the most dangerous. These people . . . ' But then she was distracted. 'Ah,' she said, and the fish hit the table. The sauce on which it lay was half soaked into toasted slices of bread and the rest served in a dented silver-plate jug. Madame Tournier gazed upon her serving in worshipful silence then said: 'These people, aren't they called the family Falcone? Birds of prey! There is nothing for it but that they should die. Or else they will take it into their heads to commit the same crime again.'

'My wife is a fundamentalist, Essington.'

Then the mussels arrived, great dishes of them, heaped, and the lemon and butter sauce in an open bowl.

It took a while to comprehend fully the import of what Tournier had told me. Moulay, working more or less on contract, had taken it into his head to kill these people. Yet, as I responded to the horror of this information, my mind understood the implications of that conclusion: if the bodies were those of the Falcones, and Tournier seemed in no doubt, then there'd be no point in leaving the woman to keep her side of the story alive.

The woman was not old, probably under thirty. Most likely she was also dead.

Why should I bother with the obvious questions about checking the identity? Hadn't Tournier told me he had a friend in the police up at Briançon? Briançon wasn't so far away from where the two corpses had been found.

I had a responsibility for the deaths, sure. Yet after the initial shock it didn't worry me so much. The idea of them shot had so much justice sticking to it. Perhaps I was encouraged by Madame Tournier's simplistic view of what was right and what was deserved: weren't we talking about the pay-back in its most ancient and uncomplicated form?

What the hell else would those Falcones understand?

I wouldn't know, I'd spent my life believing in a set of liberal ideals. Who hasn't? And nobody had got anywhere much with us all keeping those good thoughts alive. Put to the test it was dog eats dog and all right by me that it was so. No, the killing didn't worry me that much; the truth is it was the money. The fact that it had been lodged in a safe deposit box!

I asked: 'The two hundred and seventy thousand dollars?' Because I'd wondered about that. The pressure shelling out three million dollars had put on my relationship with Karen had inhibited our capacity to discuss the details of the transaction. And Danny only released the information you sought from him. He wasn't a man to volunteer anything. That wasn't the Tournier style.

He was refilling his wife's glass. He stopped. He smiled for the first time since we'd sat down.

'The money,' he explained, 'was carried from America.'

'Carried?'

'Do you imagine you can extract that much United States currency from a French bank without even President Mitterrand wanting to know why? It is a lot of dollars. No, and also we haven't wanted public interest in this thing. So I flew to New York, extracted the money there, brought it back with me — after this was arranged by a merchant bank which is here in Monaco.'

'But the customs?' I protested. 'And how . . . ? I mean to say, why not questions over there too? You coming from France to draw out so much currency?'

'It has been done . . . so many times. In the US, three million, it's not so much. Not these days.'

'An unregulated finance market,' explained Mrs Tournier, a forkful of fish hovering in front of her mouth.

'Everything for a fee, I guess,' I said bitterly, and perhaps too quickly, emphasizing the commercial nature of our relationship. And, thinking about it, who wasn't milking me? Or is that just rich man's paranoia?

Tournier's eyebrows lifted at that mention of a fee. 'For what other reason?' he asked.

Not such a bad question. Tournier, his wife, I had to face it, they were strangers who were in this for the pay.

That money got to me every time. The idea of it being passed over to Tony and his mate. I saw red if the thought entered my mind. At night, in bed, if the lost mountain of dollars appeared that was it till sun-up. I'd toss backwards and forwards, going over it, over the detail of everything that had happened. And sweating. It wasn't just the cash but the way it had distorted things with Karen. I'd even get to including the small sums as well! Because they added up, believe me.

Not bad for a middle-aged man who reckons he's more interested in the sky's dimensionless blue than in material things.

I asked: 'More wine?' The jug was empty.

'There's nobody who can trace those bills, except myself,' Tournier told me. 'Moulay appears to have anticipated that danger anyway, with the safe deposit box. He's what you get when you hire him. For such small rewards! Thirty thousand dollars! And now, Mr Holt, I shouldn't imagine you will see him for some time. Neither you nor I. He will vanish, that is the way with Moulay . . . our mystery man.'

'Go on a binge?'

'I hardly think a binge; most probably the reverse. There's something of the ascetic about Moulay Yusuf. I believe he dreams of perfection, of a state of being that cannot be obtained. The same thing may be true of a great number of people who take up death as a profession.'

Chapter 23

The London papers were going on about the Greenhouse Effect. Even the Prime Minister had changed tack on hydrocarbons. It was hard to say how scientific the politicians and the papers were being, but one thing for sure was that in London the sun had retreated behind a blanket of cloud and was signalling a firm intention to stay there, possibly for ever.

Was that a change?

Cloud suits London with its rows of white-painted buildings behind little fences of iron pikes to keep at bay a world which is altogether too close.

I'd caught a morning plane from Nice and watched out of the window the other planes full of nonentities like myself, heading off towards futility in one direction or another.

I was sitting next to a man who must have been selling something: he had a folder of computer print-outs and was making very neat notations over the top of the pale, dot matrix numerals and alphabetical codes. I didn't so much as try a nod, and I expect he was glad of my reticence.

At Villa du Phare it had been Karen in one door and me out the other. I didn't have to play policeman any more with the nursemaid, did I? The young wife could take her turn, it would do her good. Maybe if Nurse Findlay got to talking it over Karen would learn another point of view about men being tied up and treated like animals. As well as about decent Scotswomen who'd been held prisoner.

Or maybe the two of them would simply settle into playing games with Pietro, leaving hell for later.

It would depend which side up the coin fell.

So would this trip of mine to London.

Dolent . . . funny I'd developed a tendency to mispronounce

his name to myself as Dullard: there was this total greyness about the man. And yet he'd turned up a Jodie Winton living in Longmoore Street, Pimlico.

How had he turned it up?

He told me he'd got a friend who spoke 'near perfect' English to ring one of three Wintons in Mount Vernon, Ohio. They'd hit the jackpot first time. It was Jodie's father who answered. Dolent's pal explained that there was something to forward from where she'd been working out on Cap Ferrat.

The father suggested sending it straight to the States. It appears at that point the French end suddenly encountered language difficulties, and stayed tongue-tied till scoring a London address, even the telephone number, which was a bonus.

What do fathers know of daughters and their intrigues?

So that was fine.

Except it meant I had to make the trip before the bird got a call from her loving dad, and decided to fly.

Dolent pointed out that if Jodie bothered to stop and think she'd realize she would always be contactable through her family; one choice was to sever those links altogether. Unlikely in this case, was Dolent's conclusion. He had been given the impression that the father got along well with his daughter. That there was a family back there in Mount Vernon, Ohio, with which Jodie kept in touch: postcards of the Eiffel Tower on the mantelpiece, and maybe tales of pickpockets working the Champs-Elysées.

It did occur to me during the flight, watching fan-fold page after fan-fold page bare its innocent face to the attention of my fellow traveller, that Jodie might not be a key player. There is something about having a father in Mount Vernon, Ohio, that makes you ponder on the nature of evil. I mean, you don't think of bad girls as having fathers at all, do you? Even, or maybe particularly, beautiful bad girls.

At the airport I tried the telephone number Dolent had given me. Jodie's number. It was engaged. I counted to a hundred then tried again. This time the phone was ringing, and kept on like that. On and on. Just as I was on the point of hanging up a voice said: 'Hello'. That was Jodie's voice. I reckoned I knew it. I said: 'Jodie . . . Jodie Winton?'

'Oh,' at the other end. Then silence. I started to say something more but she hung up.

Screw it, and now she was warned.

Then I rang this Howard Fischmann who was working on the Makihei negotiations. I wanted to see the man face to face, and there were a few questions concerning my part of the deal that I wouldn't have minded getting cleared up. Married or not, there was a certain separation of ownership in the silk business that Karen wanted sustained. Because of the dollop of money I'd put in at the start I had a lot of equity, even though I'd never bothered to establish it in precise terms. Now it was required of me to make sure I knew just what of mine was being sold off. Funny how the sale was supposed to recover our economic position, emphasis on the word 'our'! Yet already that simple imperative had faded from view and we were locked into the fine print, crazy calculations.

Amazingly, for a lawyer's office, I got on to Fischmann first try, even though there was the hard-nosed protective secretary with a polished voice, a touch husky. I gave my name, she wasn't sure he was in, checked, then told me I was being put through.

Put through what?

I said I'd just breezed into town, that I'd like to make contact. That was fine by him, how long was I to be around? Maybe Fischmann reckoned there'd be more business where this came from.

'Here today,' I said, 'gone tomorrow.' I lied.

'That's difficult . . . let me see.' At least he was trying! 'You've caught me at a particularly bad time. Clients from Amsterdam . . . the afternoon is out, and the evening. Unless, Mr Holt, you can make it late.'

'By late you mean . . . ?'

'Tennish.'

'Tennish would be fine.'

'Then I'll tell you what — where you are staying?'

I named the hotel.

'Holland Park, splendid, I'm just around the corner. I'll be in the lobby, a quarter past. Why don't we do it that way?'

'A quarter past ten,' I said.

Cities are monuments to the human mind's capacity to tolerate sameness. London, how many of those po-faced houses does it have? Searching out Jodie I noticed that an increasing number were abandoning their vocation as rooming joints and getting reconstituted into family homes for the prosperous. An exception, Jodie's house still wore a patina of grime and a couple of nasty cracks running down its front parapet from the missing one of a pair of cement urns.

Plastic garbage bags littered the street. But there was equality in that, for the pavement in front of the redecorated residences boasted as much uncollected rubbish as I had to wade through when approaching Jodie's front door.

I wonder if, on the plane from Nice to London, my fellow passenger spent as much time casting sly looks at what I had on my lap as I'd devoted to his fan-fold paper. If I decided he was in selling, what did he make of me looking at postcard-sized snaps of bunches of photographers?

Perhaps the most boring stack of visual images in creation!

A dissolute-looking bunch of men, with the occasional woman attempting to hold her place beside the cat-walk, or in the crush outside the marquees in the Jardin des Tuileries, but getting shoved aside. The tools of trade being wound on, reloaded, the focus ring worked. A lot of photographic brand names registered; you could have used the collection of shots to survey the success of the manufacturers' marketing strategies — maybe that would have been a start-up for conversation with the man at my side.

But it was so hard to make the kind of positive identification I wanted. The job was made more confusing by the fact that there were several hundred prints in the bundle. I tried. The note that Makihei had included with the collection indicated that he'd had a secretary search the strips of film over a light table, marking down edge numbers of shots that might be of interest to me, and avoiding repetitions produced on account of the motor drives. There was a coding on the back of the shots which specified where they had been taken. They were only images that might relate to me, to my attendance, or my bursting out through the door of the apartment block as a newly found media sub-star.

Hard to concentrate on the shots while the Bordeaux–Paris flight cut across our bows, maybe a kilometre away. It's the child in me, I've never really got over the zap of flying.

Because the shots were in colour and there was a limitation on the speed of the film and the degree to which it can be pushed without losing quality to grain and burnt-out chromatic values, a large number of the subjects glimpsed were blurred, too much so for recognition. In others the photographers had used flash which does its own thing to the human face, turning it to a death-mask.

And then there was one with the head mostly turned away, the guy fiddling with his camera I guessed, but there was a shape to the head, and something in the hint of profile which felt familiar. Just one head among the several in that shot, but it caught my eye. When searching, particularly if you are going at it too hard, you can kid yourself, no doubt about it. I guess I was kidding myself with that particular shot, wanting it to be my man. I put it to one side, closed my eyes, emptied my mind of the images piled up inside there. I still had half the stack to peruse. The one shot I'd found so far had the Makihei specification on the back. That meant it had been taken at my friend's parade. If it had been one from the Sixteenth Arrondissement, at the time of our grand departure in the three scarlet Rolls-Royces, it would have been marked accordingly: two red crosses.

Clever, when you come to think about it, posing as a photographer, if you want to keep an eye on somebody. Nothing attracts attention more than the person hanging about with nothing to do; we of this work-or-be-damned world notice the underemployed, they stand out. Unless of course they happen to be sleeping beneath a pile of newspapers — that's true invisibility.

As I was taking my break from looking at the photographs, just lying back, eyes closed, the plane's engines droning in my ears, I was trying to force my mind to exit life for a few minutes. But the old thoughts started to run free, their unattractive rodent's feet scampering hither and thither. If that shot was of the man with the built-up shoe then, definitely, me becoming a magazine-cover image had nothing to do with subsequent events. Because the guy had to have been watching me already. So, I would have been in line to be snatched before the photograph was published. There was the possibility that if I was right about that then the baby had never been the target. It was always me. Because generally I didn't carry Pietro around in my arms as I had on the day of the cover photo. And if the baby had been their aim, and my hunch about Jodie being involved was right, they could have taken him away at any time. Surely the best moment would have been when Jodie was on her own with him at the apartment?

Unless of course, that would put too much suspicion and pressure on her. They would have to have considered the question of how she would stand up under police interrogation.

How, for that matter, would any of us?

Before the publication of the cover photograph, if I was in line to be snatched, or if in fact it was the baby they wanted, how had it happened that strangers were aware of my existence?

Who knew of the wealthy Australian who lived out on Cap Ferrat? The truth is that I live a private life and have a limited circle of friends. There was Molena. OK . . . but Molena! He was my friend, no question about it.

Yet instantly I began to test that assessment. Then stopped myself before it was too late.

I mean, Mr Paranoia, welcome aboard! For Christ's sake, Essington! Would Molena go along with something like that? Playing it careful, being off in New Caledonia for the main event?

You can watch Paranoia approach, can't you? Slouching, hat brim pulled right down, you can observe the way his untrusting hands are shoved deep into the pockets of a stained cotton gaberdine overcoat. Slit mouth twisted into something like a grin. Try and shoo him away, but the bastard will take up residence and from then on be as hard to budge as possums in the roof. And he'll piss on your brain too, like it was the ceiling, take the word of one who knows.

Yet isn't it Freud who tells us that Mr Paranoia is often right?

Where do you go from there?

Because, well, where I went was to thinking of Makihei himself. Of his men, too, the neat executives with the glasses who upset Farah sufficiently to cause her to resign.

I missed Farah. I'd lost my finger, I'd lost her. The finger was one thing. But her beauty, I'd fed off it, hadn't I, used it like a drug. Not for sexual fantasy, but more for its own unique self. Farah, so exquisite that you hardly imagined such a creation to have thoughts.

So, Makihei? Fine! It was a crazy notion though, one of the big designers, really big, deciding to organize for me to be kidnapped so he could do a save operation, take over the silk business. And get a Gauguin at the same time.

My fishing friend, Makihei! Up there in the sky I was starting to think more and more about him. What better way was there to find out about a man than sitting for several hours at a stretch, fishing? Yet, for my part, during those times together, I'd discovered nothing of him. Or didn't that say a lot about me?

Next thing I'd be suspecting my own dead mother.

I opened my eyes, kept on going through the stack of photographs. My companion was punching numbers into a pocket calculator, comparing the answers with figures on the print-out.

Molena, Mr Paranoia tried another go at him. I resisted this time. You've got to have something to cling to, faith of a kind, and trust.

I found myself going over the lines —

> 'He who would valiant be
> 'Gainst all disaster,
> Let him in constancy
> Follow the master.'

— as a nonsense round-song, while I found a couple more shots of interest in the bunch.

Chapter 24

The first thing I see is a black face, its expression uncertain.
It is female.
I'd been conscious some time, but in the dark. And kicking, shouting myself hoarse. Nobody coming. Well, they wouldn't would they? Not right up to the top floor. And a bit of a kerfuffle doesn't attract attention in the heart of great cities these days. The people just don't want to know.

She is large and her face broad, wonder is written across it. Caution too. She's wondering if it's some kind of game I'm playing. Or there could have been the drug angle with me.

The cupboard door is open, and across the landing, at the back of my saviour, another door, that one open as well. Through it I can see stairs leading up.

He'd come out through that door. The picture is clear in my mind. Me, how many steps had I climbed? I remember coming in the building's front door which had been unlocked, finding the pigeon holes for mail, going through them, looking for the name of Winton on a letter, or on any of the large items, mostly real estate brochures, stacked on top. Nothing there for Winton. Which didn't teach me anything. The important thing had seemed to be to get to the address as quickly as possible. I'd done that. Next the steps. Up I went, those bloody endless London stairs! You go one flight, a landing, poky doors shutting off poky bed-sitters. Another flight. Visiting in London takes the breath out of you. Particularly if, like me, you run the whole way up.

At the top I'd felt stuffed: my heart was pumping, I was hot and out of breath. Not the old Essington at all. I was panicky too, because what was it I was going to get Jodie to admit? And how would I go about doing that? By beating her up? Was that on the cards? Somehow I didn't see punching Jodie as my kind of act.

Then, preoccupied about how to question her, I'd confronted the door which, surprisingly, stood open.

I'd been working out what to do next when a figure came down the stairs, fast. Expectant, the look on his face. But the eyes were beads. The guy with the built-up shoe had just had himself some kind of a high.

I was reacting slowly to the shock of recognition. And still pulling myself together from the climb up those stairs.

Suddenly for me there was one of those freeze frames. Like the other one of Jodie herself with Pietro in her arms: Jodie who would forever look out of that Paris door, who would turn, yet somehow in a sequence of stills rather than as fluid motion.

A hand came out of his jacket pocket. Before I could react his arm was coming around, with something in it, in his clasped hand.

I recall now that somewhere inside me there was the surge of satisfaction at knowing I was right after all.

How long did it all take, the registration of what was there, the hand swinging? And him such a little guy. I should have been able to handle him.

I remember, too, recognition of the fact that it was a gun in his hand; then the blow, like an implosion.

She is putting her questions to me in a charming accent — West Indian I suppose — asking if I'm all right.

At first I'm not answering because I know that the phone call I'd made from the airport had been a mistake. Though just then I didn't realise how great that mistake was.

And next thing I'm staring at the open door, asking myself if the visit is too late.

Next comes regret that I have got it all wrong. Standing there with the woman who's let me out of the cupboard, I can't believe it . . . believe myself, the stupidity!

It was the woman who went up first, who discovered the body. She let out a shrill cry, crossed herself. Till then I hadn't seen a thing, the woman was in front. Then it was my turn. I came around. I saw.

Mount Vernon, Ohio, Jesus! What a long ride that must have been for Jodie. And there she was, in her bed-sitter. There was the parapet wall blocking half the windows; I could see the edge torn away where the cement urn should have been standing, and the cracks, which went right through.

Jodie had a David Hockney poster on the wall. There's a song like that: 'Would You Like to Stay Till Sunrise' it's called. A girl trying to sound casual, asking a stranger to stay the night, because she doesn't want to be alone.

For Christ's sake, who does.

But Jodie was alone. She was dead too. Her throat had been cut.

And most of her body was naked.

Curious: the naked, the nude. There's a difference, isn't there? Naked we all look pretty much the same. Dead, even Jodie didn't have one element of centrefold fantasy about her. Instead, I was looking at another of us poor mortals who'd lived inside her own world while we, the rest, built false images of her in our minds. And I guess there had been a soul somewhere. Almost certainly a soul.

Next thing I was asking myself why I was thinking like that — considering aesthetics, metaphysics — when confronted by this death.

I got the answer. Because there was something arranged about the body, even the degree to which it was naked, how it was naked. There was blood on the bed, on the pillow. Yet she was over the other side of the room, in a corner. Her legs were wide open, her head hanging back so that where the knife had sliced through the throat there was one enormous wound, gaping. Jodie's eyes were open wide, her mouth, curiously, was almost smiling.

She was stripped from the waist down, and her blouse had been pulled up towards one shoulder.

Blood on the pillow? How was it possible? You wouldn't have been moving about much with your neck cut through like that.

The woman with me fainted. Thump. Fell like an axed tree.

But, oddly, it didn't really give me that much pain knowing Jodie was dead. The fact that it was so demonstrated something, that my speculation, some of it at least, hadn't been too far off the mark. Because I'd seen the killer's face too, hadn't I? It was the same man, no doubt about it. And I had a photo of him back in my hotel room . . . several of them, two that were clearly recognizable.

He was marked. But for whom? For the police?

I still had to think about that one, work out where I stood, what I'd risk by spilling the whole story.

I had the other woman's head between her knees.

It was odd the way I was reacting. Cool, responding to what confronted me. Even with the right side of my head throbbing from the blow I'd received, and pain inside as well, the sight in one eye flickering a little.

Yet I was collected, purposeful.

This woman who'd got me out of the cupboard, she came round, looked at me, uncomprehending, then turned to the body. I put an arm around her shoulder, whispered sweet nothings.

I went for the phone down on the next landing; you paid to ring out. I paid.

After that the woman and I sat around chatting, keeping our spirits up, waiting for the cops to arrive and cart us off. My new friend's name was Joyce. She'd been visiting a friend whose door gave on to the next landing, the one where the phone was located. While waiting for some response to her knock she'd heard my rumpus and decided to come up and investigate.

We were swapping life stories outside the bed-sitter, away from the grotesque corpse, when a pair of police, a man and a woman, came up the stairs. They were polite, playing at being efficient. Even with me in the hot seat, having been knocking on that particular door and then slammed across the side of the head with a revolver, their touch was light. They were a holding squad, uniformed; we were waiting for the heavies to arrive: someone in civvies, a detective from the local nick.

That was when I met Inspector Morgan and his side-kick who scratched his ear all the time, an action which gave the impression there was a nicer man inside somewhere trying to get out. What an innocent, me wanting to believe in some kind of essential goodness like that!

Later there were more people: experts in white coats, men carrying stretchers, others taking photographs, checking the contents of the room. God, wasn't there something pathetic about Jodie's junk? Death makes property look like so much vanity. I was thankful once the body was rendered decent with a sheet. Those eyes, up till then they'd seemed to follow me around, accusingly.

Accusing! What in God's name had *I* done?

Is there a police station in the world that's different from any other police station? I wouldn't think so. Maybe in South America you get more screams and out of the window the view is broken by the bodies of the defenestrated dropping past. South Africa, it's supposed to be pretty wild there too. But essentially they're all the same. Put a human being in the force, give him a badge, a chair to sit on, forms to be filled out and he, she or it is going to devolve into pretty much the same kind of animal every time. It's in our natures.

Joyce finished up going one way. Me another. We gave our versions. I even went so far as to explain that Jodie had worked for me, well, for my wife actually—lots of emphasis on the wife side of the story to keep it clean. I was in London, thought I'd do the right thing, drop in.

'You thought you'd just drop in.'

'That's correct.'

'Nice thought.'

'Why not?' I asked, but keeping my head. The first rule is don't let them get under your skin.

'For a cup of tea perhaps, you and Miss . . .' He was pulling at his ear.

'Winton.'

'Intimate.'

'Inspector!'

'Detective Sergeant, if you want to get it right.'

'Detective Sergeant . . . I don't have to take this shit, not from you, not from anyone.'

'We'll decide what you'll take, Mr Holt. You happened to be coming up the stairs . . . blah, blah, blah . . .' The voice droned on. You score people like this one I'd scored: low IQ with just the rudiments of a rational thought process, but proud of what they have, of how they can put it into action. Looking into the eyes of my detective sergeant, you could get a glimpse of the small brain beyond, see the rusted ill-formed wheels turning. One of those faces that have devoured so much pudding they've come to look like one. Not young either, slow to make it up through the grades, possibly bitter from having watched younger and better-dressed men slip past him, heading for the top.

And at the start I'd thought he was all right!

'I asked what time would that have been.'

He was going to have to keep at it because they weren't getting another word out of me. Screw them.

That was something I owed to Tony, to Built-up shoe, to the Falcones . . . you chain a man to a wall for a while, cut his finger off, it starts to make even the London police look like a bunch of pansies.

My bloke was shouting, a pulsing vein standing out on his forehead. I fixed my eyes on his eyes, smiled. 'Kiss my arse,' I said.

Which may not have done me a great deal of good, except in that it did, spiritually. I felt as though inside me there was a landscape: flat, dirt and burnt grass, and me, I was walking slow and steady all the way in from the horizon. Feeling proud. What was it that had been written on . . . was it the Texas flag?

'Don't Tread on Me.'

Essington Cowboy. The Lone Rooster.

Not the hint of an inclination to spill my guts. Certainly not to that bastard. And they didn't have a thing on me. In fact he'd got it all arse about, hadn't he? I could have helped them, sure, taken them back to the hotel where I'd stuffed all those photos into a drawer beside the queen-sized bed rather than cart them about. Show them the guy they were after, what he looked like, tell about the bung leg. Except there didn't seem to be a way to do that without getting into deep water in the territory of the kidnap. Not to mention its aftermath. And I didn't want Interpol sticking their nose in where it wasn't wanted, the French and the English comparing notes on the Holt clan and its movements.

All my sweet detective sergeant could figure out from my passport was that I lived in Sydney, Australia — I have an address there. As far as France is concerned I have a residence permit that has to be renewed each year. There wasn't much to make of anything from the passport since it was a new issue, dated the European autumn; fresh as a daisy and not too many marks in there either. My right to reside across the Channel for twelve months didn't look like anything of great moment.

I beamed. He didn't.

He tried another question. I stayed buttoned up. In the end he went off after his superior: the Inspector Morgan who'd also turned up at Jodie's bed-sit. A different type.

But first the detective sergeant decided on a man-to-man exchange: 'You reckon you're smart, don't you?' Nothing but nastiness in his eyes now, the nose right out of joint.

I wasn't falling for any of that children's playground crap: him trying to get me going.

'Let's see if you're smart enough for me not to kill you next time I see you, squire.'

Funny, there was the old *déjà vu*! I'd been told exactly the same thing by a cop when I was a teenager. That time I'd believed what I was told, took off, never went back to that town.

But you don't have to take off in Merry England, do you? There's the Queen and her corgis who'll look after you if all else fails.

Inspector Morgan was Welsh, like corgis are Welsh. I guess his barrel chest must have developed from all that competition singing they go in for.

He had an accent like Mrs Gandhi.

Chapter 25

I told the Welsh Inspector Morgan that Jodie had been into the stars. Which wasn't true, but he made a note anyway. And then he asked me if I'd like a cup of tea!

Treating me gently from then on and not even wanting to know why I'd stopped hearing the detective sergeant's questions.

I told him anyway, they have to learn. I explained that I could fill them in on Jodie. Or I might decide not to. It was up to them. They were looking at a crime I had nothing to do with and that was clear cut, wasn't it? Me being in the cupboard, just as Joyce had told them.

The Welshman went over the Joyce bit, as though making sure it wasn't some group effort we'd embarked upon: cutting up beautiful American citizens in their bed-sitters. You could tell the colour of Joyce's face hadn't escaped his notice.

I told him to get stuffed. I said they ought to pull their finger out, give up the bigot shit, go and find the killer.

Being a bit aggressive paid off with the Welshman. He said to go back to my hotel.

I was at the western edge of town. You go down Bayswater Road, I think it is, to where they call it Holland Park Avenue to keep you confused. I was at a hotel at the far end of Holland Park. You can go across the road and a roundabout, via an underpass, and there you'd be in Shepherd's Bush.

Walking in a strange city at night is always a bit of a sensation. Particularly the evening after you've discovered a girl with her throat cut. Which tends to get the imagination going, puts the nerves on edge.

I dismissed uneasiness as the effect of the day, and of the underpass, its smell of urine. Yet there was a feeling of . . . well, you couldn't say for sure, could you? I glanced around several times to catch somebody following.

Up and out at the far end I still looked behind trying to outsmart the phantom at my back. Each time all I saw was the street I'd passed along, poorly lit, and people all over the place, but not like the living: even with its dense street population Shepherd's Bush had a quality of being deserted.

It was purgatory!

There was a wind blowing, litter flying on it.

I found a place to eat in Shepherd's Bush. Smarter places in the other direction from the hotel, towards the city, had been booked out. It was Friday night: gentle folk coming out of their holes for a touch of fun,

Well, Jodie wouldn't be joining in, would she?

And I wasn't any the wiser. Though there was stuff to think about. Like could it be a coincidence that she'd got killed on the day I arrived? And if not, why then had it come to pass?

I went over that while shovelling curry into me. I'd asked for it mild which apparently meant no kick at all. Lamb, pappadoms, side-dishes, condiments, I guess the food had devolved since being lifted out of its geographic origins.

I had beer with it.

How the hell could he know I was going to head for Jodie in London?

Or that I would be in London?

Answer: because she rang him immediately after I rang her. Or he was there anyway, just happened to be.

I called for one of the side-dishes I'd ordered but which hadn't turned up. And at just that instant it hit me that maybe this guy already knew that the Falcones were dead, and that there'd been a deal. But in that case how could he have found out?

Who knew to tell him?

There was Moulay. There was me. And, of course, there was Tournier as well: what didn't Tournier know?

And Molena, because he'd been in on talking with Giulio.

But that was it, had to be. Nurse Findlay, she didn't know much, and she wouldn't have had anybody to tell — Renardo would see to that.

I might not be a judge of character, but I knew Moulay wouldn't be working both sides, it wasn't in him to do something like that. Anyway, there would have been some ancient wisdom warning him against the practice.

I went for the kufli and after that, coffee. A bit before ten I exited the restaurant into a less populous street and headed for the hotel. I was looking forward to some sanity; was it too much to hope this Howard Fischmann could provide it? And I had stories to relate of my tangling with the police; maybe he could be of some help. For instance, in assisting me to get my passport back from the good Inspector Morgan who simply wanted to make sure I didn't do a bolt for the antipodes.

I paused at the entrance to the underpass, looked around, searching in the shadows for a tail. Why should there be a tail? There was a Ford Sierra ticking over at the kerb, maybe twenty yards distant; I could pick up a hint of condensation around the exhaust. The night was cold for the time of year, the wind bitter; at least it wasn't raining.

Close your eyes Essington — into the tunnel I went.

Who the hell thought up underpasses? They are the worst of a pretty dreadful set of solutions to urban design problems. I'm big, and I'd have to say fairly confident, yet they give me the creeps. Even with the litter of paper and stuff the echo of my footsteps got to me, had me pumping adrenalin, sweating. It's not so much the living you fear in a place like that, as the dead. They ought to be materializing out of the grates on top of the drain running the tunnel's length on one side — so you don't drown down there in a cloud burst.

I was running as I got to the Holland Park end and went up the stairs, two at a time, head down.

They were standing shoulder to shoulder.

'Mr Holt.' I knew the voice, of course I knew the fucking voice!

'Detective Sergeant,' I responded.

This was a pay-back for my cheek, my non-co-operation, I knew it.

Talk about sensitive, and vindictive!

Maybe my pudding-faced cop had had his head chewed off by Inspector Morgan for going in too hard on me, for stuffing it up. That would have been it. He'd received a dressing-down and the man who was responsible for spoiling his day was now going to pay the price.

I stepped back, keeping clear. They didn't move. 'Not so smart now, Mr Holt?' A sneer in it.

What do you reply to shit like that? Nothing, that's what you reply.

The detective sergeant's friend moved in. The Brits, they like a scrap. Everybody in Europe knows it. You see them all over the place with their Union Jack T-shirts on, blotchy skin, hair cut short, maybe an earring for fun. They like those big boots too, Doc Martins, for kicking poofters in the head. They do it in memory of the Empire.

The detective sergeant's mate didn't throw a punch — hell no! — he kicked. There was a railing at my back, fencing off the top of the stairs. I stepped aside, the kick missed. But next thing he was turning, bending forward: a charge! Funny animal, a cop. I sometimes wonder why we have them. And the detective sergeant wanting to watch the Christ beaten out of me.

Suddenly I got it — intuition! The one attacking wasn't with the police. It was a favour he was doing: some street hood sucking.

That blind charge!

I was proud of the timing, I just about broke my fist on his mouth. The force of the punch straightened him up. Then I connected on the side of his head with a haymaker, just above the ear. He stood like a zombie, turning slowly to face me as I moved in a semi-circle. When I hit him between the eyes he was back-on to the underpass, but instead of falling the way a post would fall, he sort of crumpled at the knees, dropped on to the cement, turned over once and then, amazingly slowly, he was rolling down the steps.

Quick, I went for the other man. Bending low, he was bringing out a revolver but I caught the hand in both of mine, slammed it back against the railing. The weapon dropped. I scooped it up. The detective sergeant wasn't a fighter, certainly when the advantage was gone. Which, I guess, was why he'd brought along his little mate.

'And a gun! We're free-lance tonight? Nothing regulation about carrying that, pal. You were intending to use it?' I asked. Reasonable, see. I mean that really was the question, wasn't it?

He said nothing.

'Then I fucking shoot you down there.' I pointed into the abyss that would hold the report of the shot, jabbing at him, getting him really scared.

It was strange, a confrontation like that, cars whizzing past, nobody stopping. No foot traffic though, not a soul in sight.

Real fear sounding: 'Don't shoot!'

Once I'd slipped the safety catch I was all energy the way you have to be. That was Moulay's trick, to have every atom of your body squeezing on the trigger, your mind there too, and be aiming at some arsehole's chest.

The detective sergeant knew I'd hooked into the feeling.

And into the pleasure of it.

That's what power is: it's being sort of crazy, off your tree. As we say back home: Kangaroos in the top paddock.

Chapter 26

I thought about the detective sergeant's Ford Sierra. I didn't want us to end up in that confined space together. Opening car doors, bending over — you can get into trouble that way. I'm at my best in the wide open.

Instead, I made to steer him towards my hotel.

'The motor's running!'

'You have to be kidding, Detective Sergeant! You hire someone to beat the shit out of me and now I'm expected to cry over the petrol bill. So, who's your little mate, anyway?'

Silence. Just him standing there facing me, refusing to move. And me wondering: What now?

I kept on talking at him. Proof, I guess, that I was losing my nerve. 'A pro off the street?' I suggested. 'Favours, that's what police work adds up to, am I right? Just like banking: calling in the paper when life gets difficult. The Mafia, only on tax payer's money. That poor sod had to attack on command.'

He said: 'You any idea the noise a gun makes . . . and when you're shooting a copper?'

That was the moment he made his move. Clever when you come to think about it. Giving me a little time to cool off first, to get over being trigger-happy. I could have sworn there was the ghost of a smile on his face as he walked to the car.

'See you around,' he said. Then shut the door and drove away.

Leaving me flat-footed. That's how it goes, Essington.

A man, I assumed Fischmann, was at my hotel reception, asking for Holt. I butted in, introduced myself. We shook hands and I steered him into a bar off the foyer — international-hotel decor, the odd cigarette burn marking the carpet.

I was talking like a man gone crazy. But talking not corporation law so much as street attack.

Fischmann was a London gent with a hell of a lot of style. A mane of black hair was swept off his dome forehead; he had a posh voice. Natty dresser too, with a dark blue overcoat draped across his shoulders. He was tall, and had a big proud nose like a horse.

The voice was so loud it made me cringe. He wanted scotch with ice. I took the same. Out came a thin cigar: 'Do you mind?' Why bother to enquire?

I kept on telling him about the attack, the police, the girl with her throat cut. Of the different ways I'd been handled by the inspector and by the detective sergeant.

Fischmann sucked in, blew smoke out; it hit me that he fancied himself, enjoyed his life act.

He had these dark brown eyes, big with bags underneath them; they never left my face once we'd sat down either side of a glass-top table.

'God this is awful,' he said.

I was up to the man who'd rolled back down the steps of the underpass.

'I mean to say . . . the furnishings!'

'Am I wasting my breath?'

'Good God no! Keep on, I'm listening.'

I followed instructions.

At the end I said: 'I understand you people specialize, and this isn't your area.' Then, for laughs: 'Believe it or not, you're the first human being I've met since the attack.'

'No need for flattery, old boy.' He laughed as though he was on stage, trying to make sure the sound carried to the back of the dress circle. A waiter rushed across.

'Another?' Howard asked. He'd downed his first.

In the lounge it was just us two and the pall of smoke surrounding the table. He sucked on his cigar with the vigour of a man in need of weaning therapy.

Next I was being moved out of my room, lock, stock and barrel — we reckoned it was wise to do so — Howard Fischmann chatting nonsense about having to go down to Shropshire for a game of cricket at some character's place. 'Wouldn't like to tag along, would you?'

Fifty feet away the man on the door looked round to check that the invitation wasn't intended for him.

'Cricket,' I responded, 'why not?' Trying out that sort of conversational delivery for myself, as though we were all on the point of nicking across to France to save a coachful of deserving aristocrats from the Terror: 'We seek him here, we seek him there . . . ' Or is it 'they' who do the seeking — like in any paranoiac's fantasy?

Fischmann lived in a house of grand proportions not so far away and facing Holland Park. We arrived there by taxi.

An outside light came on as we approached the door and when we entered someone who had to be Mrs Fischmann was hovering a little way off, a nervous grin on her face. The thought struck me that she looked as though she'd been caught doing something naughty, this short woman with untidy hair of no particular colour at all.

Ruth, it suited her, though not on account of the alien corn.

I got the impression it was the suitcases as much as anything that had her off balance.

'Is it the cricket?' she asked.

'A waif.' Howard had turned the volume down for his wife. She folded her arms across her chest. 'That blasted cricket,' she said, and then flashed another nervous grin as though it had slipped out, an accident, not what she meant to say at all.

'Are you the keeper?' I asked.

Peals of laughter, high-pitched, one might have been excused for suspecting a touch of madness in there somewhere. We were standing in the lobby, as though we'd lost the will to move.

Too many lines on Ruth's face for her age, etched there by the acid of nerves.

'Did you have a good day?' Howard asked.

'We won,' she said.

'Splendid.'

I said, trying to be funny: 'It was your cricket today then?'

'After a fashion, Mr . . . '

'Oh, I am so sorry, Ruth . . . Essington Holt . . . my wife, of course.'

'Of course, of course,' she said. A bitter tone.

'No, darling, that is splendid. What now?'

'Nothing I imagine, if they don't appeal.' She turned to me. 'Talking shop, how rude of us. Do come in, Mr Holt.'

A reception room, large, but decorated in that comfy British way, pale gold carpet which would stain under the strain of fun. Several of those paintings — of barges, peasants forking hay, lads chatting up lasses on stone bridges — filled spaces on the wall. There had been a pair in the lobby: one a chap jumping his horse, the other a spaniel with a bird in its mouth.

Over the fireplace was a fine portrait of . . . it had to be of Ruth! Very good, though quite unflattering with a sense of blue veins beneath pale skin. A powerful painting, and I saw another Ruth in it. Not this timid woman but a creature whose eyes were filled with intelligent anger.

'Mr Holt is in a spot of bother.'

'You just picked him up, an . . . '

'An Australian, careful,' I said, 'no racism.'

'Actually he's a client of mine.'

'Financial trouble?' Ruth asked, a hint of a smile lifting the corners of her mouth. And then, sitting, she added an invitation for me to follow suit. I obeyed like a trained Jack Russell terrier.

'A drink?' Howard Fischmann asked.

I said yes. My hand was shaking, shock of a sort taking over from the exultant calm I'd experienced for the full hour that had passed since I'd knocked the attacker down the stairs.

I think she saw the hand, how it was out of control. Did she notice the missing finger too? And the bruising across the knuckles where I'd connected?

Ruth declined a drink. I noticed that Howard didn't light up, not at home. Well, there was the carpet, wasn't there?

'Criminal,' he said.

'Oh . . . so why you, Howard?' She didn't like her husband, did she? They didn't like each other, but there was a pact. And no doubt children away at boarding school.

'It's half and half,' I said, 'complicated.'

Watching my hand, willing it to be still, I noticed the skin was broken.

'Then Ruth's your man,' Howard said.

Even if you've been brought up in the anglophile atmosphere of WASP Australia it's hard to believe how faithfully the British stick to their traditions. Cricket in Shropshire was no exception.

I'd been put in last wicket down because one ancient codger, who actually had his creams held up with an old school tie, had been so polite as to insist that he couldn't run between wickets with his hip the way it was.

'It's plastic, you see, Rupert had it put in two months back; blamed the need for repairs on riding to hounds, a fall at a hedge ten thousand years ago.' That was information from a stout woman whose plaid skirt was covered in dog hair: Lady somebody-or-other.

A Jeremy Irons look-alike at deep leg got under my one big hit, caught it, let it slip through his hands.

It's great to be nice to a stranger, another to pretend to drop a catch off the first ball he's delivered. I walked. Our side were all out for eighty-six.

As far as my criminal life was concerned, Ruth insisted it was well in hand. She'd already taken certain steps, among which would be a complaint to the chief constable who happened to be a fair-minded 'bloke, isn't that what I should say?

'And there's the possibility we can turn our detective sergeant around, point him . . . if you see what I mean.' This was another Ruth entirely, better with distance between herself and Howard.

'Now, now, now,' said our country host's wife, walking towards us, draining a silver hip-flask down her throat. 'We are not masons, business will not be done. Ruth, you really are too wicked.'

Eating was next. Cricket was a pretext for the lunch. The trick it seemed was to bat first, get it over with. With drunks bowling after lunch the game became considerably more dangerous.

We sat at a long table set under spreading linden trees. At my back was an imposing house in a state of decay, before me the roughly mown paddock where the cricket was being played. I was next to the hostess, being instructed. She was quite unaffected by huge quantities of what I presumed to be scotch.

As a barrister, Ruth pleaded in court, specializing in nasty cases. Despite an unprepossessing manner it seems she had quite a reputation. On my behalf she contacted solicitors who in their turn did this, then did that . . . I couldn't have followed the action even if I'd tried. But the upshot was I was heading home on the Tuesday following the cricket weekend, after having invited half the population of Shropshire to drop in next time they made it to the Côte d'Azur.

Oh, they'd all pretended to find that spectacularly chic, the Côte d'Azur!

There had been a meeting with the detective sergeant, in chambers in the city, somewhere off Chancery Lane near the Law Courts, with Ruth Fischmann and a man called Johnstone present. I gathered Johnstone was working in the law as well. The purpose was to trade: my information for the detective sergeant's promise of peace in our time. Mind you, Ruth had used a big stick on the man: he had the option of not agreeing and risking her pushing the matter of his treatment of my good self. She actually appeared genuinely concerned about members of the force carrying handguns that hadn't been signed out in the proper fashion, particularly ones that weren't police issue.

During the confrontation I guess I was the belligerent one. My policeman had already been brought to heel. I dissembled. I gave out more vague description, hinted at the possible involvement in other matters of the man who'd clobbered me at the door of the Pimlico flat. For luck I added a bit about the lad called Tony with the deck-hand eyes. In fact I muddled the two up, making it so the one man could have been the other, just possibly.

I got myself into a mess performing this trick. Me and the rest of them. Next thing I was backtracking.

The detective sergeant, whose name turned out to be Mutton, which probably explained a lot about his personality, asked: 'What I don't follow is the *why* of it all.'

Ruth Fischmann: 'The why?'

Mutton: 'Think of it. All right I'll admit I've done what I shouldn't have, but consider the facts. Here we have a man, your Mr Holt, he's locked in a cupboard on the landing. We've been asked to believe this!'

'How do I lock myself in a cupboard?' I protested. 'You saw the handle, the set-up, it isn't possible; there was a bolt on the outside.'

Mutton: 'Point taken.' A crooked grin across his unattractive features.

Ruth Fischmann: 'Your question changes nothing, Detective Sergeant Mutton. The fact remains you've assaulted my client and . . .'

'And we've been through that. There's police work, if you don't object to me pointing it out. And then there's pussy footing about the place.' Mutton had lifted his act a fraction. There he was playing Mr Clean, but sticking to basic arguments about reality, how we didn't live in a perfect world.

Ruth was not giving the bastard an inch.

Mutton pressed on: 'It turns out, doesn't it, that there's some connection between your client and the dead woman.'

'How many times must I explain that?'

'But, the coincidence!' he insisted.

Me, my hands clenched in exasperation: 'I don't control coincidence.'

'I'm certain,' observed this Johnstone character, his voice neat as a pin, 'if you tried . . . there'd be the causal connection, wouldn't there?'

Mutton took some heart from Johnstone. 'What I'm trying to say is that Mr Holt here is not telling all. I can feel it. He's bloody holding back, if you'll excuse the language. He is not what he seems to be, either. It's a lot of rubbish, everything he says. Doesn't make sense. Not logical, if you take my meaning.'

'What isn't?' I asked.

'For starters,' Mutton said, addressing himself solely to Johnstone, 'the gun. Why does he keep my gun? If I should be carrying it, put that aside for the minute, it's another question. But is keeping it what you'd expect from some blasted innocent off the street? Of course it isn't. Can't be.

'Next, how does he know so much about a man who he sees for the time it takes to get clobbered over the skull?'

'A good question,' Johnstone admitted. He turned to me, eyes behind the horn-rimmed bifocals demanding an answer.

'I recognized him, or thought I did. From Paris, I was up in Paris . . . I've been over that already.'

Mutton: 'You were up in Paris. Jesus, what a life! In Paris, in Nice . . . where next? Why not the bloody Bahamas?'

'Why not? Anything to get away from your kind, Detective Sergeant.'

'This,' said Ruth Fischmann, 'is getting us nowhere. Please, Mr

Holt, do try. After all there are two sides to this agreement. You are understood to be offering assistance in the matter of Miss Winton's death. Detective Sergeant Mutton is eating humble pie. Now it's your turn to make some effort. If you have previously seen the man in question, enough to identify him, perhaps then you could do better with your description. And you most certainly ought to be able to fill us in on his Paris movements . . . why he was there. How, for instance, he came to know Miss Winton.'

'Exactly,' chirruped Mr Johnstone.

'And there's my gun,' insisted Mutton.

'Fuck your gun.'

As it happened I hadn't done that to the gun. Instead I'd checked the weapon into a bank, put it in a deposit box. 'It's the family jewels,' I'd told the mask-faced young official. I'd purchased a tin box with a little handle on top, exactly the right style.

He'd said: 'Heavy.' And giggled unexpectedly, as though I ought to feel caught out.

'But well used,' I had assured him.

What I didn't tell any of them was how I'd been chained up in a shed. That side of the action, which had been outside the law right from stage one, had to remain that way. Apart from anything else, with the Falcones blown away, there was Moulay to think of. Caesar's law doesn't give a stuff for the justice of the soul.

Nor would that same law have been tolerant of my plans for continuing in pursuit of what had been lifted out of my keeping: the cash, and the Gauguin painting of a Polynesian girl.

Chapter 27

On the flight back I was sitting beside a nervous man who'd worked most of his life in a General Motors factory in Detroit. Only now was he able to visit the beaches on to which he'd been landed as an eighteen-year-old in the US army.

He couldn't get over me being Australian. He'd seen the film *Crocodile Dundee*, on the tube. One day, he reckoned, he wanted to go to Australia, to what he called 'the last frontier'.

It struck me then that this automobile worker shared something of Gauguin's dream: the notion of there being other places where it feels better just to be alive.

In the middle of my companion's description of the allied landing on the Côte d'Azur I got a flash of something else. Suddenly I saw the bit of red that was on the sand beside the sitting Polynesian girl in the painting. There was the sand painted yellow, the colour of a free-range egg yolk, and the sea shell which was painted in white and tinted greys, a leaf in light orange shaded off with black; then this flower, the splash of red.

It was the wrong red, wasn't it? Not in the fake Gauguin I'd been smoking age on to at the Villa du Phare, but in the original that had been used to buy my life. When producing the forgery from a photograph I'd allowed for colour values being unreliable. The thing was, however, I had permitted the reference material I'd put together to eclipse my memory of the original.

Till that instant in the plane, when I suddenly knew it was the wrong red! I could see it in my mind's eye.

And I would never have picked up the problem if I hadn't produced my version of the painting.

'These kangaroos stand taller than a man?' my companion asked.

I liked the guy for his worn face, for his plastic peak cap. He didn't give a damn, he was alive, wasn't he? I noticed the hand on the arm rest, a worker's hand.

A finger missing!

Would you believe it? Shot off, maybe, all those years ago as he went charging through the waves into paradise, rifle above his head to keep it dry.

Our plane was banking over the Iles de Lerins for the run up over Cap d'Antibes to Nice airport. Maybe my neighbour was thinking of his buddies who never made it back to a life of work in a factory.

I said: 'You get little kangaroos too, the size of a mouse.'

'A mouse, you're having me on.'

'A mouse,' I said.

I did like this pilgrim from Detroit, Michigan, even sensed something eternal about him. There I was getting about in this glorious world, and missing the highs, concentrating on losing fingers instead. Being totally pissed off with more or less everything. Over the previous few years hadn't I come to represent a lot of ideas and attitudes at which the young Essington Holt would have curled his lip?

I would once have asked: What's capital?

And answered: It's being alive, that's the only real capital you have.

Hadn't I allowed myself to be argued into hitting the art market for speculation? Well, that wasn't what poor old Gauguin had been on about, he'd wanted to live, that was all. He was like my Detroit automobile factory worker: going for it, for life! While, in Gauguin's case, at every turn the tight-arsed bastards running the islands for France were hounding him; misunderstanding, ignoring what he had to say. How is it? The Christian farewell at Atuona, from the bishop who saw Gauguin buried: 'The death of a painter called Gauguin, a pathetic man, an enemy of God and everything decent.'

Gauguin'd only been searching after a union of man and nature.

The colour was wrong, the red in the bottom left-hand corner. Big joke.

We were taxiing to where the plane was to park. My fellow passenger was looking out the window, at the other planes, at the tarmac where it ran to a breakwater of rock. At the aquamarine sea beyond.

A British Airways flight was next to where we pulled up. Its steps were in place, a hostess standing at the door. She was watching a figure run towards her, a late passenger.

I was watching as well.

It's interesting, a man late for the plane.

Then: wasn't it Tony? The man had a light springy run; he carried a soft bag in one hand, and in the other a boarding pass held out in front like a runner's relay baton. I shoved my body across, pressed my face to the window.

'Hey, hang on buddy.'

I was being pushed back gently.

'It's just that . . .'

'It's me should be going over the top, arriving. I thought you said you lived here?'

'I do.'

'Then steady on, why don't you?'

I looked at this American's face, the flesh puckered like a baby's, red veins on his cheeks, his nose; his ears were big and out of shape like a boxer's. 'What's your name?' I asked.

'Carl,' he said.

'Well, Carl, have a nice fucking day.'

We were unbuckling ourselves. God it was slow, getting out. I couldn't wait to make it to the telephones in the terminal building. I had to get through to . . . to where? Arrange a welcome for Tony if I could.

He deserved one.

Ours was a flight with more than the normal quota of non-EEC passports. Our queue was long, and slow. I couldn't believe how slow. There was somebody up the front with a wrong something. They were arguing.

Carl was at my elbow telling me how he was going to stay at the Provençal. Did I know the Provençal?

Yes, I knew it.

They were still arguing up front. It's hard to escape the feeling that tormenting tourists has become the latest global sport. When possible I avoid the confrontation, stay at home,

203

teach Desdemona to throw sticks so I can run along the beach fetching them for her. Entertaining the canine mind.

'Is it clean, this Provençal? Is it a nice place?'

'It's fine.'

'Close to the water? I said when I booked I like to look at the sea.'

'In Detroit?'

'No, but that's why . . . it's the trip of a lifetime. I think of it that way. What is it they say? See Europe and die.'

'That's Naples.'

'Naples, Europe, what's the difference, buddy?'

'There's a good chance you do die if you see Naples, that's the difference. It's the Calcutta of Italy.'

'You don't say . . . Calcutta?'

Carl was first, I prayed he had his visa. He did. I was stamped and waved through after him.

Next to discover where that British Airways plane was heading. That meant finding an official since the departures weren't listed in the arrival area, and the plane would have gone anyway. So it wouldn't be written up on the telly screens any more.

There was the customs check to come, that was after the luggage made it on to the belt. The trick is not to look edgy, or impatient — you do that and they'll unstitch your jacket and shove a fist up your arse just for the sadistic pleasure of it.

Carl found me again in the crush. 'I wonder,' he asked, 'this language barrier . . . ?'

I said: 'It's real. But if you've got a booking at the Provençal that's it, your name will be there.'

'My problem is how to get to the dump.'

'It's no dump.'

In the end I wrote a series of messages in French, and at the top put in English what they meant so he'd know when to use them. Doing that kept me sane. Then out came the bags.

Carl's, but not mine. I couldn't wait any longer, I'd pick it up later. Together we approached the customs, through the 'nothing to declare' lane. Carl got flagged down; with only hand-luggage I was let through. That fitted — my coat was better cut anyway, and pure linen. Maybe they reckoned he'd stashed the contraband in the battered cardboard suitcase with the rope tied around it.

At the British Airways desk I established that it was a London flight I'd seen Tony running to catch.

Next for the long-distance call. If I managed to find a vacant phone.

There was one vacant . . . because it didn't work.

Airport phones: people must love the feeling, leaning against the soundproofing, stuffing coins into the slot, blah, blah, blah. I hate it.

One came free over the far side; I ran and got there in front of a gum-chewing kid with a knapsack.

I didn't have Ruth's number on my person. Finally I got through to Howard Fischmann's office. The efficient lady on the reception, that husky voice: Mr Fischmann wasn't in, wouldn't be for the rest of the day.

Could he be reached?

She wasn't too sure which was the ideologically sound response to that one.

'I am not going to ring him, I promise, all I want is for someone to get a message to him, and quickly. It's important.'

'Who's speaking?'

'I told you, Essington Holt!'

'And, Mr Holt . . . '

'Can you get it to him quick?'

'I can try.'

So I told her about the flight, about who was on board. I had a description for her as well: the earrings, the sea-snake tattoo, the haircut. And that his name was Tony.

'Tony who?'

'Tony. Now, Miss . . . there's Mrs Fischmann as well, if you could call her, let her know. And there's this man in the police, a Detective Sergeant Mutton, Mrs Fischmann knows him.'

'Mut . . . what?'

'Mutton . . . T . . . O . . . N.'

I was stuffing the coins in like a day-tripper playing the poker machines at the Monte Carlo Casino. I told her the flight only took about an hour, that they'd need to hurry if they wanted to nab him,

'For what?'

A good question.

'Just do it,' I ordered. Then the light started to flash and my pocket was empty of legal tender.

Chapter 28

Carl had been standing there when I emerged from the airport after making the call to London. And I was lathered with sweat by then, from the frustration of getting to a phone, of trying to convey some sense of urgency to Fischmann's secretary. Then a mix-up with me going back inside to fetch the case I'd left getting giddy on the baggage conveyor belt.

Just one small man in a plastic peak cap standing beside a suitcase tied shut with a length of rope, Carl had missed the bus that would take him around the coast to Villefranche and the Provençal.

Talk about Ulysses getting a raw deal when he returned!

Everything, even the trees, looked chic by comparison with this battered figure, this factory worker. When God created the Côte d'Azur he'd never considered that such types would turn up either in battalions or singly. I wouldn't have thought my Carl stood much chance of getting a taxi. If he approached a native with one of the pieces of paper I'd written the questions on they would have turned and run before he got it into their hand.

Missing a finger wasn't all that smart either. It looked bad, as though you'd done manual work at some time.

I hailed a cab. Took Carl along with me. We crawled with the traffic, bumper to bumper, on the Promenade des Anglais along past the Hôtel Negresco, at which point I caught myself looking up at the windows of the refurbished building where Farah had bought her apartment. Which was Farah's window? I looked at that wall of identical glassed rectangles and got a tingle, the ghost of a thrill from knowing one of the cubes of space within was hers.

Funny that.

Carl was saying: 'Hell, like I have to pinch myself.'

Then the lights changed, the cab was off again.

Carl didn't even have a camera. 'What are you going to do here?' I asked.

'Hang about . . . you know. Maybe walk a bit. I don't swim. I'm not the body beautiful any more.'

'These things pass.'

'To tell you the truth, I never was. Say, you know, coming in, taxiing, and you diving for the window, I decided you'd been bullshitting me. People do that, if they pick you for a mug on holidays, a guy who wouldn't know the difference anyway. Next you're telling this driver where to go like you was General de Gaulle.'

I asked the cab to wait, helped Carl up the steps of the Provençal, and with the checking in. He had a room facing the North Pole.

'You wanted the sea, didn't you?'

'And I haven't got it, don't tell me. Never mind.'

'Hell, mind,' I said.

'No.'

People like Carl stay poor because they simply aren't bastards enough. Yet, on command, they'll come wading through the sea under enemy fire and for a minute and a half the world pretends it's grateful.

I asked for the manager. Carl walked to the door; embarrassed, he gazed fixedly out at the cab.

I explained about how my friend wanted to see the sea. How he'd been booked that way, or understood so. They are polite at the Provençal, there's an old-world charm to the place. Carl got a balcony and from it you could see my place, the Villa du Phare. Only I didn't point it out, somehow just it being there made me feel ashamed.

I told him I'd ring, never dreaming he'd be mixed up in my life before I got around to not doing that.

Like it or not people were coming for dinner. Nothing elaborate, but since I'd phoned in before leaving London Karen had taken it into her head to invite Molena. Which meant Dawn as well to keep the numbers even, male and female. Karen is worse at that than I am, making sure there's a man for every woman as though

Rebecca was out there in her kitchen pouring aphrodisiacs into the sauces.

Nurse Findlay joined in for the drinks, bringing Pietro with her, keeping him in check while putting him on display.

It was small talk, deliberately so. And that got on my nerves because I felt I had so much to say,.

Nobody bothered to ask about London. It was just old Essington who shot off from time to time and was now returned. Let's hope he hadn't picked up anything nasty.

'I met a man who was missing a finger.'

'You didn't?' Dawn gazing at me in mock seriousness.

'American.'

Desdemona was there. I reckoned she was more interested than the rest. She went into a crouch beside me, placed her muzzle on my shoe.

'Molena . . . it goes?' I asked.

'This weather is perfect, Essington. The sun brings people.'

'For you to fleece?'

Molena's latest scheme was a block of holiday apartments in behind Beaulieu; he was advance selling them at discount prices. That way he used buyers as a bank. Good weather, a pressure of tourists all in a dream of retirement planning, that was Molena's idea of a perfect world.

'I might have one for you, from Detroit. He's the conqueror returned. Nice little man. He'll feel comfortable with your low ceilings.'

Because she'd come across to pat the dog, Dawn and I went from drinks into dinner together. I asked her when she'd last seen Farah.

The curious thing was it had been only a few days before.

'That was when?'

The answer: the day I'd headed off to London.

When we were seated I asked her: 'You didn't happen to mention me to Farah, did you?'

'Why should I?' Turning: 'Your husband's out of control, Karen, it's . . .'

'Farah, don't tell me. Fantastic, isn't it?'

'Why fantastic?' I asked.

'That you don't even try and hide your obsession.'

'Karen . . . "obsession" — isn't that too strong?' I objected.

Dawn was laughing at my discomfort. We weren't exactly a *ménage à trois*, rather, I suspected, a *ménage à deux* with me locked out.

I pressed on: 'Obsession or not, Dawn, did you mention to Farah that I was off to London? You have to believe it, the question's important.'

'She asked,' Dawn said. 'It struck me as odd at the time. In fact, Essington, it went through my mind that the two of you were up to something, a dirty weekend perhaps. Funny, though, to describe such excursions as "dirty", isn't it? I mean —' she screwed up her nose,' — dirty doesn't really fit, does it?'

Karen was talking next about Makihei's men, the demands they were making. I got the feeling that the loss of total control over the business was more of an irritant than either she or Dawn had envisaged.

I told the assembly about my friend Carl while Rebecca removed the plates.

The phone rang.

I whipped out and took it in the front reception room. The instant I exited I heard a ripple of laughter, as though the atmosphere was suddenly relaxed.

It was Danny Tournier. He didn't want to talk, only to say that Farah had been found dead, in her apartment.

I asked how he knew, how it could be?

'I have had Dolent watching,' he explained, 'for some time now . . . following a feeling of mine.'

Funny, in the taxi I'd had some kind of feeling too, but confused. I hadn't known if it started in my head or my heart.

'Watching, why?'

'Tomorrow. Right now I thought you should know, that's all.'

He hung up.

I stood in the reception room. I looked at the Modigliani crayon drawing of the caryatid. From that my eyes roamed to the Sisley with its poplar trees. Then to the bay windows which reflected me back to myself, an image set against the dark of a moonless night.

Farah was dead, Jodie was dead too. Beauty falling off the perch. I'd asked Dawn, hadn't I? And Dawn had indicated that Farah put the question about me.

What did that mean?

Reminded of Tony rushing to catch a London flight I dialled London: the Fischmanns. I counted to fifteen rings then hung up.

It can drive you crazy, not knowing.

They were still laughing when I came back into the room. Karen caught my expression: 'Something's wrong, Ess . . .'

'No,' I said, 'nothing.' I took up the wine bottles, one red, one white, and charged everybody's glass as Rebecca entered bearing a large earthenware casserole — *paupiettes de veau Clementine, une specialité de la maison*. She, as artist, looked about her, eyes gleaming, expecting the response.

But I'd taken on board a terrible beast, it clung to my back, whispered evil at my ear. Together that creature and I killed the atmosphere. The lot of us remained silent, eyes down.

Picking up a bottle of Bordeaux I set myself to refill the glass I'd drained at a swig. But then I put it down again. 'Excuse me,' I said. The breath was coming hard, I was hunting after it, gulping. My body turned itself up to boil. I ran from the room.

Dolent was there, but not Madame Tournier. She was out. I didn't bother checking the composer of the music on the piano.

Tournier was still the same man: the cardigan, that sense of the gentleman in his chambers.

I asked: 'Why was Dolent watching?' As though he wasn't in the room with us, able to represent himself. 'What was it you had in mind? And, anyway, I didn't think you liked work that much, Danny. Isn't it supposed to be the occasional big job with you, then whiling time away at the keyboard?'

'It's true, Essington. But, you see, there was an intellectual reason for my continued interest. There has always remained the question of why? Why these people pick someone to kidnap . . . in this case, why you? From the start I have believed that there is inside information of some kind. Just, I suspect, as you've believed. So, it's natural, once you had employed our friend here to do some work for you — and let us not forget it was myself who pointed you in his direction — why shouldn't I make some suggestions? If they were on the right track it might help satisfy my curiosity.

'The question, who is on the inside? And there follows another question: why would they do such a thing? You tell me the girl minding your child has been killed. Of course, it's obvious why she is killed once we know who has done this thing. You also tell us of the man coming out of the flat, how he hit you across the head, and what followed. He has been there with this girl . . . you say she is very beautiful! We must not underestimate the power of such things. Beauty, it destroys man's capacity to think.

'Let us assume this one is obsessed with Jodie Winton. Let us imagine he is so intense in his ardour that he frightens her, just a little bit. At first she is interested, perhaps even flattered. She could also pity him since he has a problem with his leg. This is a girl who is looking after children. It is not unreasonable to assume she has a sympathetic character. I have seen him, you have seen him. We are not talking about a screen hero.

'Next thing, it is too late, I think. Our Jodie has told him what he wants to know. But it is too late for him as well, he can't get her out of his thoughts.'

Tournier holding up both hands as though stopping traffic: 'Speculation, I know. But, all thought is speculation . . . we have the choice to try out our ideas or let them evaporate.

'All right . . . Dolent here has found this girl. It has been easy for him to do so. What do we make of this? That she is not hiding. Therefore she does not feel particularly involved, particularly guilty of anything. Further, this is most likely the truth as well. Jodie has done nothing more, perhaps, than be indiscreet, maybe give away . . . well, not family secrets surely, for I believe you have never directed her in any way, never warned her not to speak of what is happening in your household. Why should you do so? No reason.

'And we know how little she has been told of what has happened since you suddenly vanished; she was kept in the dark. What was she to think? That you had run off with a chorus girl? It is likely that since the exchange I have carried out Jodie has not seen this cripple. On the other hand there might well have been some communication, perhaps a telephone call, a letter. Also we should not forget that there were . . . shall I say "incidents"? . . . which led to her quitting her job with your family. Treatment, from what I understand, that she is not going to have relished. True, Dolent?'

A rhetorical question.

Dolent shrugged: 'Who would?'

'No,' Tournier continued, fiddling about with his pipe at the same time, 'of course she is not going to have liked that.

'Time passes. Our friends are becoming more easy because not so much is happening. There is no hue and cry. In fact it's better than can be believed because the police are still not involved. Such good luck. And the next thing, suddenly you and Moulay go off on that crazy mission! Moulay, the man who does the disappearing act. Surely our friends, this Tony, the other one, know that the game is now turned upside down when they hear about it from . . . who? With Moulay in control the Falcone exchange goes as planned, it is perfect even down to the detail of the hostages being killed after the money is handed across. What is the expression? A state of the art exchange.

'Now *you* have applied real pressure. Note *you*, Essington. It is not me, not my idea. Yet there is a propriety to it since the central elements with which we must deal are death and money. It is a trade, one for the other; and nobody meaning what they say, never a contract that can stick. Except the bottom line: the inevitable execution.

'Moulay, remember this . . . Farah knows him as well. A coincidence, don't you think so?

'One death, in London. Why does our man kill Jodie? Firstly he is edgy. We assume he knows about the Falcones. He, I am supposing, is interested in Jodie, maybe already he has started to visit her over there. Before that he would be stupid to do so, wouldn't he? But, in the period of calm, and they still wait for all possibility of trouble to pass, knowing how the world forgets . . . mightn't he then, this well-spoken man, mightn't he then dream? He has money. Why do we want money? For power. Power is to do what you want to do. For Roman Emperors it is to kill . . . killing being the ultimate luxury. But a man who is maimed, who is small, his skin is bad . . . what might he dream of? For him, mightn't power equal having this Jodie, who you say is so beautiful?

'And Farah, she is beautiful as well, isn't she?'

I nodded agreement.

'Then there is Essington Holt who has arrived in London, visiting our Jodie!

'The man is coming down the stairs, the door is open. He

appears calm. Except he does have a gun in his pocket. But, he is a criminal after all . . . he likes guns perhaps. He sees you standing there. It is lucky for him you're exhausted from climbing the stairs. He hits you, knocks you unconscious. But in that moment his dream of power vanishes. He must eliminate this girl, because he knows she doesn't see herself as . . . not as a bad girl. Imagine, she hears him shout. Or she descends the stairs, observes him stuffing a body into the cupboard on the landing. What is her response to this? Imagine Jodie, from . . . where is it again?'

'Mount Vernon, Ohio,' Dolent doing the honours there. He'd been stuck on that 'Ohio' detail right from the start.

Tournier: 'She is not going to be involved in killing people, even in carrying guns. She suddenly sees truths she has not seen before. At last she understands what this man is. But she fails to comprehend that she should have pretended to take his side. Instead she tells him how she objects. That she wants nothing to do with him and his criminal life. For suddenly Jodie is staring reality in the face. In all her innocence she has never understood that life must contain tragedy, even death. That the next death might be her own.

'There's no choice in the matter, it's become himself or her. That is the equation. He kills Jodie, arranges the body in such a way as to make it appear a sexual murder. Then he is off. He could not discharge a gun, it will be heard, so he has slit her throat. And, Mr Holt, if he opens the cupboard on you . . . then what? You are a big man, you could be crouched to spring. To fire a shot would be to send an alarm out to the world. And possibly you are already pounding on the door, shouting for help. In fact because you are doing these things he must get out of there, and quickly too.'

'In which case he didn't have to know I was going to London?'

'Of course he didn't; how could he have known?'

'Because there is Farah as well, isn't there?'

'Yes,' Tournier said, 'there is Farah. And she is dead . . . why? I suspect for the same reason. Or something similar. She has allowed herself to be compromised. Which of us doesn't? In everything we do we agree when we should say no; we bend our own fixed rules, simply to avoid conflict, to make life flow more easily. Is Farah an exception? I do not think so, do you?

'Yet, Essington, you being in London — had our man expected you to arrive there looking for Jodie he would have been prepared, wouldn't he? Therefore I don't think any message about your movements had been passed to him. I think he had been obliged to improvise, quickly, possibly frantically.'

Tournier had been over that one as well, his suppositions were based on what he'd been able to string together out of what he already knew and Dolent's observations. Farah's death had been a very different affair.

I had the terrible feeling my desire to look at the windows of the building where she lived had been to do with the inexplicable. Had Farah already been lying on her bed, dead? Of course she had. For I'd seen Tony running across the tarmac at the airport at Nice. He had killed her, suffocated her, shoving a pillow into her mouth and down hard across her nostrils, while her arms and legs thrashed about in an attempt to swim up towards the light of life.

What sin had Farah committed? Would I ever know? Chances were I wouldn't. For, first thing that morning before heading off to visit Tournier, I'd been back on the blower to London. That time I'd connected with the Fischmanns' house in Holland Park. I'd been asking about Tony, where he was held, what pretext had been used to grab him? Asking those questions before Ruth Fischmann could get a word in, before she could ask me who Tony was.

'Who is he! What are you trying to say?'

'Tony who? Essington, calm down.'

Calm down all right. Even Desdemona, who'd never managed to understand about telephones, about the voice going down the wire, even she had taken two steps backwards to avoid connecting with my agitation.

'Tony who! Ruth, how do you mean? I told Howard's secretary . . . whatever . . . the woman. THAT FUCKING WOMAN!'

Desdemona was out the door at that.

And Karen belted in from the shower, standing there dripping, naked, wide-eyed.

'Do you mean to tell me you never received a message?'

'What message?' Ruth asked.

Hope, they say it springs eternal. 'Then she must have got through to Mutton, to our detective sergeant.'

'About what? Essington, do try and make yourself clear.'

'Mutton, to collect a man from the Nice plane . . . she didn't do it, did she?'

Eventually I did settle down, I did spell it out. And Karen listened as I did that. She sat on the end of the bed, still dripping, her hands clenched in front of her breasts. She didn't move a muscle. Ruth was taking careful note of what I had to say, making me go over things. I added the fact of Farah's death, for emphasis.

Karen gave a little cry at that.

And Ruth got the full import of the secretarial oversight.

'There's one thing left, the flight lists; maybe you can have someone check those, to get a name at least and pass it on to Mutton so he can work off his guilt, get on the side of the angels.'

Straight into the domestics, role reversal time, Karen collapsed in a heap.

Accusations at first, and demanding to know why I hadn't told her.

What could I answer? There wasn't an answer, except that I'd been keeping the whole thing close, with the hope of recovering the money, everything. I hadn't wanted her to know, or to be involved.

It was my thing. Like it was my finger that was missing. Of course I understood how it must seem to Karen, us having Pietro, the answer to our prayers, our baby. Yet happy families had to be held over for later. All I could think about was catching up with the men who'd chained me to a wall.

'Surely, by now it's gone far enough. Drop it, Ess, let go. Oh, for God's sake, nothing can be worth these deaths, this hell you live in.'

'I can't drop it, particularly not now. Even if you don't agree, please sympathize. It's to do with a reality I have, we all have, right down inside . . . I lose hold on that and what's left? There's Farah as well, whatever she did, contributed, it wouldn't have been for me to be chained to a wall. I know that . . . I knew

Farah; you did too. Like, Karen, why did she leave? Was it the Japanese? I don't think so. Wasn't it more that she'd done something . . . suddenly realized that she *had*? Something to put her outside the family, beyond the pale. So she cut herself off, bought the apartment . . .'

Bought the apartment, but with what?

Chapter 29

Danny Tournier had developed his own ideas about Farah's apartment. What didn't that man try to know? He was a living advertisement for piano playing improving the mind. I guessed it was spending so much time sitting still, going over the fingering of a few bars, getting it right.

The building on the Promenade des Anglais had been turned into apartments by a consortium close to the civic fathers of Nice. Molena was always going on about how it was a club all along the coast; when an outsider tried to muscle in they resisted.

Because of his own line of business Tournier knew the developer of Farah's block; it was a prime site overlooking the sea and you don't get your hooks into that sort of thing just by dressing well and turning up to practice. Hell no. You send decapitated rats to people through the mail, you fit concrete blocks to the feet of thine enemy, that's how.

So Tournier knew the man who'd put that one together. And already he'd discovered that there wasn't any Farah apartment, it had been bought off the redevelopment plan by a man named Horne, English.

'Can I use the phone?'

'But of course, Essington, go ahead.'

It was the London number again, Howard Fischmann's office. I got the same woman. I asked for Howard.

'Who shall I say is calling?'

'Just put me through.'

Objections to that.

'Do it!'

She did.

I told him who it was.

'I've a client.'

'Did Ruth say anything, Howard?'

'About your wild-goose chase? Well, yes.' I heard him say 'excuse me this will only take a minute' to whoever was on the other side of his desk plotting a leveraged buy-out.

'Not a wild-goose chase . . . what's got into you?'

'What possible legal status do you imagine, Essington, attaches to you seeing somebody running for a plane? Ruth and I have talked it over. The question I keep coming up with is, why me? Of all the rotten luck, for me to get involved in this mess of yours. You must realize — Ruth will tell you this as well — people are allowed to run for planes, they may enter at airports without others ringing through with unfounded accusations against them. That's why we have law, why we have a legal system.'

'Even murderers?'

'Even murderers while presumed innocent, of course.'

'And it's also written into your legal system that police can beat up people in the street because they decide to hate them, is that right, Howard?'

'We've already seen to that, haven't we? Things happen, we all know that, we live with it. An imperfect world, old boy. Still, the fact remains that you can't grab individuals stepping off planes without a very good reason. We are not in Iran.'

'More's the pity.'

'As I said, I have a client.' They do that, put on their office masks, take them off at weekends. Except the day arrives when the mask stays put, they join the ranks of the living dead. Maybe I'd caught Howard's day for that to happen: a moment in history.

I said: 'Before you hang up I think the name's Horne, note the "e" on the end of it.'

'I'll tell Ruth.'

'And could she pass it on to our pet policeman, Howard, to the good Sergeant Detective Mutton?'

'Detective Sergeant.'

I stood corrected. I told him I'd see him when I returned to give evidence to the coroner.

Was that good news for Howard? I don't think so.

'Oh, and Howard, better practise your defensive shots on the leg side, your batting's weak . . . you know that?'

*

Tournier was waiting, sucking his pipe. Neither he nor Dolent saying a word, just watching me.

Tournier had his theory off pat about the death of Jodie; one about Farah's death as well. He'd convinced himself he'd got it right.

'Now where Farah is concerned, perhaps there has been some depth to the intrigue. Still I don't imagine that Farah has been made aware of the whole plan. More likely there's been a great deal of talking, this man — let us say this Tony — is interested. He asks a lot of questions. Maybe he talks as well about the difference: Farah being the working girl who is serving in a shop, despite her beauty! As well she is staying with one of the partners, with Dawn . . .'

'Who wants to fuck her.'

'*Alors!*' Dolent exclaimed.

Tournier continued: 'Suddenly there is a man who will offer Farah everything. This is difficult to refuse. His gesture of good faith is the apartment on the Promenade des Anglais, she can live there. Maybe he tells her he has a business deal coming up, after that they can take a holiday, enjoy themselves. Hormones again, Essington. These are the ways in which the world is made to keep turning. Little patterns of ongoing compromise.'

'And with Jodie delivering Pietro in Paris? You believe that?'

'This is possible. People, they can convince themselves of anything. Maybe she imagined it to be so simple. But, more likely still, Jodie was coming downstairs, she had just been called on the telephone perhaps . . . a voice, her friend, please come down, there is something I must tell you.

'Lovers, they do these things.' Tournier talking to me as though I was past the stage of romantic love! I wasn't so sure I liked that. After all, hadn't I even dreamed of Farah, of her being the sky?

'And she has seen you approaching the door at that moment. You too have seen her. Something feels wrong, she retreats. As I have said, essentially not a bad girl.'

'But Farah, she knew more?'

'Yet I don't believe she would have wished for what happened. In fact the tragedy of these two girls is that neither of them was actually taking part in the plotting. If they had been more involved they would surely be alive today. For they would have been partners in the crime. This pair of men were using them to gather information, so that they come to know everything: your movements, the business, the money, even the money! Because Farah would have been able to discover so much through living with Dawn Grogan, who as you said wanted to . . . '

'*Alors!*' Dolent, like a chorus in a Greek play.

'And,' Tournier continued, 'the real sadness seems to be that our friend, Moulay, he now has an interest in this great beauty — Dolent, while watching Farah, has seen them together. He has known her from these meetings of SOS Racism where he's part of their defence against attack from anti-Arab groups. Possibly Farah is why he has entered into an agreement with you to work for a percentage of the ransom you manage to recoup. He has found love maybe and now for the first time he wants money. Then he goes away, suddenly. Why is this? We don't know. But that too, I think, has something to do with Farah.'

'Moulay and Farah?'

'He was in love with her, I believe.'

The idea took me by surprise. Stated outright like that.

Tournier: 'That is why God painted the wings of butterflies.'

No need to explain about the wings of butterflies to me. I already knew: it was the power of beauty, one of the unsolved wonders of this world.

Leaving Tournier and Dolent I walked down the rue Berlioz, heading in the direction of the silk shop. It seemed to me that things were at an impasse. Dolent was instructed to continue keeping a look-out while at the same time doing what he could to catch up on the police investigation of Farah's death. If possible he was to urge them into regarding that as something more than yet another of Nice's unsolvable sex murders — pimps exercising their right to discipline, crazies after some kick higher up the scale.

There would be questions asked. And I stood quite a chance of joining the ranks of the interrogated, but since I was in company from the moment I'd stepped off the plane at Nice airport there seemed no possibility of the law expecting anything more from me than background information. And that was where I might be able to nudge them along the right path a little.

Of course the kidnap still had to remain a closed subject.

From the instant I stepped out from the entrance of the Tourniers' apartment building and into rue Berlioz I had a feeling akin to the one that had acted as a warning to me in Shepherd's Bush. And yet part of the mind mistrusts hunches, it is trained into doing so. Hadn't I emerged from Tournier's apartment into the scream of a sander ripping at the reshaped panel of some crumpled car, and the smell of automobile paint acrid on the air? That was enough to wake Mr Paranoia from sleep. On the corner where rue Berlioz crosses rue de France there's the Musée Massena; it's an Italianate villa sitting in a garden which goes through to another frontage on the Promenade des Anglais. The villa is now a public art gallery and the aged of the town take advantage of the seats placed under the trees outside. I crossed the rue de France, entered the garden, placed myself behind a barrier of oleanders and watched back up along rue Berlioz.

What did that achieve?

It got me nervy, that was for one. Also it caused two old women to move from where they had been sitting and go into the museum, most probably to alert an attendant that there was a weirdo behaving strangely in the bushes.

I was summarily warned off by a red-faced official. But not before I'd proved a point to myself, that I needed a holiday: maybe half a year in Australia drinking beer, catching waves, fucking or shooting everything that moves.

I dropped in at the shop and paid my respects to Madame Cuntz who was wearing her gold-rimmed glasses on the tip of a finely sculptured nose and reading off the exact fraction of a metre of printed silk for a pair of German holidaymakers.

I envied them, Madame Cuntz, the customers; I got the feeling that the length of silk was at that moment the extent of their worldly woes.

I was told that Madame Holt and Madame Grogan had left.

To the question 'where' I got an exasperated hand gesture, a charming smile.

Even signalling a taxi on the waterfront, I had this feeling of eyes upon me. It made me want to take a shower.

Instead I decided on the Bar Plage — that's where I pass the time. The cab turned off the Corniche Inférieure at the Villefranche soccer ground to crawl down past the citadel and along the wharves in the direction of the beach. There were crowds walking, and in the sea a lot of people bathing. Out in the bay a Russian cruise ship stood at anchor. Which meant full restaurants. But not the Bar Plage with its uninviting shabbiness where it huddled against the wall at the back of the beach. I paid the cab, tipped him for his trouble in negotiating the town's narrow streets and was just in time to commandeer a freshly vacated table slopped over with beer froth.

The patron and Desdemona have this thing going between them: 'Where is your dog?'

'At home.' I shrugged, I guess trying to offload those worries I had no right to carry about with me. Then I gave a whoop. It was spontaneous . . . I don't know why. If you'd asked me had I wanted to see Carl from the London–Nice flight again the answer would have been in lower key, certainly not a whoop.

Carl didn't respond, he kept on walking, the saddest, the most out-of-shape figure in sight. A celebration of polyester. Why didn't somebody tell him about the plastic peak cap? It was lime green! His shoes were imitations of imitation Reeboks.

'A minute,' I said to the patron. I belted after my little monolingual pal. We were the lost finger club, or about to be. I grabbed him by the shoulder. 'How are you doing?'

He squinted, piggy eyes in the time-worn drinking man's face. He recognized me. But, Christ, it took time! The seconds had ticked past with me waiting for the signal to register in the brain.

He said: 'Hi.' And I realized he was well under the weather.

There are people who think that to be drunk is to be close to God. I am one of them. I sat my little saint of a mate down and introduced him to the patron, who had watched our meeting without moving from where he was standing wiping the beer off the vacant table.

Carl reached out his hand, eyes blinking like a koala bear; he said, very badly: '*Bonjour monsieur.*'

And I laughed. But Jesus, doesn't it make you feel good to laugh like that?

A couple of hours later we'd walked around the sea side of the citadel to the boat harbour and dry dock that sits in behind a long breakwater. That was after a couple of hours of munching on the salad Niçoise the patron's wife or aunt or someone stuffs inside a round bread roll covered in poppy seed. And in the salad tiny local olives. Combine that with the *rosé de la maison* and if it's not paradise, what is?

Anyway, that was Carl's opinion.

It is very pretty over in the boat harbour. I don't know but I'd guess it had been sending out fleets of warships since the sixteenth century, building them there too. We were in a mood to appreciate it. Standing on the wall formed of well-fitted rectangular rocks, we gazed through the oil on the surface of the water at schools of small fish and, below them, a litter of bottles, cans, car tyres, rusting lumps of steel. The nautical atmosphere was strong, that distinctive smell too; owners worked on their boats; a huge yacht with 'Guernsey' written across the stern was hauled up for repairs to be carried out on the hull. There were sporty cars, aged men in seafaring dress, as though hired from a theatrical agency to add to the feel. We walked out on the breakwater to watch for a while as an old couple cast their lines, observed the floats' bobbing motion, then struck — all that concentration to reel in fish the size of home aquarium species.

There was a blue yacht there, moored among the others, a single mast and a canvas tarp over the boom. Forty, forty-five feet long. Written in fancy lettering on the transom: 'Top Hat'. There was a top hat painted after the name. And then underneath that: 'USA'

Carl liked the idea of a yacht from home.

'Hey,' he said, 'They sailed right on over!' He shook his head in wonder at the feat. The boat looked so small. It wasn't in the neat condition of most of the others. There was an accumulation of bird shit on the weathered deck; close up you could see the blue paint was peeling in places and tendrils of weed were growing out from the hull below the water-line.

The boat's abandoned look, combined with the wine, I guess, not to mention the fact that with 'USA' writ on the back it represented a little chunk of home, these things beckoned Carl to put a foot on deck. Just for the feel of it.

Hell, if you're in the missing finger club, and you saved Europe from itself, then you can put a foot on a neglected yacht. It's reasonable.

You'd reckon anyway.

Except you'd be wrong, and surprised.

Because the boat lurched a little with Carl stepping on to it like he did. A voice inside there, below deck, it called out: 'Fucking hell!' And then: '*Arrêt* . . . get off . . .'

'Carl!' I hissed in the instant before I turned and ran. I don't know, maybe he paused for a moment, but by the time I was belting past the entrance to the yacht club like a boy close to being nabbed for pinching apples, little Carl was at my heels, and calling out for an explanation. But I wasn't providing one. Instead I headed straight across an area of rank grass, trees and rotting hulls. All I wanted was to be out of sight of the man who'd been below decks on *Top Hat*.

Because I'd recognized the voice.

Wasn't it strange? Carl had been the catalyst twice. Point him in a direction and up would pop a kidnapper, like a mushroom in compost.

Chapter 30

There was a gale blowing. I'd told them while we were driving around past Mont Boron: 'A man and his son went to market to buy a sheep and the boy watched, fascinated, as his father felt the tails of all the animals . . . ' That story.

'And?' Tournier demanded.

'But you must already know . . . it's Moulay's, after all. The father kills the neighbour.'

And I wished Moulay was in the back of the black Citroën with its Maserati motor. I guess I still do wish it: that he'd been there with us.

Instead of . . .

The harbour with its boats is a very different place at night. There's a prohibition against living on them, because of the pollution. Villefranche is proud of the efforts taken to keep the bay clean: they publish the results of tests every day so people feel confident to swim there.

We were three men who had to shout to be heard above the noise of the wind.

It was after midnight and there was no sign of life at the yacht club, or anywhere else. Even apartments back up the hill had switched off their lights.

No moon. The sky was covered in the heavy cloud that had rushed down from the Alps in the late afternoon. It could come on to rain if the wind was to drop.

Dolent had gone first. Right up on the sea-wall, bending low to keep out of the way of spray from crashing waves.

Perhaps it would be all for nothing. If our prey had made too much of Carl's intrusion he'd have bolted. But then, Carl, what was there about him to connect with me?

Provided I'd been out of sight before the man we were now after had appeared on deck.

Man? But would he be alone?

Everything pointed to that being the case, still . . .

I'd wanted to go next, after Dolent, to be the one to leap on to the boat, to charge down below. Hadn't I made a pledge that I was going to kill this man?

Tournier insisted he'd head the charge. In the end I'd even tried jokes about keeping his hands out of harm's way, saving them for the piano, for Bach fugues.

'They are used to harm's way, as you call it. It can do no damage.'

So I was bringing up the rear. It was mostly worked out back in Nice while Tournier went over the action of the gun he'd given me, as though convinced I was short-changed in the head. I'd complained: 'You flick off the safety, pull the fucking trigger!' High on the memories, and on the approaching moment when I'd take my revenge. That's why I wanted to be the one to go down there, to blow his face away.

Yes! I wanted to blow his head right off his shoulders.

They'd got an electric torch for me as well. I missed out on being instructed on how to make it light up.

Tournier must have sensed the madness surging inside me. Thinking back, it's amazing they took me along at all.

I had talked all the way in the car as we drove down to the harbour, going over the whole thing out loud. I'd described Jodie, dead, her legs open as though the killer'd wanted to make some weird point. I went on and on about her. Because that was something I'd never understand: her role in the whole affair. As I talked I clarified what I had chosen to believe: that Jodie was just an innocent from the Midwest of the USA. But compromised by that innocence. How she wouldn't have had a clue who was up to what. Hadn't she simply been used? And so skilfully used. Her beauty shielding her from any understanding other than what it was like to be wanted. So, believing herself wanted, she was content to be manipulated. Just as I needed to think of her as an innocent, she must have wanted to set herself apart from whatever compromising acts she might have committed.

Who judges us, anyway, in the last resort? And who knows? Which of us understands what was a good act, and which of all the things we did was bad. Jodie, I guess she just had her head down and was trying to maximize her sense of living. While into that sweet ear, my kidnappers, or one of them at least, had poured their souring words of adoration. Coaxing her to venture down paths she might have preferred never to have found on the map.

Oh yes, I rambled on about Jodie while Dolent and Tournier never said a word.

Maybe they weren't even listening.

And I rattled on about me being chained up, airing all that mind garbage as well. I'd hold my hand up to Dolent's face, shaking the missing finger before his unblinking eyes. I was shaking nothing, wasn't I? That's the absurdity of losing a part of you.

And I told them over and over that story of Moulay's about the boy and the sheep. Maybe I told a few more . . . stuff about oranges and bananas, too.

Every moment I was conscious of the weight in my jacket pocket, the little Rossi .38. Eight inches long, six rounds in the cylinder. I was going to hold it in two hands like I'd done up there in that cursed shed; go in firing. Watch the petals, from roses of blood, unfold. I was going to be down below deck, up close, breathing in the cordite as though it was incense.

Sometimes Tournier and Dolent would make eye contact with each other, as though trying to communicate, but not wanting me to know about what.

I caught them at it. There we were coming around the Boulevard Princess Grace, me nattering ten to the dozen, them exchanging looks. Was that a recipe for success? Were we a team?

I wasn't so sure.

I even started to take it up with Tournier about the fee! I told him how he never worked, didn't he remember that? Wasn't he working now?

He said we'd go into it later. Now wasn't the time to talk about money . . . Tomorrow, Essington. Putting me in my place on money, on everything.

Telling me, as well, my place was to come behind as we made our way along the wharf, as we passed in front of the yacht club, as we watched Dolent go up on the sea-wall, head out beyond the boat, his body bent over double so he couldn't be seen against the sky.

There were portholes in *Top Hat*'s side but no light showing. There wouldn't be if you weren't supposed to be living on board.

Then Tournier was standing there, still, just a faint silhouette in the dark about thirty yards away from me. His gun was in his hand, held out in front of his body. He stepped on board as though he'd been invited, then he moved all the way forward, fast like a cat. He vanished.

I leapt on board, following, impulsive, breaking the rules.

Did I hear Dolent shout something above the wind? That could have been at me, I guess. But I kept on, down through the forward hatch which was pulled back, open.

Tournier was an arm's length away; he had his torch on, the beam was shining on Moulay's face. The Moroccan was alive, I could see that, but he'd gone quiet like he had when hit up in the mountains. His hands were clutching the beloved assault rifle the way a sick kid might cling to a rag doll.

It was such a tight space in there, with the width of bunks and only that much room again between. My torch picked up the shoe first, there was a foot in it and the body was mostly hidden beneath the bunk on which Moulay lay.

I said: 'Danny!'

'Moulay beat us here, Essington, somehow he knew.'

Chapter 31

Morning at the Villa du Phare, the storm had drifted off to the south-east, leaving us sun and the bright blue sky.

Karen was already out of bed. I could bank on it that she'd be disgruntled at knowing nothing, at having me return home a couple of hours before sun-up like I'd been putting it about with the ladies; or lost at a poker game with the boys.

How long had she been roaming the house, shuffling around in the debris of our relationship?

Jesus, Moulay — who didn't like me using the name of Jesus like that — he knew about what was real. Maybe that was why he'd always talked so little, restricting himself to the repetition of wise saws, and quotations from the holy men.

In the end though, he'd talked, to Danny Tournier. He'd felt something about Tournier, an equality perhaps.

Dying, Moulay letting his recent history trickle out a word at a time, just as the blood was trickling out of the three bullet wounds in his torso.

Dolent had headed off along the wharf in search of a telephone that worked.

We needed an ambulance.

Tournier had insisted that I search through the yacht, see if I could find the painting, anything connected with the kidnap. He wanted them out of the way before the police arrived. Even the money, he had hopes for the money as well!

I went through from stem to stern, locker by locker. I reckoned the bilge was out, there was too much water down there anyway. I felt between the folds of sails: big heavy slabs of cloth roughly put away in the locker forward of the front hatch. I checked the head, the galley, under the bunks. Assisted by

Tournier I even shifted the body of the dead man, both of us startled by the clatter of a handgun falling and sliding across the slatted floor. We left it there, it was evidence.

I kept on with the search.

I could feel it in myself, particularly as we dragged at the dead weight of that body: I was one of those people who rob tombs or go over corpses on the battlefield.

The beam of the torch was my prodder. I'd stir the recesses of the vessel with its illumination. And finally I found the Gauguin wrapped in plastic and face down on a sheet of thick cardboard, shoved in a locker, underneath a pile of rope. Not really the way to treat a painting. But fair enough for a fake with the flower the wrong red.

No money though.

Tournier led me up on deck, leaving Moulay in some peace for the dying process. He told me to piss off. If there was no money, he said, then there weren't serial numbers as a lead to the bank transactions he'd made to get the three million in the first place. Tournier's view of things was that it didn't matter which side of the Atlantic you were on, once corpses started to show up on moored US-registered yachts there'd be a hell of a lot of investigation going on.

He insisted I disappear with the painting.

Like a child about to be abandoned: 'Go? Go where?'

'Vanish!'

'The police find me wandering with a Gauguin under my arm? What am I to say?'

A groan below decks. A sound which had come out of the centre of nothingness.

So I went, fleeing death as it stalked in the storm.

Taking the picture with me.

The last thing Tournier said to me was: 'It's the money he regrets, Essington—desiring it. Moulay has said he wanted his ten per cent for her. He entertained a fantasy of them going home. With the cash, he said, he could have set himself up as a rich man in Morocco. He and Farah could have had children. You see, he failed the wisdom he had cherished for so long, those truths he had polished up like a collection of precious stones.

'And when he woke to his mistake he felt suddenly he was so poor, that spiritually he had nothing.'

It was weird, the fact of the yacht, my kidnappers hanging around so close to my home. Probably watching, checking out every move I made, especially after the Falcone killings. You don't pay too much attention to the characters down at the marina, they are all sort of the same anyway. So it was a good place to blend into, even if you were taking a risk by sleeping on board. The money, well it could have been anywhere. England, I wouldn't have thought you'd fly it across there just in case the customs men took a fancy to you. But any of the car ferries would have been safe.

I told myself the bundles of US dollars were a lost cause, and repeated that message over and over while rowing *Top Hat*'s tender across the sheltered marina waters so I could jump ashore at the steps at the end of the walk around the sea-wall of the citadel. Going that way had been Tournier's idea. He reckoned it was safe. It was certainly dark. I clutched the painting, felt it flex from catching the wind that was whipping a salt spray into my face.

While I'd been hunting the Gauguin, systematically working my way along the interior of the yacht, Moulay had continued whispering a reconstruction of events into Tournier's ear. A fragment at a time. Telling how he'd realized so late that it was Farah who'd produced and directed the kidnap performance.

Moulay had been in love with Farah, now he hated her memory. That was the real tragedy. Tournier was right about that.

Simple truths, straightforward solutions: the world according to Moulay Yusuf. The Falcones have done wrong so they must die.

Farah must have known about that world too, she'd been brought up in it. OK, she tried to step across and master the infidel's art of endless compromise; and she had failed.

Why failed?

Primarily, I suspect, because of Dolent, of him watching. While back there in the wings, hidden among the props, Moulay must have been watching us all. That was the method he'd decided on. If he was to get his hands on ten per cent of the rest of the ransom money Tournier had handed over, it would be by letting us do the background investigation while he kept tabs, interpreted. He'd observed Dolent checking Farah's new apartment. Maybe he'd also looked up the registered owner of the property, wondered who this Horne was — spelt with an 'e'.

I guess it had been Moulay I'd sensed at my back when I'd walked down the rue Berlioz after my meeting with Tournier and Dolent.

Moulay had forced Farah to tell him what she'd done before he had suffocated her. Then he left the apartment, continued his watching. The way I reconstructed things Tony'd turned up pretty soon after that. Because Tony had done his balls over Farah . . . it had been the two of them working together, plus the man with the built-up shoe. Tony would have stayed for the time it takes to identify death. Then off, in a panic. Grabbing a taxi, bolting for the airport.

'She was playing these games with everyone.' That had been Moulay's final pronouncement on beautiful Farah. Tournier told me how it went.

Moulay was dead by the time the police and the ambulance arrived.

There I was with the morning's warm light. That's what the dead don't enjoy, the warmth of it. OK, they've got flowers, and on one day of the year the Latin world stops for them and remembers. There's something in that.

But it's not the warmth of the sun.

'More milk?' It was hot, the milk, served in a solid white ceramic jug.

Karen sipped her coffee out of a bowl with a flight of birds painted around the rim. She held it in her hands, brought it to her lips. *Café au lait*.

There were croissants as well.

Life can be tough at the top end of the economic scale. Even going bust it can. For instance, the flakes of a croissant might catch in the hair on your chest. So you lick the tip of a finger, dab them with it, pick them off the finger with your tongue.

Unconsciously I was licking where a little finger used to be. It surprised me, it being missing.

I said: 'Finger missing good.'

Karen shook her head, not getting my meaning,

'Like with Kentucky Fried Chicken.'

'The mystery man,' said Karen. Only she wasn't looking at me then. She might as well have been addressing Colonel Gadaffi over the sea: that's how far her gaze seemed to reach.

'Who?' I asked.

At that point the good Scotswoman came out of the nursery, holding Pietro in her arms.

Pietro was saying: 'Da, da, da.'

Nurse smiling as though Pietro saying 'da' was the greatest thing in the world,

Me thinking: Essington, you've got to get into domestic life. It's the future. Or there's nothing. And saying: 'Morning.' Rising on the second syllable, as though there wasn't one thing but joy in this world.

Standing, Karen had taken Pietro; she had his little feet resting on hers, hands held in her hands. They were walking across the balcony towards me, Pietro smiling.

Desdemona wagged her tail in approval.

Happy families. It's a conspiracy.

I held my arms out, took the baby on my knee. Bounced it up and down, trying out Nurse Findlay's little song for the first time: 'I want someone to buy me a pony,' I sang.

Pietro closed his mouth hard, his eyes popped and he let out an unholy howl.

'The wee pet's got wind.' Nurse Findlay rushed forward.

As I handed him across I caught Karen watching me.

Nurse and Pietro vanished to prepare for the next round of let's play with mummy and daddy.

I asked: 'Who's the mystery man?'

'You are, who else? Nights out on the tiles, or you're locked in your studio like some alchemist. Telling me nothing of what's going on . . . when I know something is . . . has to be.'

I took a gulp of coffee.

'We have to talk about it,' she insisted. 'The painting, for instance, Essington.'

'Oh,' I said.

She changed tune. Out of the blue, suddenly: 'I'm sorry,' she said, 'I didn't understnd.'

'What?'

'How you felt.'

'What do you mean?' I asked.

'I was talking it over with Dawn, Ess. She said there's a form to it.'

'To what? A form. Oh hell! Some new theory?'

'Ess, you know as well as I do that Dawn's sharp.'

'Too sharp.'

'And as often as not what she says is a . . . '

'Metaphor.'

'Exactly, Ess. The stars, for instance . . . it's not so much that she believes that garbage, but it's a way of acknowledging what we can't speak about. Perhaps because we don't have the means. Because, I guess, we aren't supposed to. What will happen . . . ? You can't help but think about fate, wonder. Who can? So, to make the future bearable, people have developed systems, games if you like. They're as useful or as useless as you want them to be.'

I shrugged. I wasn't going to be converted to the stars, no matter how reasonable they made it sound.

'Essington, Dawn's interested in all that, in trying to understand the difficult bits. Art as well . . . she says the Gauguin was a mistake.'

'Hell, you don't need the stars or a ouija board to cotton on to that. The cost . . . '

'I know, Ess, I understand. And I'm trying to say I'm sorry. Art isn't money.'

'Often it isn't even art, Karen.'

I was looking at her now. At her face. I realized it was a dear face, to me at least. I got up.

Desdemona followed suit.

'Maybe,' I started out, 'we could get used to this, to the way we are. You and me, Karen.'

'Get used to what, Ess?'

'Well, it's not exactly easy going, is it?'

Then she said: 'I think I'll find a cigarette.'

How about that for a piece of non-conversation?

At lunch Dawn was there.

I'd known a rich man back in Australia. He'd made a pile out of minerals and then set himself up in a style he reckoned was about right. He told me: 'The trouble with servants is you have to interface with them.'

It's true: servants, business partners, nurses, even children, there are times I wish the lot of them would vanish and leave Karen and me to feel our way back together.

Dawn said: 'It's fatal.' She was looking directly at me.

Nurse Findlay was picking over the flesh of a mackerel, trying to avoid the bones. She kept a lump of bread close at hand in case one got caught going down.

Poor Nurse Findlay.

'What's fatal?' I asked. No choice in the matter.

'Beauty,' she said.

Dawn was one of those women who reckoned she didn't have beauty. Maybe she'd regretted it too much as a teenager. A lot of girls eat their hearts out gazing at photographs in magazines, not realizing that it's the women picked up by photographers who are the freaks.

Like boys who decide they've got small dicks, and suffer.

'Gauguin hunted beauty, look what happened to him . . . he's dead,' I said.

'No, Essington, I mean what I say,' Dawn insisted. 'Think about it for a minute. Jodie, Farah, both killed. How many girls would have given their eye-teeth to look like them? Like either of them. And with Farah, it was just too much, too extreme.'

'You'd know,' I said.

'Essington, you are so thick, and bloody-minded!' Dawn looked to Karen for support.

Karen said: 'There's more to it. Essington, maybe she should know what you've told me.'

It shouldn't have got to there. The story had to be contained. I cast a look across the table at Nurse Findlay who had shoved most of the mackerel to the side and was concentrating on Rebecca's potatoes.

'Oh, never mind me,' Nurse Findlay said.

'Why not?' I asked. And then as an afterthought: 'What is it you're writing about this time, Nurse?'

'Oh, this and that,' she replied; 'it's trash I write.'

'Then you won't mind not knowing.'

She shrugged, her face coloured something terrible. God, talk about girlish blushes.

'Can it do any harm?' Karen asked.

'Fucking oath!'

'Mr Holt!' objected Nurse Findlay, rising.

'Dawn,' I said, 'Moulay is dead. Like Gauguin is, only with Moulay it's a closer thing altogether.'

I slept most of the afternoon. I keep a bottle of sleeping tablets, Mogadon, in the bedside table. I took one. It slowed my mind down, caused the light to fade, led me by the hand to oblivion.

Hell, that was nice.

Awake. It was dark.

My initial thought: what were Tournier and Dolent doing? Where was Moulay? Then I remembered he'd died before the ambulance arrived. Tournier swore to me that the bastard had been grinning. As though death was a release, a friend. As though there were better things around the corner.

I'd rather believe that too. I mean really believe it, live by it. Yet I can't.

The room was darker than the night outside. I looked through open doors to where stars shone, and lower down there were the lights of Villefranche, of Nice too, illuminating the sky.

Closing my eyes on that, I tried to bring Farah back, to read details of the other being lurking behind her perfect features. But I couldn't get it. Instead I produced for myself some alabaster image, more like the face of an angel sculpted to decorate a grave. And not beautiful, corny would have been the word, a cliché. No life to it at all.

I was going over what Tournier had told me on the phone before lunch. Just the bare bones of it, but it wasn't too hard to fill in the gaps.

Farah had got the timing wrong. There'd been a vacuum in her life. She didn't want Dawn to fill it, that was for sure.

Instead, hate of some kind must have got in there and occupied the vacant space.

Moulay had told Tournier that Farah had thought up the kidnap . . . after meeting this man who had sailed his yacht into the marina at Villefranche. Farah, always resentful it seemed, feeling that economic inequality was dooming her to an existence at some other being's beck and call. Yet sensing that fate could hold something more for her. All fate needed was a little help to achieve its purpose. There she had been, living, showing nothing of this worm which ate into her heart. And just as Moulay had wanted his ten per cent cut of what he retrieved on my account to fund a life with Farah, so she had earlier conceived the idea of kidnapping me to fund an escape with Tony the sailor.

Afterwards Farah had used Moulay, that was what he'd concluded, used him as a source of information about what was going on at the Villa du Phare. So they were always one step ahead.

Except nobody had suspected I'd suddenly up and take off for London. Screwing it all with the accidents of that journey.

La Voix du Sud ran a front-page article about the yacht, *Top Hat*, and its dead. One, Gerard Berger, the paper's fearless crime reporter, had decided that it was to do with drug running, and even hinted at some link up with child prostitution along the Côte d'Azur, the killings being the result of a territorial dispute. Thus Berger. The photo had come out badly so that the yacht looked a bit like the *Flying Dutchman*, sort of semi-transparent. I guess it was unlike the *Dutchman* in that there was the image of an underclad girl showing through from the back of the page. Tournier was mentioned. In fact Berger gave him quite a coverage, almost an edge of hero-worship to the journalist's tone. I got the feeling that the drug thing had been Tournier's inspiration. His red herring. It went with the boat.

And not a bad idea either since drug running, as a subject, tends to focus people's minds wonderfully. And that's good. It stops them looking about to find out what might actually be the case.

I suppose the same principle applies with scantily clad girls.

Drugs I had on hand: the sleeping tablets, for instance. Reading the paper I could still feel whatever chemical it was massaging my soul, instructing me to stay quiet.

Get through to lunch thus soothed, and well, all that could follow would be the rest of the day. And a reasonable prospect that the boys in blue from the *préfecture* might find no reason to pay me a visit.

Chapter 32

I couldn't bring myself to explain to Karen about the red in the Gauguin, about how it was the wrong colour. My knowledge of that was the last straw.

Only in reasonable moments did I fail to blame her for me buying a forgery. There weren't all that many reasonable moments.

As far as the forgery I'd manufactured was concerned, Karen didn't want to know too much about it. Rebecca had had a word to her concerning the smoke chamber. And my vanishing to the back of the house, to my studio, didn't pass unnoticed either. But Karen seemed determined to distance herself from the activity.

Even when I held my exhibition she was reluctant to attend the *vernissage* — that's what the French call a private viewing.

But Karen came. A patient smile on her face, me hamming it up.

'Sherry?'

She smiled wanly.

It wasn't sherry, it was dry vermouth; I dumped an olive in the glass.

'Cheese?' I suggested. A million years ago that was what you got at art openings, wino's sherry and lumps of mouse-trap cheese. Maybe toothpicks stuck into the cheese for the sake of hygiene.

I didn't have the toothpicks, but hell, aren't we husband and wife? Fingers ought to suffice.

'The other guests?' Karen asked.

'This is it, the invitation list.'

I'd spent half a day getting the studio cleaned up, hanging the two paintings on the wall.

Karen wasn't going to state the obvious.

It was left to me: 'A leitmotif,' I explained: 'you dream up one, you stick to it. Sort of a habit.'

'So it would seem.' Looking from one Polynesian woman to her twin image.

I recharged her glass. The olive bounced about like a mooring marker.

'Why from the back, Essington?'

'What are you trying to say?'

'The rear view?'

'Oh,' I said, 'it's a preference, like with horses. Wasn't it Queen Victoria who enjoyed watching stallions covering the mares?'

'I don't think so, no.' Karen took a chunk of cheese. It was cantal, the closest the French get to a cheddar. 'Definitely not Queen Victoria, Essington. She was German, her pleasure was to watch the Scots mating.'

'Did Nurse Findlay tell you that?'

I could see we were going to have a time of it, sparring, keeping off the subject of the paintings. The truth being that I hadn't yet admitted I'd repossessed the Gauguin I'd bought.

Indeed, keeping everything to myself had become a habit. And feeling guilty because of it a habit too. Very much like childhood.

A week had passed and still I'd kept events on the yacht to myself, having added nothing to that one scrap of information: Moulay was dead. Of course Karen might have read an account of it in *La Voix du Sud*. But she wasn't going to let on if she had. That's the way we play it: Anglo-Saxon, each soul locked in a private hell.

Meanwhile there'd been more misgivings over the Makihei silk deal, Karen and Dawn now constantly banging their heads together trying to work out what was best. All I could gather was that there were a lot of second thoughts on every side.

And, to top everything off, the stars had come down heavily against the deal.

You know how it is with the stars.

Me, if anybody'd bothered to ask, I would have said to drop it.

Like Karen would have warned me to drop what I had in mind as well, if I'd let on. So I didn't.

The *vernissage* was me offering her a chance to participate unconsciously in my plan. There was still a lot more work to put in on our relationship if we were going to produce that *de rigueur* series of photographs of our boy growing into the world, a loving couple looking on, hands on his shoulders, faces grinning with pride.

'The question, Karen, is will the real Gauguin please stand up?'

I was proud of what I'd produced. Never a finer copy made of anything. I would have thought its production signalled my reaching the top of the profession.

'Neither.'

That shocked me.

How the hell could she know they were both fakes? It had taken considerable research for me to prove conclusively to myself that the red flower in the lower left-hand corner of the picture was done in a pigment non-existent in Gauguin's time.

'How can you tell?'

Playing the game, Karen stepped back several paces; she had put her drink down on my work bench. She shut one eye, then the other, tilted her head. Even held up a hand, screened part of the composition. It was as though an aesthetic judgement was about to spill out of her mouth.

'Because,' she said, 'the real one was passed over to those bastards who kidnapped you, Ess.'

'Good point.'

'The real question is,' she went on, 'what in God's name do you think you're playing at?'

'Reasonable.'

'So?'

'I retrieved it.'

'Not possible.'

'Maybe not, Karen, yet that's exactly what I did.'

She reckoned she needed her drink again, picked it up. I offered yet another tiny cube of cheese.

Munch: thinking. Knitted brows. Next she was tapping her foot like a swing-era saxophone player.

'Quite something, isn't it,' I said, 'picking the difference?'

'Firstly, I'm not certain I believe you, Essington. Though I'd have to admit it's clever what you've done. Very clever. Yet I ask myself, why two? No answer. You see, I'm confused.'

'You're meant to be.'

'And I'm also worried, because I've some inkling of what you must have in mind. What I say is: don't do it, please. For my sake.'

'Don't do what, Karen?'

'Don't try and sell a forgery. They will put you away forever. Property is not something you tamper about with. Sell your sister, drown her if you like . . . '

'I don't have a sister.'

'You know what, Essington, I do believe that's part of your problem.'

'You got that from Dawn, Karen . . . the improving qualities of the human sister and other crap by Dawn Grogan, D-Y-K-E.'

'A sister, Essington, might have made you more sympathetic.'

'I resent that. Jesus, unsympathetic! I'm doing this for you, believe it or not. To get the money back, shore up the business, that's all I'm doing it for. And I'm proud of myself. But tell me, let's just suppose that, sister or no sister, I'm at least capable of telling the truth from time to time. Then play my game, please. At least try, Karen!'

'I'm not endorsing anything by doing it?'

'Nothing, I assure you.'

'You promise you're not going to sell it?'

'That's another thing, Karen. Put it to one side. Right now, one step at a time. Anyway let's assume, for the form of it, let's assume I'm telling the truth. And if one of these is the real thing . . . I got it back. Then what's the harm in selling it? I mean, you were right, there's a boom on. Minor work that it may be, it's still a Gauguin; the value might have doubled in a few months, could be it's even done better than that. The whole world's convinced itself there's a recession coming, a slump in commodity prices . . . but they believe nothing can stop art. The fact that I happen to think they're wrong doesn't make one iota of difference.'

Karen shrugged: she couldn't give a damn about my economic predictions,

Neither could I, really.

Karen was playing my game, that was something. She moved from one painting to the other, checking on details, examining the sides as well, the condition of the canvas where it turned over, what the brown paper stuck around the edge looked like. We'd talked about all that hundreds of times; she'd kept up with my obsessions on our visits to the art galleries of Europe, grinning each time another attendant asked me to move further back from the surface of a masterpiece. I mean, if you can't look up close you might just as well buy books or prints, enjoy the reproductions.

I topped up the drinks, ate my olive. Placed the pip on the work table.

'Want to examine the backs?'

'Forget the backs, Essington. I'm sure you've taken care of them.'

She knew me, I was on my home ground.

And then she picked it, my Gauguin, the latter-day fake! She took it to be the one I'd bought.

Like winning a tie-breaker at tennis . . . I broke ranks, wrapped her in my arms.

'Careful,' she said, the vermouth splashing, 'my lipstick.'

Did I really convince her about the Renouard family heirloom painting I'd paid six million US dollars for being a fake? I don't know. Still there was some progress made, we were getting back on to normal terms. Whatever they were. And if she did think it was a fake was Karen less opposed to me selling it than to me selling my own work?

Question three: did she really believe I'd painted both pictures, and that it was a ruse of mine to get the money back, with her approval?

A couple of days after my little exhibition opening I took the leap: I contacted a British auction house that was arranging a big international sale in Monte Carlo. What I really had in my favour was the provenance of the Gauguin. With that it didn't matter too much which one I sold. A buyer would be totally confident, they'd be picking up a work with an impeccable history. With, in fact, the history I'd purchased when making my big mistake. The only addition to that story now was my own records of purchase. I mean, with bits of paper like that what speculative buyer is going to look too closely at the picture itself?

Answer, hardly any. Most of these people have some little smoothie working for them anyhow, checking the work out, examining the documentation — mostly the latter.

Everybody in that world deserves the rest of us, like at a crack dealers convention.

I didn't need any convincing as to how seedy the whole thing was, and therefore I wasn't agonizing with myself about the morality of shoving my Gauguin back in there, palming it off on to some fresh sucker.

Screw them.

What I did worry about was getting found out and locked away for years to pay for my crime. I'd already demonstrated to myself how badly adapted I am to confinement. I had a nasty feeling that just the threat of it would cause me to leap off one of the coast's shonky condominiums.

I calculated that the way to stay clear of prison was to sell the painting I'd already made the mistake of buying. It would be an innocent act; how was I supposed to have found out the thing was valueless? Cashing in, there's no law against that, in fact it's supposed to be the only sensible thing to do.

So I'd be left with my little number as a memento of the unhappy story. And the Holt coffers would once again be overflowing.

As in a fairy tale.

A decision is only a decision in as much as it has been made to be broken. The sporting half of the primitive Essington Holt mind wanted to test the water with its own masterpiece. How well had I performed? A forgery is only a copy till you drag it into the market-place and try it. Any mug can produce a copy. Forgers are the master rogues of our age — of any age, I guess.

Imagine the pleasure of selling what I'd produced? Surely the effect would be the same: it still fitted the paperwork. I could claim it was the one with that watertight provenance which I'd bought. Complete with the history of Renouard family ownership. What then was the problem?

Only that with one false Gauguin, if there were to be investigations into its authenticity, I'd be telling the truth. With the other I'd be lying.

What the hell difference did that make? Would I blush like Nurse Findlay was wont to do? Would they wire me up to a lie detector?

I didn't think so.

Thus I changed my mind, I firmed up on selling the masterpiece produced by my own hand.

*

The sale was big.

Plush location, gilded rooms in a neo-classical monstrosity across from the Monte Carlo casino. Salukis on solid silver leashes, flash shit like that. Ageless women with lacquered hair piled above lifted faces. Little guys with over-shot jaws and barrel chests; tall willowy chaps with red-veined cheeks. Curious how we looked a set, like a sub-species. The useless rich.

Me there as well, oh yes. Not ashamed. I mean I hadn't worked for my wealth, had I? Nothing vulgar like that.

And at the auction I was going to claw my way back up through the ranks of the top ten per cent.

For the viewing day before the sale my Gauguin had been given pride of place in the rooms. There was a tiny Monticelli beside it, and on the other side a bland work by Utrillo who I reckon ought to have tried painting while sober, just to see how it turned out.

Other nice stuff, all minor. This was not the really big league — generally you have to go to London for that. But a picture like my Gauguin, you'd have some trouble I'd reckon getting a permit to cart it out of France. They don't like their art being exported, the French.

Of course, there're ways around the export problem, like there're ways around everything.

Or let *la belle France* cling to the fine Essington Gauguin on offer.

Which was how I was thinking of myself right then, as Essington Gauguin. What was it Gauguin and I had over the rest of the crew at the art auction? Surely our extensive experience of the *Pacifique Sud*. We had, in fact, both walked down the same Sydney streets.

But not together.

I liked it, Gauguin and me: little Paul, big Essington.

Sale day. We'd been through close to twenty items by the time the Gauguin came up. It's amazing how quickly the pictures pass under the hammer at an art auction. As though all those people with nothing better to do are in one hell of a hurry. Yet you can tell when the star work turns up. A silence falls. Even the lap dogs go quiet, the nervous Italian Greyhounds, too.

People recross their legs and there's some discreet glancing about as they try to pick who might be primed to bid. The fact is most of the mob are observers. They could be a hired crowd for all the effect they have on proceedings.

It was my Gauguin held aloft, done by the Holt hand. And big on a screen behind there was a rear-projected slide of it just so nobody was getting anything wrong. A lion-haired Englishman with hand-stitched lapels and loud stripes decorating his shirt calmed us down with the briefest introduction to the work.

My heart was going. The body heat rising.

A pair of women were on either side of the auctioneer; they were holding on to phones. I hoped that meant we had at least two buyers from outside the room. These women were smiling as though posing for a toothpaste advertisement.

There were the spotters as well, with their hands clasped behind their backs. They'd pick out the bids from us lot.

Good.

All the currencies were displayed on a computer-operated board. You bid in francs, up the value would come in yen, in marks, in US dollars, sterling. It's nice.

The man with the mane of hair was asking what he was bid. He wanted to know did he have a hundred million francs.

Funny, I wanted to know that too.

Did he have seventy-five million?

Fifty, what about fifty?

No go. He looked bored as he set to telling us how Gauguins were rare as hen's teeth. Rent a crowd stroked their dogs, scratched their necks, looked over their shoulders.

If I looked over my shoulder I saw the room's back wall.

'Do I have fifty million, surely?' He was letting us know that was the bottom. And that he was buggered if he was going to waste his precious time running all the way back up again from below that mark.

They'd valued the thing for me. They'd put their estimate on it. We were under the estimate.

Fifty million francs, that would have recouped me around seven million US as the exchange was that day. It varies, particularly lately, currencies going up and down like kids on a see-saw.

I'd be a million up.

We ought to do better than fifty million francs.

Unless some arsehole picked that it was a fake, and had passed the word around the professionals.

Those telephone women were up there like the thieves on either side of Christ, clutching their handpieces, showing off their teeth. Even if there was nobody holding on down the other end. The charade sort of keeps up the spirits of all concerned. That's what speculative bubbles are, collective high spirits.

He got fifty million. One of the spotters pulled it out from somewhere, imagined or real.

We were still under the estimate and therefore under the reserve. Someone else bid.

Healthy.

Big leaps.

The women were talking into the telephones now.

The movement was upwards.

We were at sixty-five million. Over nine million US.

We got our first bid from the phone.

We were at seventy-three million. I was nearly choking from the excitement, my body heat going over the top.

How about if I'd died of a heart attack then and there? Good one!

I left. I went to cool off on the grass outside.

Then I popped over to the casino. I joined the bus crowd playing fruit machines, lowering the tone, taking the poetry out of gambling.

Molena reckons fruit machines are an argument against democracy.

Well, yes and no. I got a jackpot. Money pouring out of the thing.

Your luck, see, it can turn around.

Chapter 33

Is it part of the metaphysics of things which causes events to group into threes?

Go to the bottom of the class for that question.

Next I'd be into the stars. Yet people do talk of a lucky streak. Perhaps, though, we put ourselves in the way of luck, push it a bit. I remember that if, when young, I fell in love with a girl I'd keep on bumping into her. As though by coincidence. The thing being that I didn't even comprehend how I was setting those situations up for myself.

In London. I'd attended the coroner's court that day. I'd been there on the previous day as well. It was a longish affair because of the police having no particular lead. And because of the presence at the scene of the crime of my own good unco-operative self. We had gathered up on the corner of Kensington High Street and Earl's Court Road, opposite the Commonwealth Institute where well-dressed ladies worry themselves sick about how all us lot out there in the wider world are making out.

I think Ruth Fischmann called it a spill-over court. That meant there wasn't room elsewhere, the British were killing each other too fast. Which is progress. We were in a police building. The coroner was a shabby man with a charming smile which he put on at the most unlikely moments. The jury were all unsmiling. Looking at them I decided I didn't like my chances and it took Ruth's frequent pep talks to keep me up with the fact that I wasn't on trial, nor was I liable to be.

My friend Joyce made an appearance; she said the right things as though we'd spent the previous weekend rehearsing our lines.

It was apparent that Detective Sergeant Mutton had already taken it upon himself to go his own way. He'd leapt at an early retirement, and was now working in the north, in Manchester. For a private security firm. He chose to look right through me. I was happy to leave the relationship like that.

I still had the bastard's gun. In fact it was back at my hotel. I'd popped along to the bank, opened the tin box, extracted the family jewels. Then I'd checked the box, empty, back in under my name. I reckoned just having the box there might turn out handy.

And no knowing when you need a gun — needless to say, even before I spotted him in London, Tony was very much on my mind.

The pistol was most certainly not police regulation issue, it had Benelli stamped into the metal. There were eight 9mm rounds in the magazine. I deduced it was from Mutton's private arsenal.

I saw Tony before the jury had retired for what eventuated as a decision that Jodie had been murdered by person or persons unknown. That wasn't too bad, considering.

Suddenly there he was, large as life.

Of course, every day in London I'd been watching out for him, hoping. Searching through the faces which passed me on the streets, those which packed the underground. But I'd been frightened of finding him as well. And then there he was.

Tony, surely unable to let go!

That's the way it is with our psychology, we can't leave things alone. Commit a crime and you get to be like a dog with a bone, turning it into your life's obsession.

He was hanging about at the back of a rag-tag group of spectators, slack-arsed mugs filling in yet another day. He wore dark glasses and had a scarf pulled up half-way across his face, like he'd just been to the dentist, or his glands were up. But I guessed the scarf was to avoid recognition. What he didn't gamble on was the way that sensory deprivation, like I'd endured at the end of the chain, urges the mind to compensate by making a lot of the little it has to take in to itself. I would have picked Tony at half a mile if I'd caught a glimpse of his eyebrow.

Trapped in there with the law, and its procedures, I just about went mad knowing Tony was so close. And me not being able to act.

Would I have another chance, ever, to get at him? Yet I couldn't set up a hue and cry because that way I'd be ensnared in the middle of something that might have no end; certainly would have no legal end. And, anyway, who was going to believe me if, out of the blue, pointing a finger at a face I'd picked out of the crowd, I randomly accused this innocent bystander of murder.

You have to have some basis for that sort of act.

Certainty of mind just isn't enough. You require proof.

Then I spotted him a second time. He was walking quickly along the crowded street, heading away from where I'd been testifying; his head was down, he was thrusting himself through the crowd of people. A man in a hurry. Because he knew he'd taken too big a risk? Because, maybe, he'd registered the flash of recognition which must have lit up my features back there in the coroner's court?

Yes, there he was. It had to be him. I was already in a taxi — no point in hanging about, my legal representatives having bolted the minute the jury retired. And I felt in need of a drink, maybe of a bottle . . . or two. I was agitated; and that first glimpse of Tony being most of the reason for my condition.

I told the taxi to stop.

'Stop?'

'Yes.' I was paying, wasn't I? What difference if I'd only just got in the door?

We were a hundred yards past Kensington High Street station. I hopped out, left the driver with a five-pound note to wrap around his troubled soul. Next I was belting back in the direction of the station entrance.

I reckoned that was Tony up ahead. He was going through the ticket check, the scarf knotted around his neck now. It was Tony's way of holding himself, yes, his build too. As for the rest, well there'd been some changes made. He wore an expensive dark suit with a pin stripe. The same rugged-looking head though, the hair cut short on top, long at the back, in the style of Rod Stewart.

Rod Stewart put a date on Tony.

He went down to catch the train, direction Victoria.

There wasn't yet a big push of people. We were in the lull before the after-work storm. Still enough bodies around for me to keep out of sight. Not that he looked edgy or anything. Cool as you like now he was underground, feeling safe. Which was strange since he must have had a fair bit of stuff on his mind. On his conscience. Or didn't Tony score one of those?

Of course, then, me being me, it didn't enter my mind that Tony might feel he had yet to get one more person out of the way. That he could have been keeping tabs on me for some time, waiting for the moment, working it out. If that was the case then me spotting him, even me following like I was, as a dog might follow, could have been part of something he already had in mind.

But right then I wasn't thinking that way.

I stepped on to the platform at every stop, which wasn't many, checking on who was getting off. My fellow passengers observed this performance with contained interest.

Tony's destination turned out to be Sloane Square.

From the station he headed straight down Sloane Gardens. Not a bad address. No problem working out where at least some of my money had gone. Into the sink of London real estate.

I was hanging back a long way when he went into a house, but I was confident I'd got the right number.

I left it ten minutes, watching, then, cautious now, I went along to check the details. From the pavement I couldn't be sure if it was a flat or if he lived in the whole joint. Either way it was solid class. Even a fraction boring, perhaps. Which is correct.

I didn't want to be seen. So I hurried back to the other end of the Gardens. I spent most of the rest of the day there, just watching.

Ruth, Howard and I were to have supper together. Ruth had insisted, saying that Howard would want to see me, to have a chat. Then she'd added, with less self-assurance: 'If he manages the time.'

As though we couldn't bank on Howard, not for anything.

We were going to meet at eight-thirty at a place Ruth had picked out on Holland Park Avenue.

Wasn't it going to be nice?

I had just enough time to make it back from Sloane Gardens to my hotel for a scrub-up, before grabbing a cab to arrive at the restaurant a quarter of an hour late. There was a weight in my pocket, I hoped it didn't show. Unfortunately it wasn't really overcoat weather.

I'd wrapped a couple of handkerchiefs around the gun to soften its profile.

As I sat down it bumped against the back of the chair. Ruth didn't seem to notice. She was fussed enough. Talking about how she wasn't sure where Howard could be. But, I guessed, knowing nevertheless. It's a funny world.

The conversation was hard going once it strayed from the inquest. I kept things alive with my fund of stories of life in the Australian bush, how we fought crocodiles, ripped trees up with our bare hands, surfed on cyclones using corrugated iron roofing sheets for boards.

Ten-thirty we were through. Ruth wanted to know if she could drop me somewhere. I told her I liked to walk.

She didn't mention the bill for the legal work. You don't talk about money over supper, not if you've got it pouring out your ears.

A balmy night.

Thinking back I find it strange to examine my thoughts. Well, at least to examine the question of whether I had them at all. It was as though I was driven by instinct, by a fundamental understanding of what must be done. You hear about people who get that way, often it's before they carry out some amazingly altruistic action, like striding into a burning building to search for a child. They do it like zombies walk the Haitian night, as though goodness has nothing to do with reason, with decisions, as though it comes from some deeper source.

I was not on my way to do good. Rather I'd made a promise. Now I had no choice but to fulfil that promise.

I walked. I got lost walking.

I suppose it should have taken no more than an hour and a half to cover the distance. I didn't have a street directory and I'm not particularly familiar with London. So it was more than double that. God knows where I went as the city shut down around me. As the streets emptied of traffic. There was just me and the milk bottles and the garbage. The occasional cat. One or two homeless people making do with cardboard boxes.

Not a light on in the houses along the row at Sloane Gardens. Funny, I felt a bit like Peter Pan, out there and all alone while the good people were snug in their beds.

Peter Pan with a 9mm Benelli in his pocket.

Which wasn't in his pocket, not any longer. It was feeling snug in his hand. I slipped the safety catch, checked that there was a cartridge in the breech. Nice. I enjoyed the weight. I pulled a cotton glove on my complete hand, wiped the Benelli all over with a handkerchief. Jesus, I'd got this right, hadn't I? It felt so good. Even the details.

Details like the fact that I was chewing gum.

Next I held up my other hand, the one without the little finger. I kissed the air where the missing tip ought to have been and drew on the second glove. I took the gum out of my mouth, stuck it over the peep hole in the door. I hunted around for a bit of rock, a brick. Found what I wanted! A chunk of wood in the street outside, just along the road. It was perfect for what I had in mind. Well, the thing is that it wasn't in my mind. What I was doing, how I went about it, everything was given to me direct. Which is why it felt so right.

I rang the bell.

A minute or so later I rang the bell again. I wondered about that place being really mine because it had been my money that must have bought it. It even struck me as funny that someone might inherit it from Tony . . . from Tony Horne! Spelt with an 'e'. I wondered what his name was now. And did he light candles for his little mate. Or for Farah, or Jodie. For all the beauty squandered.

An outside light came on, illuminating where I was standing.

I pressed the bell again.

Wasn't it a weird sensation to watch the door open, just a crack, just far enough for a person to peer round?

Tony was peering round. No mistaking those eyes. Not so much as a question about it in my mind. Nor any mistaking that he knew exactly what it was visiting him so late at night. But too late for knowledge. Surprise written all over what I could see of the face.

Sure he knew.

Too late, like I said.

The problem for Tony was I'd kicked my bit of wood into the gap between the door and the jamb. Not being able to close the door stuffed up his reflexes: the safety chain wouldn't let it open any wider and my chock prevented the thing from closing. While his sleepy brain was processing that one, and his eyes were still on me, I started firing the gun. Quickly, seven shots. The first one angled up at his head, the rest following where I reckoned he was falling.

With the last round I shot away the chain, opened the door, checked on a job well done.

I placed the gun on the stoop and headed briskly for Sloane Square. I didn't want to be a witness.

Particularly if the law found out it was Mutton's gun.

Mutton's gun! It was too late to go back by the time that thought hit me.

Which nags at me. The stupidity of it. Yet I wasn't thinking at all. I'd given myself over to that other, perhaps external form of direction. Can you be stupid when not thinking?

It seems the Benelli was never traced to Mutton. And certainly not to me. That night was also a tribute to the property owners of the western world who like to stay tucked up in their beds. Even after discharging a pistol eight times I didn't hear a police siren sound while I was moving away through the London night. By the time I did it could have been headed for anywhere.

The reality of killing the man didn't strike me till I was back at Cap Ferrat. And then it shocked me. Not because I'd done it, but that it had been so easy.

I was shocked as well to discover that I didn't feel remorse. Not even at the idea that I had some dark secret to carry to the grave. Instead it was as though a weight of responsibility to myself had been lifted from my shoulders.

I was free for the first time since entering unknowingness outside the apartment in the Sixteenth Arrondissement.

There was still one thing unsettling me. That was the documentation on the Renouard family Gauguin. How had it come to be faked? I had kept photostats of everything initially provided to prove to me that the picture was genuine. Of course there was no record of the family making the original purchase, but there was an early photograph, taken around 1910 judging from the mode of dress: two men in a room and the painting hanging in the background — the painting out of focus.

There was mention of a Gauguin in an inventory of household items dated 1921 and again in a similar list dated 1936. This was a family which liked to make lists, in elegant copperplate writing.

I was gazing at the painted surface, wondering if this was a forgery done by a genius of immense patience, or one who had propelled the work into the future confident in the knowledge that eventually the mischief of his craft would upset some too-stable apple cart. I noticed something curious which had previously escaped my attention. Something about the appearance of the picture in the background of the early photograph, the one with the men in front of it. It was down in that corner with the shell and the flower . . . !

What a fool I'd been not to have examined the evidence more closely. What I'd had on hand I'd simply taken as proof of the painting's existence at that time. It was in fact proof of something more. Because in the photograph the Polynesian woman was higher in the composition, there was more space between her buttocks and the picture's lower edge. I was sure I wasn't deceiving myself about that even though the variation was small. And what was painted down where the shell and flower and leaf should be was different in some kind of way. But the image was too blurred to identify that difference for sure.

I set to considering what this could mean.

Then to examining the painting itself. Whatever the outcome of my investigations I was going to have to get it out of the way anyhow, since officially it was sold. The only value it could have for me now was as a souvenir.

I placed it face down on the work table, examined the canvas where it had been turned around the lower edge of the stretcher, and beneath where the brown paper was stuck on.

It's terribly exciting, exploring a painting from the back, because it is from that side that you learn so much about a work's history.

Suddenly unable to contain myself, getting wound up, working faster, going at it.

The next thing, rubbing gently at the front surface with a cotton bud, I tried a touch of solvent on the red flower. It takes a long time for old paint to dissolve, and you can't speed the process up without risk of damage to what's underneath. If there's something to be discovered underneath, that is. I was working down to the lower edge and already finding something dark hidden there, a sense of a flowing outline to it.

Maybe a bird's leg, and a tail of some sort!

Then I was finding that not just the flower but the leaf as well was painted over this shape.

I couldn't believe what was happening.

But one thing was for sure: I was convinced it *was* a Gauguin that had finished up in my possession! Now that I was getting rid of that false red pigment, and slowly revealing underneath what appeared to be an owl holding a lizard.

Couldn't have been anything else. Cause for thought. So I put the old brain to work. I propped the painting up in front of me, together with the photograph showing it in the background, and the two gentlemen, in sharp focus, still gazing out at the camera. Some kind of explanation began to form in my mind. Well, maybe more what I was doing was speculating. With eighty years separating those men and myself it could be nothing more than speculation.

A Gauguin, I thought, in, say, 1910. What would have been the status of such a painting? And what attitude would these two men have had towards the work? They couldn't tell me, could they? Those eyes caught, forever open, in the photographic emulsion. The mouths that would never speak again. But Gauguin, not the man, nor the artist, rather the product name, the gilt-edged investment, that was something of which those two men would never have dreamed. The painting they were standing in front of had been made by a man, by an extraordinary man, and it had come into the possession of this family. They would keep it, perhaps as an historic document relating to the French presence in the Pacific rather than as a work of art. But, even as a work of art, why couldn't it be changed, if it offended taste. If the possibly barbaric and mystic message of the owl and the lizard offended someone why not paint it out? Not these men, the change hadn't been done by them. But perhaps the next pair of hands into which the painting fell wrought the changes on it, for pious reasons, or for reasons of taste. Since the beginning of time the paintings we poor mortals have created have been modified by subsequent generations: a disgraced relative removed from a family portrait, fig leaves added over genitals, the pagan and the profane revamped.

All I could suppose was that something of the kind had happened with the Gauguin, and that the hint of pagan ritual in the owl and lizard had been obscured by the more predictable shell and leaf, the former object's sexual reference unrecognized.

*

Karen knocked at the door.

I said to come in.

'What's that smell?'

'Solvent,' I replied.

'God!' she said. 'If that doesn't kill you . . . '

'Nothing will, because, Karen, take a look at this.'

'Which one is it this time?'

'Here, look and it'll tell you.'

So she did.

'Essington . . . what is it?'

'If I'm not wrong that's an owl, Karen, a white owl, and it's got a lizard in its talons. See, there . . . the lizard's head.' It was showing up from under the shell and I was working right around now to where the canvas had been turned over on the side of the stretcher.

'You see what it means?'

'Essington, where's the other one?'

'It's sold.'

'The forgery . . . Essington you sold the forgery!' Her voice too loud. 'What for? You must be mad!'

'I'll tell you what for, eighty-two million francs.'

'But Essington, that's . . . '

'It's a fact. And you're going to have to get used to it, because if you don't, and if you so much as breathe a word . . . '

'And this . . . ' Karen was pointing to the real Gauguin.

'I'm afraid it's going to have to spend a few years rolled up in a bank vault. But not too long, I wouldn't think — people forget.'

Karen's expression changed; well, I guess you'd have to say it travelled through a range of emotions.

She came up smiling.

She said: 'People forget, and people remember.'

'While for us oldies,' I said, 'distinctions fade, the mind gets to be more of a jumble every day.'

'Oldies . . . spare us! Essington, please spare us!'